Sasha opened her eyes ⬚⬚⬚⬚⬚⬚⬚⬚ingly. "What's wrong?"

Her voice was so low he ⬚⬚⬚⬚⬚⬚

"Nothing," he said. "I ju⬚⬚⬚⬚⬚⬚⬚⬚⬚⬚⬚ what you're doing." He stare⬚⬚⬚⬚⬚ into her eyes.

"What do you mean?"

"How much did you have to drink today?"

"Just enough," she replied.

"Enough for what?" He examined her closely in the dark interior of the car.

"Enough for me to forget my three-date rule." She reached over to the ignition, shut the engine off, and removed the keys. Then she unbuckled her seat belt to get out.

Sexton unbuckled his own seat belt and walked around to Sasha's side of the car. He opened the door and held out his hand to help her. Once her car door was shut, she handed him his keys and deliberately strutted in front of him, swaying her hips more than usual, toward the entrance of her apartment. Behind her she heard the beep of Sexton's remote as he activated the alarm.

MOMENTS OF CLARITY...

MICHELE CAMERON

Genesis Press, Inc.

INDIGO

An imprint of Genesis Press, Inc.
Publishing Company

Genesis Press, Inc.
P.O. Box 101
Columbus, MS 39703

All characters in this book have no existence outside the imagination of the author and have no relation whatsoever to anyone bearing the same name or names. They are not even distantly inspired by any individual known or unknown to the author and all incidents are pure invention.

ISBN: 13 DIGIT : 978-1-58571-330-1
ISBN: 10 DIGIT : 1-58571-330-9
Manufactured in the United States of America

First Edition

Visit us at www.genesis-press.com
or call at 1-888-Indigo-1

DEDICATION

I dedicate this novel to my sister, Sherrie,
because she is truly my best friend.

ACKNOWLEDGMENTS

I would like to acknowledge my deep gratitude to my executive editor, Deborah Johnson Schumaker, Sidney Rickman, my line editor, and of course Brian Jones, Valerie Dodson and Diane Blair of Genesis Press.

CHAPTER 1

Just before dawn, Sasha opened her eyes. The incessant sound of the running toilet from the adjoining bathroom had awakened her. Groaning inwardly, she turned over and buried her face into her pillow in an effort to block out the noise. Then she peered at the still body lying next to her.

In the light that made its way through the slats of a broken blind, Abdul stirred restlessly. Fascinated, her eyes followed the sweat trickling to his navel. She studied the marvelous man. Abdul was one of the Greek heroes from the Trojan War movies come to life. The only significant difference was the color of his skin, which was a smooth cocoa brown. He had a chiseled face framed by sleek, wavy hair that fell to the base of his neck. The rise and fall of his chest had the solid rhythm of a talented drummer playing an African drum. A flattened stomach wet with moisture heightened her awareness of his sexuality before her eyes rested on his shaft. It lay limply to one side, spent from hours of lovemaking.

Suddenly Abdul opened his eyes and they connected with hers. Immediately aroused, he reached for her.

Sasha closed her eyes as he pulled her toward him.

Abdul kissed her softly on her neck, then moved his mouth down to her breasts. The lingering smell of the incense burned the night before reminded her of the pleasure they had shared. Sasha playfully slapped his wandering hands away from her body and whispered, "The toilet is running. Please go and jiggle the handle to make it stop." Her voice always had a throaty sound to it, but the combination of Abdul's mouth and hands as they explored her from hip to breast made it sound even huskier.

"Ignore it," Abdul ordered, attempting to turn Sasha over.

Resisting his movements she responded, "It's distracting."

Abdul stiffened. He pinned her eyes with his. "You're breaking the mood. After all this time with me you still don't know when to be quiet?"

Sasha began to maneuver her body from under his, and dragging the bed sheet along with her, stood up.

Abdul lay back with his arm cradled under his head, looking up at her.

"Now I'm not in the mood." She grabbed her overnight bag off the floor and began pulling clothes out of it. Quickly she donned a shirt and shorts.

"You're throwing a temper tantrum just because you didn't get your way," Abdul said in a disgusted voice.

"I'm not throwing a temper tantrum. I'm just getting a little tired of you being so selfish," she returned hotly.

"Selfish? Why are you calling me selfish? You're the one leaving because I didn't jump up and do what you told me to."

"I'm leaving because this argument is so stupid!" Her voice was a few decibels higher.

Now Abdul sat up in bed. "Are you calling me stupid?"

His eyes were narrowed, and she knew from previous experience that this was not a good thing.

"No, I'm not calling you stupid," she denied, "but all you had to do was go and stop the toilet from running. If you had, we wouldn't be having this fight right now." Exasperation was evident on her face and in her voice.

"Why didn't you do it since it was bothering you so much?"

"Why should I?" she said slowly. "This is your place. Besides, it's always something. Either the toilet's running, or the faucet's leaking, or the sun awakens me early in the morning through those broken blinds after I worked a late shift at the hospital. You need to fix this place up or something."

"You're too materialistic," he replied with derision.

Sasha stood next to the bed, her hands on her hips, in a confrontational stance. "Is that so? You know, Abdul, I'm really tired of you acting like everyday conveniences don't mean anything to you. I didn't see you turning down that leather coat that I bought you last December," she paused for effect, "and you say that you don't cele-brate Christmas."

Abdul chose to ignore that but said defiantly, "There's nothing wrong with this apartment, Sasha. Everyone hasn't been raised in the lap of luxury with doting parents that gave them everything they asked for."

"I wasn't raised in the lap of luxury, or given everything that I asked for, either. But my parents did teach me that hard work and perseverance pay off in the end, and I'm very grateful that they did." She tapped her chest with her index finger. "The problem is that you think it's cool to look poor." Sasha's eyes were narrowed in anger because of the crack he'd made about her family. "Being poor never has been fashionable, and believe me, this," she pointed at the raggedy furniture in the room, "is getting old."

"So in other words my apartment isn't good enough for you." Abdul continued to glare at her.

She pointed at the air conditioner in the window that had been broken for months. "The least you could do is to fix that. Maybe I wouldn't be so irritable if it wasn't so hot in here all of the time," she said before she scooped her overnight bag off the floor and stomped out of the apartment.

Sasha hurried down the New York City street with her head ducked to block the glare of the sun. There had been a heat wave for over a week, with the temperature reaching record highs. At nine-thirty in the morning, the sidewalk felt scorching.

She weaved her way in and out of the throng as she headed for the subway station. Stopping at a booth to purchase sunglasses, she looped one arm through her overnight bag and began trying them on. The booth's mirror reflected the face of a five feet, nine inch woman with bronze skin wearing a scooped neck white shirt that contrasted quite nicely with red short shorts trimmed with white piping on the pockets. The eyelashes framing her dark eyes were so thick and long they always looked as if she was wearing mascara.

Recently her beautician had highlighted her black hair with streaks of gold, and it cascaded to just below her shoulders. In her haste to leave Abdul's, she hadn't taken the time to put on a bra or underpants and now began to feel uncomfortable as she became aware of the vendor eyeing her apple bottom as he stood behind her.

Hearing her name called, Sasha swung her head around and saw her friend Tiara sitting with two men at a small bistro table outside a café. She was waving her arm at her. Sasha recognized her companions as Tiara's brother Calvin, who was an athletic trainer for the Knicks, and Sexton Johnson, a point guard for the team. Quickly she handed the vendor a ten dollar bill, perched her new sunglasses on top of her head and, dodging cars and taxi cabs, crossed the street to join them.

Tiara stood up to greet her and they gave each other a big hug.

Sasha affectionately planted a kiss on Tiara's face and smiled at the men, who had also stood when she reached their table. "Hello, how are you doing?" She smiled at them. Sexton and Calvin seemed to dwarf her even though she wore a pair of four-inch wedge sandals.

Taking her overnight bag from her, Sexton slid it under the table, then pulled out a chair for her to sit next to him. She sat quickly because she was acutely aware that with his height he could easily get a bird's-eye view of the twins through the low cut décolletage of her shirt.

"Girl, I almost didn't recognize you. You've changed your hair. It looks fantastic," Tiara said.

Tiara possessed a bubbly personality, and Sasha always had a good time when she was in her company. Sasha automatically smoothed her hair with the palm of her hand. "Thanks, but I changed it out of necessity. Since my promotion to head nurse at the hospital I sometimes wear a nurse's cap, and it doesn't look right on a curly afro."

"I must say I like this better. What did Abdul say about the change?" Tiara teased.

"Oh, you know how he is. He said that I'm trying to blend with mainstream America." Sasha's tone was droll and she wrinkled her nose at the memory of the conversation.

Tiara laughed good-naturedly. "I figured he would say something like that." She turned to Calvin and Sexton. "Sasha's boyfriend is a Muslim. He can't stand anything that conforms to what he considers the establishment."

The two men looked at Sasha and then Calvin spoke. "He should let you be what you want to be and support that." Calvin gave Tiara a pointed look and a short silence descended on the group.

Sexton broke it. "You'd be beautiful no matter how you wear it." He held her trapped within his gaze.

She looked down partly from embarrassment, but also to avoid the sensual liquidity of his eyes.

Calvin said to Sasha, "I haven't seen you since last year at Tiara's party."

"I know. When I saw you guys sitting over here, it was such a cool surprise."

On the table were various breakfast items, eggs, bacon, waffles, hash browns and coffee. Just then the waitress, a gorgeous, leggy blonde, walked up to the table. Her short, black waitress skirt revealed the fact that she had no cellulite and was proud of it. "May I get you anything?" she asked, looking at Sasha.

"Sure, I'll have a ham and cheese omelet and a cup of coffee. Low cal sugar and cream."

"Right away, ma'am." Before she headed to the kitchen she gave Sexton and Calvin a come-hither look.

Tiara gave a low whistle. "Well, I must say, she's a looker," she grinned at the men at the table, "and obviously looking."

"Not my type." Calvin gave a small laugh.

"Mine, either," Sexton said, still staring at Sasha.

Tiara turned to Calvin. "Peter is out of town on business again. When he gets back I know that he wants to see the Knicks when they play against Dwayne Wade. He just loves him."

"Will do. That's in two weeks. Do you want some tickets also, Sasha?" Calvin looked at her inquiringly.

"No, thank you. I don't want to put you to any trouble." She didn't want to admit that Abdul refused to watch any sports live or on television because he felt that black athletes were being used and then put out to pasture if they didn't perform well or got in any trouble whatsoever. She herself was an avid sports fan and had played basketball while in middle and high school. Her brother and father had taught her to play aggressively and their tutelage had made her a formidable adversary.

"It's not a problem at all," Calvin replied.

"Can I let Tiara know if I want some tickets? I never know what shift I'm going to be working from day to day."

Tiara looked at Sasha. "I would think that since you are in charge of things down there you could work up any master schedule you want?" She took another sip of coffee.

"You'd think so, wouldn't you?" Sasha countered wryly. "It seems as if I'm in charge of the grunt work, and still don't get the good schedule."

"I thought that a decent shift was one of the perks for being in charge."

"It could be. But right now, I'm helping someone out by covering her shift until she gets her life in order. It was an unexpected snafu, but I'm trying to turn it into a positive experience by trying to learn all of the facets of each job in my department. I think that might help me be a better administrator later on down the road."

"Beautiful and unselfish. Those are two very admirable traits." Again Sexton's eyes pinned hers and Sasha felt herself blushing.

As if on cue, Tiara and Calvin started chuckling.

Calvin stopped long enough to say, "Man, just go ahead and ask her out. But before you do, please wipe the drool off your lips."

"I asked Sasha out last year at Tiara's 'Get Rid of Your Loser' party. She took my number and said that she would call, but she didn't."

Sasha felt decidedly uncomfortable being discussed as if she were not present. Clearing her throat she explained, "I would like to apologize for that. You didn't ask me if I was seeing anyone so I didn't know what to say when you gave me your card and asked me to call you," she tailed off lamely. "I don't date more than one person at a time. It's hard enough for me to find the time to devote to one relationship, let alone try to juggle two."

"If that's the case, you did the right thing by not calling me because I don't share, not that it would come to that," he replied without rancor. "After one date with me you would forget all about Arnold."

"His name is Abdul," Sasha corrected him.

"Whatever," Sexton replied smoothly.

Tiara hid a smile behind her hand and Calvin pretended to have an immense interest in his menu.

"So you think you're all that, huh? Don't you have a steady girlfriend?" she asked, curious about him in spite of her protestations to the opposite.

"No, ma'am." He drawled his words.

"Why not," she teased, "if you're all that?"

"I'm picky." Again he watched her.

9

Even though they were in a public place, Sasha felt as if they were alone on a desert island.

"When you didn't offer me your number at the party, I kind of figured that you were involved, though I am surprised to find out that you're still dating the same guy. I thought that you weren't in a serious relationship or you wouldn't have been at the party at all, considering the theme of it."

Upon hearing this Tiara chimed in. "I insisted that she come. She's my best friend and we needed a certain number of beautiful women to pull it off. And I resent you calling it my 'Get Rid of Your Loser' party. She mildly glared at Sexton. "All of those men there were eligible, intelligent, and looking for the right woman. Maybe you guys didn't get the hookup, but I hit pay dirt by meeting Peter. My husband is perfect," she ended with satisfaction.

"No man is perfect," Calvin corrected his sister.

"It depends on what your criteria for perfect are," Tiara retorted sharply.

Calvin's answer was only to roll his eyes.

In an effort to quell what appeared to be the beginning of an argument, Sexton leaned forward and beckoned the others to do the same so that the people at the next table couldn't hear him. "I think I come pretty damn close to being the perfect man. I'm handsome, rich, and fantastic in bed." He paused for emphasis and then finished with, "I hear it all the time."

"Don't leave out the word humble," Sasha piped in with a laugh, knowing that he was joking because of the teasing glint in his eyes.

"Anytime you want to find out for yourself, Miss Sasha Diamond, you have my number," he declared, suggestively giving her a wink.

For the first time since sitting at the table, Sasha really looked at him. She was sitting so close to him she could feel his breath fanning the whispers of hair just below her ear. Sasha wished the sunglasses she had purchased were covering her eyes so she could mask her expression.

Sexton Johnson undeniably had an air about him. His skin looked smooth and was an unusual coloring of smoke and charcoal. But he was no pretty boy with facial hair that included a thick mustache. On his chin was a neat, round circle of black hair. His eyes were so dark that the pupils were indistinguishable from the cornea and he wore his black hair in rows of thick braids tight against his scalp. And then there was his body. Sasha loved the bodies of basketball players. Whenever she watched a game, she was in awe of their physical perfection. They were thick, but not fatty because of their constant running up and down the court. Today, Sexton wore a casual tee shirt and a pair of basketball shorts that stopped right above his knees. The muscles in his calves were prominent even though he was sitting.

His body was absolutely perfect. Additionally, he possessed a sensual quality that could not be manufactured.

She dropped her eyes in embarrassment. What she had meant to be a sly assessment had turned into a long perusal of him from head to toe, lingering too long in the area just below his stomach.

Sexton sat quietly observing Sasha size him up and he was pleased. Her lips said she wasn't interested, but her eyes said that she was.

Suddenly, Calvin looked at his watch and exclaimed looking at Sexton, "Man, we have to hurry or we're going to be late for conditioning."

Sexton glanced down at his Rolex and agreed, "You're right. Why don't you go and hail a cab and I'll take care of the bill?"

As Calvin stood and adjusted his clothing, Sasha realized how much he and Tiara looked alike, except for the fact that Calvin was much taller and shaved his head. They both were strikingly good-looking with full lips and slanted eyes. If you slapped a wig on Calvin they could double as twins. He leaned over and kissed Tiara on the cheek. "I'll come by sometime this weekend and drop your tickets off." Smiling at Sasha he added before he walked off, "It's been too long. Don't be such a stranger."

Sexton reached into the pocket of his shorts and pulled out some bills held together by a gold money clip fashioned into the shape of the symbol of a dollar sign.

"Ladies," he said smiling at them, "breakfast is on me." He placed a folded bill on the table, and then, looking pointedly at Sasha, said, "Let me know if I can do anything else for you," before he winked at her again, smiled at Tiara, and went to join Calvin as he stood waiting at the curb with a taxicab.

"Whew!" Tiara breathed deeply, playfully fanning herself with an imaginary fan as she watched the cab merge into the traffic and Calvin and Sexton disappear. "The sexual tension between the two of you was so thick you could cut it with a knife. Sexton is really smitten with you. Heaven knows how you could resist his obvious invitation. He's so damn fine."

Sasha blurted out her next words without thinking. "If it weren't for Abdul, I would have taken him up on it."

"You should have. It's not as if the two of you are married or anything. In fact, you're not even engaged." She gave her an encouraging smile. "You're allowed to go out with other people."

"I didn't encourage Sexton because I don't want to take him up on his offer out of spite."

Tiara gave her a questioning look.

"Abdul and I had a pretty nasty spat this morning. I had just left his place when you guys saw me. He made me so angry I stormed out."

"Is that why you're running around without a bra on? I noticed," she added dryly, "as did everyone else at the table."

Sasha half-laughed. "I don't have on any drawers either. Abdul's place is such a dump. Anything that breaks doesn't get fixed. I mean that it's literally falling down around his ears."

"Then why doesn't he get his landlord to fix it? That's what they're there for."

"I told him that weeks ago, but he said that if he did, the landlord would go up on his rent and he doesn't have the extra money. He rents on a month-to-month basis."

"Bummer. Why don't you two get together at your place? Your loft is so beautiful."

"I suggested that, but Abdul said that my hours are too crazy and he's not going to sit around my apartment waiting for me like he's a house husband."

"Well, I know that there has to be give and take in every relationship in order to make it work."

"I realize that. But lately I've been doing all of the giving and Abdul has been doing all of the taking."

Tiara looked aghast. "You don't mean to tell me that you're giving him money?"

"Abdul never asks me for money, but he never has any either. Anytime we do anything out of the ordinary, I have to pay."

"Why is he so broke? He does own his own business."

"He does, but he's barely eking out a living. His storefront is expensive. Harlem used to be cheap, but ever since Clinton moved in, property values have gone out the roof. You know, it's sad to say, but a lot of times black people don't support each other's businesses. I'm sort of ashamed to say it out loud, but I don't even buy that much from him. How many wooden elephants or bowls do you want in your house or give to someone as a gift?"

Tiara smothered a laugh. "Not too many. That's the kind of gift you give to your nosy mother-in-law or adult stepchildren who just won't go away. Just kidding," she amended hastily because of the look Sasha gave her.

Deftly shifting the conversation back to the problem at hand she said, "Sasha, when you met Abdul you knew that he had a fledgling business."

"I know, but there comes a time, or should come a time, when some of those idealistic dreams that we have when we're young change into reasonable goals. If that pie in the sky crap ain't working, it ain't working."

Seeing the woebegone look on Sasha's face, Tiara couldn't able to hold it in any longer. She laughed so loudly the couple at the next table stared. Once her laughter had subsided, she looked at Sasha and, with a serious edge to her voice said, "Sasha, you met him on New Year's Eve handing out leaflets in Times Square. You knew from the beginning that he wasn't the CEO of a major corporation."

Sasha didn't say anything for a while, just sat absently stirring her lukewarm cup of coffee. She said slowly, "It's not just that."

"There's more?" Tiara stared at her as she took another sip from her coffee cup. With a grimace of distaste, she set it back on the table.

Sasha now spoke very slowly. "He's different from when we first started going out." Then her next words came out in a rush, as if she had to say them in a hurry or not say them at all. "In the beginning, Abdul seemed very passionate about things. We would talk for hours about what we wanted to accomplish in our lives. He followed politics and we could discuss every current issue that was going on here or abroad. Now he doesn't watch the news because he says that everything you see on television is propaganda by the mainstream media in order to show Muslims in the worst possible light. Even though I didn't have the same religious beliefs that he had when we met, I felt that he truly believed in his faith. Now, sometimes I think that he uses it as an excuse not to do the things that I want to do or to have any fun."

"I've never heard you talk like this before. If you feel this strongly, why are you still with him? Girl, if I were you, I'd jump that ship as if it was the *Titanic*. It's not as if you owe him anything."

"I don't leave him because I know that he's faithful to me."

"How do you know?" Tiara looked at Sasha with a raised brow.

"If your man was cheating on you, he wouldn't give you a key to his place," she answered. "I can show up at Abdul's anytime I want, and I don't have to call and tell him I'm coming. Also, when I get there he's always alone or with his cousin." Sasha gave Tiara a tired look. "I've been cheated on before, and even before I found out for sure, I knew something wasn't quite right though I couldn't put my finger on it."

"I guess you would know then," Tiara acknowledged.

Sasha continued, "Fidelity is a big thing for me. Because of his upbringing, Abdul doesn't believe in fooling around with a lot of different women." Sasha drew in a deep breath. "As a nurse, you don't know how many times I've had to stand in an examination room while the doctor told a woman that she has a communicable disease or had tested positive for AIDS. It's heart-wrenching to watch. There's denial, and the patient declares that there's been a mix-up in the lab and insists that the doctor redo the whole testing process. After the second round of tests with the same result, the tears begin to fall, and then comes the anger. For days afterward I watch the news anxiously, hoping that a murder doesn't result from the information that I helped to deliver." Looking at Tiara, she added quietly, "And that's why I stay."

Tiara waved her ring hand at her and said, "And that's why I got married. It can be dangerous to be single in today's society. I can't believe people are still taking chances by sleeping around. It's like playing Russian roulette with your life. But Sasha, Abdul isn't the only man who doesn't cheat. There are others. Maybe you two should take a break."

"I can't leave him right now, not after this morning. It would be too cold. He would think that it's because he's poor." An image of Abdul's hurt yet angry face before she walked out of the apartment came to mind.

"I hear what you're saying, but after all you've just told me, I can't believe you gave Sexton the brush-off.

You don't run into men like him every day. You act as if they are everywhere." Tiara added with a smile, "And he has money."

Sasha grimaced. "Yeah, probably too much. He didn't have to pay for breakfast for everyone."

Tiara smiled. "I didn't get the feeling that he was showing off. I think that he was simply in too much of a hurry to wait for the waitress to divide up the bill."

"I know. But Sexton has only had two conversations with me, and each time he has come on to me as if he just has to have me. It makes me nervous. I'm sure that like most men, it's all about the thrill of the chase. If I had called him like I was supposed to after your party, I doubt he would have shown the interest he did today. If we had gone out he probably would have become bored with me halfway through the date. Obviously he's just flirting with me."

Tiara scoffed. "You're insane. Have you really ever looked at yourself? You're absolutely beautiful. Even Calvin said so the first time he met you."

"Really?" Sasha answered, surprised by this revelation. "That's news to me. I didn't think he even noticed me, he seemed totally engrossed in my sister Desiree."

Tiara looked away, then looked back at Sasha as if she was going to say something but changed her mind. "I think Sexton whisked you off to a corner before he got a chance to engage you in conversation."

"Can you imagine what Sexton's life must be like with women throwing themselves at him all the time? He doesn't even have to promise them anything. There's a real demand for rich, good-looking, Black men," Sasha said.

Tiara responded, "I think it might become boring after a while. Calvin travels with the team and he said that some of the players hang out all night right before a game at strip clubs, but usually he and Sexton just chill in the hotel room, relaxing and watching tapes of their opponents."

Sasha sighed. "I don't need or want a millionaire. I just wish that Abdul would lighten up, make his business a success, and take me to see *The Color Purple* on Broadway before it closes."

Tiara reached over and put her hand consolingly over Sasha's. "Call him. You'll smooth things over."

"I can do better than that. I'll stop by his store after he has a chance to cool off."

"Be a sport and take him out to dinner." Sasha and Tiara looked at each other before they chuckled at the irony of it.

CHAPTER 2

Sasha let herself into her loft and gave a sigh of satisfaction as she looked around at the décor. Mahogany furniture and accent pieces dominated her L-shaped living room and dining room combination. A forty-two inch LCD television hung on the wall facing her brown suede couch, overstuffed chair, and ottoman.

She kicked off her shoes on the hardwood floor, then walked down the long hallway to the bedroom. A queen-size bed, covered with an ecru comforter set that matched her wheat walls was the focus of the room. Matching nightstands flanked it. Sasha picked up her phone to check her caller I.D. and grimaced. There were no calls.

She bent over and withdrew from her overnight bag the uniform that she had worn to work the previous night and threw it in the hamper in the corner next to her closet. Then she stripped her clothes off and walked naked into the bathroom.

Standing in front of the closet doors that doubled as two full length mirrors, she eyed herself critically. She was proud of the fact that she had no scars on her body. Even after years of playing sports, her body was unmarred. Since working the night shift at the hospital, she had gained a little weight and it had all settled in her butt and breasts, yet she'd remained toned. Sasha made a mental note to schedule a trip to the store for new bras. The ones she had were too small and recently, when she had bent over to pick up a box of supplies at work, one of her boobs had popped out. Thankfully no one had seemed to notice that she'd remained bent over at the waist fidgeting with her clothing before straightening.

Sasha reached for the shower cap hanging on the bathroom door, and after stuffing her hair under it, stepped into the shower. The water pressure was stinging and relaxing at the same time. As she lathered her body her mind wandered back to the morning's events. The minute her eyes had met Sexton's she'd felt irresistibly drawn to him. Because of that, she had tried to mask it by being more offhand with him than she felt.

Now that she was alone with her thoughts, she had to admit that he was a spectacular specimen of man flesh. However, she felt guilty about feeling such an intense attraction to Sexton right after the bout of lovemaking with Abdul the previous night. Remembering this, she deliberately dragged her mind away from Sexton and concentrated on how to make things right with Abdul. Admittedly, his place was a dump, but Tiara was right in saying that she'd known that early on in their relationship.

Stepping out of the shower, she quickly dried off and after wrapping a towel around herself, lightly padded over to the nightstand and picked her telephone receiver off the hook and dialed the telephone number to Abdul's shop. It was answered on the fourth ring. A voice spoke rather sharply, "A Dose of Reality, Pandora speaking."

"Hello, Pandora, this is Sasha. May I speak with Abdul, please?"

There was silence and then a curt, "He's stepped out for a moment. Would you like to leave a message?"

She ignored the antagonism she heard in Pandora's voice and said, "Tell Abdul I'll be down in about an hour."

"Will do," was the only response before she heard the dial tone in her ear.

She muttered to herself as she dressed. "I'm going to talk to Abdul about her. She always has an attitude. I know that he doesn't pay her a lot, but she needs to conduct herself better than that."

She rode the subway to Harlem and sighed in exasperation when she returned to the sidewalk and caught the scent of rain. Glancing up the sky, she saw black clouds looming overhead. She began to stride more quickly, wanting to reach Abdul's shop before she got drenched in the imminent thunderstorm.

Spying the small gray building between a dog grooming shop and beauty parlor, she sprinted towards it, barely reaching it before a clap of thunder. The heavens suddenly seemed to open up.

Sasha slipped into Abdul's shop and slammed the door, breathing a sigh of relief at her narrow escape from a drenching. She looked around, surprised tht no one was behind the counter. Then she heard a sound from the storage area and went to the door, opened it, and stood transfixed.

Abdul was sitting in a leather chair with his head thrown back. His back was to the door and she could tell from his reflection in the cracked mirror that hung on the wall facing him that his eyes were closed. The only noises in the room were the sounds that came from him.

Sasha silently moved forward.

Pandora was down in her knees in front of Abdul, pleasuring him. She too looked to be in a state of ecstasy. The sight of what she had stumbled upon made Sasha hastily step back, bumping the door. Only then did they realize that they were not alone.

Abdul swiveled around in the chair. His surprise was quickly replaced by fear when he saw the look of total disgust on Sasha's face.

Her eyes then moved to Pandora. She had a sullen look as she slowly got up, shielding her body behind Abdul's chair. She unflinchingly held Sasha's eyes with hers.

Abdul stood and slowly zipped up the fly on his pants. He avoided Sasha's eyes and looked down at the floor as if he was studying some unseen object.

The room was as quiet as a tomb.

Sasha finally spoke, and her words sounded as icy as her expression. "I thought she was your cousin?"

"Pandora is my play cousin." Abdul looked down at his feet again and then up again at Sasha. "I'm sorry that you found us like this, but it's really not what you think," he stammered. "Occasionally we help each other out, when the need arises."

"But we were just together last night," Sasha replied dully. "What need could you have?"

"Don't get melodramatic. We never said that we're exclusive." Abdul's voice was strained as he tried to explain away his betrayal.

Sasha continued to stare at them. Then she looked at Pandora, and the pity she felt for her was reflected in her voice. She spoke to her slowly and clearly, as if talking to a mentally retarded person. "What makes this so sad is that you don't have enough sense or self-esteem to know how you're supposed to be treated. Every day you have been pretending that you're only his secretary. You've been content to stay in the background, waiting for the leftovers from another woman." She paused and now said musingly as if she were alone and thinking out loud, "Your mother must have really done a job on you."

"Don't you talk about my mother!" Pandora became so incensed at Sasha's words that her eyes seemed to bulge out of her head. "What does my mother have to do with this, anyway?"

"Women usually mimic the behavior of their mothers." Sasha stared her straight in the eye and shook her head sadly. "Somehow, somewhere, you've gotten the idea that it's okay to share a man."

"I'm a grown woman. I do what I want to do," Pandora retorted.

"So you're actually telling me that this is all you want from him?" Disbelief was evident on Sasha's face as she looked at her.

"Yes." Pandora stood and defiantly glared at Sasha even though she remained shielded by Abdul.

From deep within, the anger that had been building steadily from the moment she'd entered the room spewed out. "Good, because that's all you're going to get from him. The way you start a relationship is pretty much the way it's always going to be. You will always be just a back door 'ho' to him."

The unapologetic, now even triumphant look on Pandora's face made Sasha nauseous. She felt bile begin to rise and tried to quell it, but suddenly her body lurched forward and spilled the contents from her stomach down the front of Abdul's groin area. Once she'd finished, Sasha calmly reached over and tore off some paper towels from the roll on the desk. She calmly wiped her flushed face and took in the angry look on Abdul's face. "I could say I'm sorry that I vomited on you, but I don't want to be the hypocrite and liar you are," she said to Abdul, who sat there immobile, unable to speak.

Then she turned around and walked out of the room and out of the store and out of his life.

When Sasha got back outside she looked up at the clear sky surprised to find the thunderstorm had passed so quickly. Then she turned and saw the brightest rainbow she'd ever seen.

Hours later, she sat on the cream leather couch in Tiara's living room.

"Get out of here!" Tiara exclaimed once Sasha finished talking. She hadn't uttered a word throughout the entirety of Sasha's story, but her mouth had hung open and now she reached for her untouched glass of wine. She swallowed the contents in one draught. "Diddling the secretary. Abdul gets an 'F' for originality. And to think that I encouraged you to go and talk to that jerk to try and work through your differences. I feel awful."

"Well, I'm glad that you did," Sasha said quietly. "Otherwise, no telling when, if ever, I would have found out."

Tiara had a sudden thought and said, "Aren't they kin?" Tiara was horrified at the thought and her expression showed it.

"They're not blood," Sasha answered. "They just call themselves *play cousins.*"

"Girl, that's that ghetto mess. Black people are always going around claiming that they are related to people that they aren't. They use that as a cover to be nasty, and that sex buddy idea is for the birds. If I am sleeping with a man, I'm not going to pretend around others that we're just friends." Disgust at the afternoon's revelations showed clearly on Tiara's face.

"Now that I know what's going on I understand why Pandora would be so nasty to me whenever I called to talk to Abdul."

"Obviously that was nothing but jealousy." Tiara gave Sasha a quizzical look. "What does she look like?"

"Does it matter?" Sasha looked down.

"Not really, but I'm interested in knowing."

"She's really, really unattractive. And I'm being kind in my description. If anyone ever saw the two of them together they would never suspect that they're lovers," Sasha added with disgust. "I would have never suspected Abdul of sleeping with someone like her."

"That's what makes it the perfect cover-up. Ugly women are the worst. Men say that they don't want beautiful women because they're too high maintenance, but the truth of the situation is that they like ugly women because they are so desperate they're willing to go back door. Ugly women are far more deadly when it comes to men because they go for the jugular. They are willing to sneak and put up with anything in order to have a piece of a man. Girl, women with low self-esteem are the cheating man's dream. No matter what you might say about Abdul, he is handsome. I guess Pandora really thought that she was doing something by making him cheat on you with her," Tiara finished.

"She didn't make him cheat on me. She just made it easy for him to do so."

"Well, I guess it's true what they say."

"What?"

"A stiff dick has no conscience," Tiara retorted, angry on her friend's behalf. She continued, "And to be named

Pandora. That name itself is a conversation piece. Abdul puts new meaning to the phrase 'opening Pandora's box.' "

"I feel so humiliated." Sasha began to weep quietly, wiping her tears from her cheeks with the back of her hand.

Tiara moved over and sat close to her on the couch, putting her arm around her shoulders. She said consolingly, "You have nothing to feel embarrassed about. You didn't know."

Again Sasha wiped her tears with the back of her hand. "I don't know why I'm crying. I've known for some time that I'm not in love with Abdul, at least not the kind of love that makes a person want to marry someone and be with them forever."

Tiara very calmly got up and returned with a box of tissues. She handed it to Sasha. "You're crying because you think that you've been duped. No one likes to be taken advantage of," Tiara nodded her head in understanding.

Sasha continued to cry. "To think that I wasted two years with that loser."

"Don't think of it as a waste of two years. Think of it as a saving of many years to come."

"I know. But I thought that he was basically a good person. You don't know the opportunities I've missed out on because of him. Everyone gets sick sooner or later. Working in the hospital I meet a lot of eligible men. Did I tell you that Abdul tried to excuse his behavior by saying that we weren't exclusive?"

"That does take a lot of nerve," Tiara agreed. Then she said, as a way to lighten the atmosphere, "Actually, the timing is perfect for you to find out about this. There's a silver lining in this cloud. Now you can go out with Sexton with a clear conscience," Tiara prompted with a note of encouragement in her voice.

Sasha shook her head negatively from side to side. "Are you crazy? If a man like Abdul, with absolutely nothing going for him, could lead a double life, what do you think that Sexton is capable of?"

"So now you're going to lump all men together because of what Abdul has done? Shame on you, Sasha."

"I don't think all men are like Abdul," she denied. "I just want to be by myself for awhile. No more drama."

"But Sexton seems to really like you and he's not going to be available forever. I say strike while the iron is hot. That's why I snapped Peter up."

"But Abdul has caused me to doubt myself. I've thought myself a good judge of character. Now I've lost confidence in my judgment."

"Well, I'm glad that I have Peter," Tiara said with relief. "Being single these days is for the birds."

For the second time that day, Sasha let herself into her apartment and walked to her bedroom. From the doorway she could see the red blinking light on her answering machine. She pressed the message button and heard a series of hang-ups before she heard Abdul's voice which held an obvious sense of urgency, "Sasha, I've been calling you for hours. I'm sorry about what you found out, but there's more to it than that. Give me a chance to explain. Call me."

"About what I found out?" She screwed up her face. "You're not sorry about what you've been doing?" Sasha held down the delete button on her machine until she heard the automated voice, "Messages have been deleted." Then she stripped off her clothing and headed for the bathroom to try shower away the stench of the day's events.

CHAPTER 3

St. Mary's Hospital was one of the busiest in Manhattan. There was a newly built cardiac unit and a sports conditioning unit that housed the latest equipment in the tri-state area. It had been recognized nationally for the last three years as best in customer satisfaction.

Sasha was in the process of dictating notes into her voice recorder when she felt three light taps on her shoulder. When she looked up and saw her favorite patient standing next to her, she ceased her dictation and gently scolded him. "Mr. Ramirez, what are you doing out here in the hall? You know that you're not supposed to be wandering around. It's dangerous to your health."

Mr. Ramirez answered grumpily, "It can't be more dangerous than letting some of these first-year interns work on me."

Sasha smiled at him and whispered conspiratorially, "You don't have to worry about that. Every time they leave your room I go behind them and check your chart to make sure that you're being well taken care of."

Mr. Ramirez's voice was plaintive. "Good, because that last guy had no bedside manner at all. I needed to use the bathroom while he was there and he wouldn't help me. He said that he would send for a nurse. I waited for twenty minutes or so before she got there. It was only by the will of God that I didn't pee on myself."

"You should have called for me. I wouldn't have minded coming to your aid."

"I don't want to be more of a pain to you than I already am. As it is, you stay after work an extra hour every night just to keep me company." He blinked away tears at the mention of the kindness Sasha had shown him since he had been admitted into the hospital three weeks ago.

Sasha gently turned Mr. Ramirez back in the direction of his room and once there, she steadied him as he slid onto the bed. Though he made no noise, his facial expression showed the spasms of pain he felt at every movement. She pressed the button on the side of the bed, raising the back of it until he was in a comfortable sitting position.

"Don't you dare thank me," she ordered. "I do that for me just as much as you. You're the only one that I can get a decent game of cards with."

"What about your fella? Doesn't he play cards?"

Sasha hesitated before speaking and then she said brusquely, "No, and it doesn't matter now. We broke up."

"So you got tired of him, huh? I'm not surprised. You two had nothing in common," Mr. Ramirez replied with conviction.

"That's not exactly what happened. He was cheating on me and I caught him at it." Sasha's eyes flashed fire when she thought about her previous day's discovery.

"Usually when a man cheats on a beautiful and successful woman it's because he's insecure."

Sasha shook her head in denial. "Abdul wasn't insecure. As a matter of fact, he was too secure," she added sarcastically.

"Has he called you to make up?" Mr. Ramirez asked.

"He's left some messages on my phone, but I haven't returned his calls. Without going into detail, I can never forgive him for what he's done." Sasha was quiet for a moment and then said, "And there's absolutely nothing he can say to change how I feel."

Her telephone was ringing when she entered the apartment. Giving a sigh from sheer tiredness, Sasha slowly walked over to her answering machine. As she reached to pick up the receiver she heard Abdul's angry voice: "Sasha, I know that you're standing there listening to me. You are so childish by not at least returning my calls."

Sasha stared at the answering machine with hands on hips, tapping her foot impatiently as she listened.

His next words sounded threatening, and Sasha raised her eyebrows at the arrogance of his tone.

"Sasha, I'm not going to call you again. You call me when you grow up!" There was silence before, "Then maybe we can straighten this thing out!"

The next thing she heard was the harsh sound of the phone on the other end being slammed down. She calmly reached over and once again pushed the delete button.

Sasha rolled over in bed to look at the digital clock on her nightstand. She groaned when she realized that it was four o'clock in the afternoon and she had slept away most of the day. The banging on the door that had awakened her sounded impatient, but she continued to lie still, willing the intruder to go away.

Then the banging ceased and she heard the sound of the doorbell. She resignedly got up and went to the door. Looking through the peephole, she saw that it was Tiara causing all the ruckus. She grabbed the doorknob and opened the door.

"What on earth is wrong with you?" Sasha demanded. "You're making enough noise to wake the dead."

"Apparently not!" Tiara retorted. "I've been pounding on that door for at least five minutes. Why haven't you been answering your telephone? I've tried to reach you for days, and then I began to worry. I haven't heard from you since you left my house the night you caught Abdul doing the nasty with Miss Thang. Are you okay?" Concern was etched on Tiara's features as she searched Sasha's face.

Sasha brushed Tiara's concern aside as she beckoned her into the loft. "Of course I'm fine. I've been working third shift and I've been cutting the ringer off when I get home because I don't feel like answering all of the nuisance calls from telemarketers that you get during the daytime."

"Oh," Tiara responded in relief. "Is that all? I thought that Abdul might be giving you a hard time and you were in here playing possum."

"No. He hasn't called for a week or so. He called for a while and left some not-so-nice messages."

"I know he didn't. Where in the world does he get off?"

"I think he was trying to brazen it out, girl." Sasha half-laughed. "You know how when people are wrong about stuff they try to play it off and go on the offensive."

Tiara snickered and then asked, "Aren't you going to hear him out? It might be amusing, if nothing else."

Sasha drawled, "Naw, I don't think so. I don't have the patience or the time. He's gotten too much of that already."

"You're different from me. Before I got married, whenever I broke up with a guy, even if I knew that I wasn't going to take him back I let him take a stab at it. It's always a good conversation piece for your girlfriends."

"If I thought that we could work it out, I would listen to him, but we can't, so why bother?"

"I must say that you're being very mature about this. It's obvious that you never really loved Abdul or you couldn't let it go so easily."

"I know you're right." Then Sasha walked a circle around Tiara and gave a long whistle. She leaned towards her and sniffed. "Obsession?"

"Of course. You know that's my signature perfume. It's like a fine wine, and never has a shelf life."

"You sure look mighty fine for a Saturday afternoon. What are you doing all gussied up? You and Peter have a hot date?" Tiara was wearing a silk shirt with small pearl buttons. Her short hair was parted on the side, and diamond studs accented her carefully made up face.

Tiara gave a frustrated snort. "I wish. We were supposed to be going to the Knicks game tonight with the tickets Calvin got me, but Peter called and said he's stuck in Boise. That's why I'm here. I want you to go to the game with me."

"No, thanks. I'm not in the mood."

"But you have to come with me," Tiara wheedled. "I don't want to go by myself, and Calvin put himself out to drop these tickets off at my house. Please, just for me."

"Oh, all right," Sasha gave in. "I know better than to stand around arguing with you when you get that look on your face. What time do we have to get there? I need to shower."

"Tip off is at seven-thirty, but we have plenty of time. Calvin sent the team's chauffeur, Stefan, in a Hummer limo to get me and Peter, so I had him drive me over here when I couldn't get you on the telephone. He's downstairs waiting."

"You're kidding, aren't you?"

"Now would I make up something like that? Girl, we're going to the game in style. When we show up at the stadium and get out people will think we're really somebody."

Sasha laughed. "Too bad the reality is that we're just like Cinderella, and all of our trappings are on loan."

"Well, if you get with Sexton you could live the life of Riley all of the time and I could be your sidekick."

Sasha had turned and started for her bedroom, but she stopped and looked back at Tiara. "I refuse to go if you are going start waving me under Sexton's nose like I'm some mare and he's a stallion."

Tiara laughed at Sasha's description but promised, "Okay, I'll stop."

Once they got situated in the limo, they filled their glasses with champagne from the bottle in the bar that was located behind a partition. "Some people really know how to live, don't they?" Tiara said as she sank back into the sumptuous leather.

Sasha kicked off her heels, showing off her French pedicure.

"They sure do. But don't you think that this would get boring after a while?" she asked, raising an eyebrow.

"I wouldn't mind trying to see." Tiara mimicked her friend's mannerism.

As the limo approached Madison Square Garden, traffic slowed to a crawl. While Stefan navigated through the congestion of people and cars, pedestrians peered through the tinted windows, attempting to see who was arriving in the team's signature mode of transportation.

When Stefan pulled up to the curb, he quickly jumped out of the front seat and walked around one side to open the door for Tiara to exit. Once she was standing upright, she lifted her arms high above her head and gave herself a good stretch. Then Stefan walked around to the other side and opened the door for Sasha. She joined Tiara and, with a smile, copied her.

A group of interested bystanders milled nearby. A teenage boy shouted out to them, "Are you ladies stars or something?"

Sasha and Tiara caught each other's eye and decided to have some fun. Sasha looked at him, widened her eyes, and said, "Are you telling me that you don't recognize us?"

The boy hesitated for a moment and then said, "Yeah, I know who you are now. I saw the two of you on a video. You sure looked good in those bikinis."

Sasha and Tiara looked at each other, barely able to stop themselves from laughing. Tiara said, "Thanks for making our day. Now we know that we've arrived."

Stefan had stood quietly watching the scene and with a playful smirk on his lips said, "If you ladies like, I can lead you through the VIP entrance. You're sitting in the seats behind the team, so there's no need for you to go through the turnstiles."

Nodding their heads in agreement, they followed Stefan to the side entrance. Sasha walked gingerly because she too, had donned a pair of skinny jeans and stilettos. The only difference between her outfit and Tiara's was the color of their shirts because Sasha's was a pale yellow.

Once they reached their seats, Sasha turned to their escort, reached in her pocketbook, withdrew a ten-dollar bill, and held it out to him.

"No thank you, ma'am. Mr. Calvin already took care of it."

"Stefan, you've been so kind."

He nodded his head at her and replied, "It's been my pleasure. Enjoy your evening."

The energy in Madison Square Garden was one that could not be duplicated in any other arena. The Knicks were warming up and Sasha automatically started scanning the area looking for Sexton. He was on his back in the middle of the basketball court, and a trainer had his leg raised perpendicular to his torso. Sexton continued to stretch, bending his knees several times before he switched legs. The trainer nodded at him, then walked over to another player and began bending his legs so that his knees hit his chest. Sasha turned excitedly to Tiara and said, "I'm glad you talked me into coming. I love live basketball games. I haven't been in a while, and I've never had a spot so close to the team. I feel so special."

Tiara laughed. "I know. Too bad I'm married. Believe me, if I wasn't I'd do some early Christmas shopping."

"Just look for fun, girlfriend. There's no harm in that."

"None at all," Tiara agreed.

They sat watching the teams practice on the court. Some were dribbling lay-ups and others three-point shots. Sasha studied the long length of Sexton's body as he ran around the court. With every step he took she saw the muscles in his legs tense and veins stand out prominently.

Her attention was diverted when she saw Calvin walking towards them. He was dressed in a navy blue pinstriped suit, set off by a white shirt. *Calvin really knew how to dress.*

He looked at Sasha and said, "My goodness, Peter. You sure have changed since the last time I saw you."

Sasha and Tiara laughed and Tiara explained, "Peter is still stuck out of town on business so I brought Sasha.

I didn't want to sit alone because I knew that you would be too busy with the team to pay me any real attention."

"Good idea," Calvin replied. "Where are you ladies going after the game?"

"Home," Tiara said, "why?"

"Some of the team members are planning to get together at a club later. Would you like to join us?" He looked at them.

"Sounds good to me. How about you, Sasha?" Tiara asked.

"Sure, it sounds like fun. Do I need to go home and change?"

"No, it's a private club. You have to be a member or be invited by a member to get in. We go there in order to relax. The players like it because they aren't bothered with fans who gawk and want autographs." He looked at the middle of the court where the players were forming a line. "I have to go. Meet me outside at the west entrance after the game because that's where the valet brings our cars."

~~~

After they stood for the national anthem, Sasha was looking around when she felt as if she was being watched. Her eyes were drawn to the basketball court. Sexton was watching her. Across the expanse of the arena their eyes locked.

A warm sensation coursed through her body and filtered down to her abdomen. Feeling surprised and a little shaken, she squirmed under his piercing stare. Trying to break the spell, she signaled to a vendor walking by with a tray of beverages. She turned to Tiara. "Do you want a drink?"

"Sure, why not?" Tiara began to reach into her pocketbook and Sasha stopped her by placing her hand on hers. "This is on me. It's the least I can do. I would never have been able to afford to sit here."

"These seats aren't for sale anyhow. They're reserved for special people."

"Then I guess we are really are the stars we pretended to be to that teenager outside." She turned to the vendor hovering at her side. "I'll take two beers."

Handing one to Tiara she said, "I wish I hadn't drunk that champagne earlier. I don't like to mix my liquor."

"Don't worry about it. Calvin will look out for you if you get tipsy."

"I think that he's done enough for me as it is." Sasha took a swig from the beer. Over the rim she looked to see if Sexton was still watching her, but he had sat down on the bench with his teammates and was listening to what the coach was saying.

From tip-off, the teams battled for every basket. Every time one of the Knicks made a basket the fans screamed and threw confetti. The tempo of the music was upbeat, and Sasha and Tiara moved in their seats with music that they liked.

At the half, Sasha turned to Tiara and asked with an overly casual tone, "Do you think that Sexton is going to play tonight?"

"I don't know. He's not a starter because he's one of the newer players, but I think that he does get some playing time."

"I'm going to the ladies' room before the line gets too long."

"You go ahead. I'll wait here."

"I shouldn't have had that second beer. Good thing that I'm not driving."

As Sasha stood at the sink washing her hands she suddenly felt the hairs on her neck stand up. The mirror reflected Pandora standing behind her. The look on Pandora's face was so malevolent that Sasha's body tensed up though she returned her stare.

After what seemed an eternity of silence, Sasha calmly reached for a paper towel and dried her hands. Instead of walking over to the large garbage can where Pandora stood, she balled the paper towel she had used and aimed at the can. She hit her mark and without looking back, she confidently strolled out of the restroom.

When she returned to her seat she said to Tiara, "Guess what?"

"What?"

"I just ran into Pandora in the ladies' room."

"You've got to be kidding." Tiara's eyes widened in surprise. "What happened?"

"I think that she was trying to intimidate me. When I looked up she was standing behind me staring me down."

"That chick is a real hood rat. She needs to be apologizing instead of trying to front."

Sasha agreed. "I know. But she really doesn't have anything to say or she would have. I mean, it was just like I was in high school again," she scoffed, throwing up her hands in mock horror. "Trying to look so threatening that I'm supposed to be scared or something."

"That's what they call selling wolf tickets." Tiara snorted in disgust. "You missed the halftime show, and it also was kind of interesting."

"Oh, yeah? That's unusual. I usually find them kind of dull."

"Not this time. The cheerleaders were out on the floor doing their thing and one fell. She got up in a hurry and continued her dance, but it was some kind of funny."

"I'd be so embarrassed. It's not like it's worth it or anything. I heard that these girls don't make any real money. The pay is something like one hundred dollars a game."

"You're kidding. Why would you bust your butt for chump change like that?"

"Well, I guess for the exposure. They do get seen by millions of people and get on television. They probably all want to be a model, actress, or a singer."

"A bunch of Paula and Jennifer knock-offs," Tiara laughed. "And if that doesn't work out they can always get pregnant by one of the players. If he doesn't want to marry her, she can put child support on him. You can't be a cheerleader forever. You need to have a plan B."

"I think that would be an awful way to live, totally dependent on a man. That's not the life for me."

"Me, either," Tiara agreed.

Their attention was drawn to a commotion where the cheerleaders were sitting. Sasha at first assumed that a fan had become unruly because the security guards were in the midst of the small group of people. Then they dispersed the group and a guard led one of the cheerleaders out of the arena. Another cheerleader and guard soon followed.

Sasha and Tiara gave each other speculative looks.

"What in the world do you think is going on?"

Tiara replied, "I don't know. But one of those cheerleaders being led out of here is the one that fell."

"I'm dying to know what happened."

Tiara pretended to admonish her. "You are too nosy, girl."

"Don't even try it. You know that you want to know as much as I do."

Tiara laughed good-naturedly. "I sure do. I'm going to text Calvin and see if he knows what's going on." Tiara pulled out her cell phone and they watched Calvin. When he pulled the phone out of his pocket, he read the message, looked over at them, and then texted back, "The Asian cheerleader tripped that other girl on purpose. They're fighting over Sexton and he doesn't want either of them."

"Damn!" Tiara said. "He has cheerleaders fighting over him in public. He must be a keeper!" She jokingly moved her body suggestively on the bench.

Sasha stared at the back of Sexton's head. He had never even looked in the direction of the cheerleaders. His head was tilted towards the scoreboard which showed that the game was tied.

Sexton said at breakfast that he was all that! "He must be good," she murmured quietly to herself.

The third quarter was even more exciting than the first two. Each team had two technical fouls from the referees for questioning calls and the Knicks were ahead by only one point. When there was less than a minute left, Sasha and Tiara stood with the rest of the crowd as a point guard for the Knicks dribbled down the court. As he went up for the lay-up, two basketball players from the other team rushed him and he went down.

A gasp went up from the crowd as the referees blew their whistles. The two women saw Calvin and the coaches rush to the basketball court and crowd around the down player. Sasha held her breath, knowing that the longer the player was down, the more serious his condition was. After a minute or two a stretcher was wheeled out and the injured player lifted and placed on the gurney. Calvin followed as it was quickly wheeled off the court.

At the beginning of the fourth quarter, Sexton pulled off his hoodie and joined his other team members at the foul line. He made two baskets to deafening noise from the crowd. Tension was high between the two teams, and they became even more aggressive against each other. Sasha felt mesmerized as she watched Sexton. He ran from one end of the court to the other and dribbled and passed, doing whatever was needed to score.

Tapping Tiara on the arm she exclaimed, "Did you see that? Sexton's ambidextrous!"

Tiara nodded her head, smiling at the lilt in Sasha's voice and her enthusiastic expression when she commented on Sexton's basketball skills. Tiara looked at the scoreboard and said, "There is only room for one more play if they don't go into overtime."

"I hope they can prevent them from scoring," Sasha said, mentally crossing her fingers.

Just then the point guard from the other team looked at the clock and hurled the ball towards the basket. The ball bounced off the rim and three Knicks clamored for it. Sexton took possession of the ball and began a leisurely trot down towards the Knicks basket. In the remaining seconds, the crowed stood to their feet. Just before the buzzer went off, Sexton hurled the ball towards the basket. The ball dropped neatly into the basket and the Knicks won. The fans went wild and danced to the Knicks' theme song as if every person in the arena was a champion. As the music blared and the fans filed out of the stands, Sexton separated himself from the crowd and stood alone in the middle of the basketball court. For the second time that evening, their eyes locked, and this time Sexton gave her a slow wink.

CHAPTER 4

They stood outside the arena at the V.I.P. entrance. The night air had cooled considerably and Sasha shivered slightly.

Tiara noticed and said, "I'm going to text message Calvin. His plans may have changed because of that injured player."

Just then, Calvin emerged from the side door. "Ready, ladies?" he asked before heading towards the white Lexus that was parked at the curb in front of them.

Sasha sat quietly in the back seat listening to Tiara and Calvin.

"Honestly, when I first met Peter he rarely had to travel," she complained. "Now it seems as if he's gone all of the time. He said that he was going to be only gone three days, and it's turned into five. If I had known this, I wouldn't have quit teaching."

"I don't know why you quit in the first place. You always loved your job."

"Peter talked me into it. It takes a lot to keep a household running smoothly and as a teacher I was overworked and underpaid."

Calvin frowned. "I know that, sis, but now you seem bored. Maybe you should go back to work, at least part-time."

"I would have to substitute until I got my certificate renewed. That's not even teaching. It's just babysitting. Ninety-five dollars a day isn't much for combat pay."

"How long would it take for you to get your certificate reinstated? Calvin asked.

"I need three hundred hours." She paused for a moment, thinking. "Maybe I'll pick up those hours so that I can go back to work part-time."

"That would be good for you, Tiara. That way you would have your own money and still have enough free time to make sure everything at home goes smoothly."

"I have my own money," she corrected him with a slight attitude. "Peter's money is my money."

"I know that, Tiara, but you still have to account to him for the money that you do spend," he replied without rancor. "No one should be completely dependent on another for financial stability."

"I do think that teaching half a day is the perfect solution," Tiara said, ignoring Calvin's remark. "I'll talk to Peter about it."

Calvin pulled up to a small building. Two men who looked like sentinels flanked a wooden door. Seeing the limos, luxury cars, and sport utility vehicles parked out in front, Sasha knew this must be the secret hang-out.

Calvin turned off the ignition and announced, "We're here."

"It doesn't look very crowded," Tiara said doubtfully.

"Looks can be very deceiving. This place is so exclusive they don't even have the name on the door. If you're allowed to be here, you know where it is. People walk by and don't even realize that it is a nightclub. Some actors come here in order to unwind. If they do something outrageous and it hits the paper, the owners move hell and high water to find out who the leak was and that person is politely asked not to return."

"If that's the case, are you sure that Sasha and I can get in?" Tiara looked doubtful.

"Of course you can. You're with me."

Sasha brought up the rear behind Calvin and Tiara and nodded at the doorman as he stepped aside and allowed them to enter.

She looked around in amazement when she stood inside. The outside was nondescript but the inside was opulent. On one side there were leather couches designed for two people, and in front of each there was a small cocktail table. Nearby lamps provided subdued lighting. In the middle of the room, women and men sat at high chairs at a long bar. Other people clustered in groups of two or three and still others sat alone nursing a drink and swaying to the music.

Even though the club wasn't brightly lit, Sasha recognized an up-and-coming star who the tabloids had reported was doing a stint in rehab. She unconsciously shook her head. The flushed look on his face said he had already had too much to drink, yet he was ordering another round.

"Would you ladies like to sit down over there?"

"Sure!" they replied in unison.

Calvin led them over to an area with booths. Once they were seated, Tiara pointed to the black plaque that had the number sixty-nine painted in red on it.

"What does that number mean?" Tiara asked drolly. "Besides the obvious?"

"That's our extension. If someone in the club wants to hook up with someone sitting here in the booth, all they have to do is dial that number and our phone will ring. This place is the hook-up of all hook-ups," he laughed.

"Then why in the world did you pick this booth? I'm sure Freud could come up with a psychiatric interpretation of that," Sasha teased.

"Actually I didn't think about it. There's an empty booth over there with the number three on it. Do you want to move to that one?"

Sasha and Tiara laughed.

"No, thanks. We don't do threesomes." she said as she slid into the booth, "I guess anybody can make any of these booths have an underlying message if they want to."

"Where are your teammates?" Sasha asked, sounding a little too casual.

With perfect timing, Sexton entered the nightclub. Closely following him was a cheerleader who had been at the game. Sexton quickly surveyed the room and, once he spied them, he bent down and whispered something into the girl's ear. She stood there for a second and then, with a frustrated look, stomped out of the club in an obvious huff.

Sasha gave Sexton the once-over. He was wearing a pair of charcoal gray pants paired with a black short-sleeved mock collar black shirt. Her eyes wandered to the black leather loafers with tassels he was wearing. A waitress walked over to him and she saw a flash of his white teeth as he talked to her.

He approached their table and grinned at them. Standing in front of their booth he said, "I notice that no one is drinking. Is this going to be a dry night?" He lifted one eyebrow quizzically.

Sexton slid into the booth next to her and when his knee touched hers, a feeling of excitement shot through her. She felt herself squirming from Sexton's proximity. When she looked up she saw the knowing look on Tiara's face and tried to calm her desire.

"No way it's a dry night," Calvin denied. "We had just gotten seated when you got here."

"Good. I told the waitress to bring me some Don Pérignon. I know champagne's not the latest popular drink, but I like it."

"So do I," Tiara beamed. "It reminds me of my wedding."

"Is that all you think about, Tiara?" Calvin's tone was caustic. "You did have a life before you became Peter's wife."

"I know that," she said tersely. "Don't hate me because I found my soul mate."

Sexton interceded before Calvin could answer. "Do you believe in soul mates, Sasha?"

"I don't know." She shrugged her shoulders. "He may be out there, but I haven't met him yet."

"How do you know?" Sexton countered.

"Well, if someone is your soul mate, aren't you supposed to know the minute you meet him?"

"I don't think that you would necessarily know your soul mate the minute you met him, but you probably would when you really got to know him."

Just then the waitress showed up with two bottles of champagne and glasses. She popped the cork on one and Sexton reached into his pocket. Sasha couldn't see the amount of money he slipped her, but she practically danced away from the table.

"Congratulations on winning the game. You were great!" Tiara complimented him.

He nodded his head in her direction. "Thank you."

"I noticed that you're ambidextrous. Do you get that from your parents?" Sasha asked as she sipped from her glass.

"I don't know," Sexton responded, "I was adopted."

A thick silence descended on the table. "Now, everyone, don't get all quiet on me. You don't have to feel sorry for me. The best people in the world raised me. They took a truculent seven-year-old out of foster care and gave him a good life. I doubt if I would be where I am today if it were not for them. My parents taught me that everything happens for a reason."

"It's good that you're so well adjusted," Sasha responded with admiration in her voice. 'I hear so many horror stories about the foster care system that I cringe anytime I hear that someone has been through it."

"It wasn't all fun and games, but I made the best of it." The finality in his tone indicated that he was through discussing his time in foster care system.

"How is that player they had to take out on the stretcher?" Tiara turned to Calvin.

"Anthony's going to be fine. He'll be back in the next game. He got an elbow to the eye and was temporarily blinded, but he's already feeling better," Calvin answered with certainty.

"He'd say that he feels better even if he didn't," Sexton added a little sarcastically as he refilled their glasses with champagne.

"You don't want him to be hurt so that you can play, do you?" Sasha admonished him before she stopped to think that it wasn't her place.

"Of course not," Sexton replied, not at all offended. "But I've been on the team for more than a year. I would like a little more playing time."

"Well, you're certainly good enough. I would have thought that you would be starting," Tiara complimented.

"That was the bait promised to me when I joined the team, but all the while I knew that it might not be happening right away."

"Did you play for another team?" Sasha asked in surprise.

"I played ball overseas for a couple of years."

"Oh, I didn't know that," Tiara said. "But then, why would I? I hate to admit it, but I'm not a big sports fan so I don't know all the background to basketball and its athletes."

Their attention was drawn to the fanfare on the other side of the room as other members of the team made their presence known.

Sasha recognized Anthony as the injured player because he had a patch over one eye.

He walked over to their table and he and Sexton shook hands. "Thanks for taking over for me. If it wasn't for you we might not have won."

Sexton responded graciously, "Thanks, man."

Anthony looked at the women at the table and said, "You ladies are some fine looking women." He laughed and looked at Sexton. "Hey, you should encourage them to try out for our cheerleading squad since it seems that we're going to have two openings."

"Is that the verdict?" Calvin asked.

"I guess so. I overheard the coaches talking, and they said that maybe we should try out some more girls. Any suggestions, Sexton?"

"Don't even go there. I had nothing to do with that drama," Sexton answered. "Rosemary and I dated over a year ago, and the only time that I've even had a conversation with Monique was last week when I gave her a ride home because her car was in the shop."

"Sure, man, whatever you say." Anthony looked over his shoulder. "I'm parched, so I guess I'll make my way to the bar."

Sexton watched Anthony's retreat with a not-too-pleased look. "His mouth is probably parched from running it too much. I wonder what made him think that I had something to do with that mess?"

"Then why did you come here with that other cheerleader?" The minute Sasha spoke the words she wished that she could retract them. She sounded like a jealous fishwife.

"We met at the door on the way in. That's all. And by the way, thank you for noticing. That makes my night."

She felt uncomfortable that she hadn't been able to conceal her awareness for someone she had previously pretended a disinterest in. She averted her eyes from the smirks of Tiara and Calvin and took a sip of champagne. In her haste to distract the others, she inadvertently picked up Sexton's and drained it.

He said teasingly, "That was mine, but I don't mind."

"Oh no, I'm sorry." Feeling even more mortified, she said, "Let me get you another glass from the waitress."

"I wouldn't hear of it." Sexton lifted the empty glass and put his lips on the rim at the exact spot where Sasha's lipstick had left a print.

Trying to help her friend out, Tiara asked, "Don't people dance in here? And where is the deejay booth?"

Calvin pointed. "See those stairs? There's another floor upstairs and that's where the majority of the dancing takes place."

"I certainly like the music that has been playing so far." Rhythm and blues, combined with the sounds of Motown from the sixties, seventies, and eighties, had been playing since they had arrived.

Tiara turned to her brother when she heard the next song. "I love the theme from *Soul Train*. Let's go, Calvin." She ordered Sasha and Sexton, "You guys, come on."

Upstairs there was a huge dance floor, and Sasha was surprised to see so many twenty-somethings trying to outdo each other as they jammed to the oldies but goodies.

As Sexton danced in the crowd he towered above many of the other males. Sasha was not surprised to see that Sexton could hold a beat on the dance floor because so far it appeared as if he did everything well. He was not the flamboyant dancer that Calvin was, twirling and snapping his fingers, but he was smooth and obviously comfortable on the floor.

At the end of the song, the deejay slowed the tempo and she recognized the baritone voice of Barry White.

Sexton held out his hand to her in order to draw her closer. She placed hers into his and felt herself folded into his arms. He held her tight as they danced sinuously. As they danced, she was vaguely aware of Tiara and Calvin leaving the dance floor.

"Did you ever get a chance to meet him?" he whispered in her ear.

"Who?" she whispered softly as she settled into the security of Sexton's arms.

"Barry, before he left us way too early."

"Of course not," she answered, startled by the question. "What would ever make you think that I did?" Sasha's voice was so clouded with desire it sounded unfamiliar to her.

"Because I think he must have had you in mind when he wrote a song about a woman worth a million dollars."

Sasha smothered a laugh. She knew it was a line, but still she felt flattered. She didn't recognize the scent of Sexton's cologne, but combined with sexual intensity it almost overwhelmed her. All of a sudden she felt a response from Sexton's body. It seemed as if a rod had somehow been placed between them, and she felt a surge of gratification when she realized that she had on him the same effect he had on her.

Sasha felt moistness between her thighs, and when her body jerked in response to his she realized that there was enough moisture to leak out of her thong underwear.

Sexton felt her movements and slightly eased his hold on her. He looked down. "Am I holding you too close?"

"No." She was breathless, and he had to bend his head even closer in order to catch her words.

She didn't see the satisfied smile on his lips as he laid his head on top of hers and left it there. They danced to the next three songs as if they were floating on air.

Afterwards Sexton led her down the stairs, holding her hand tightly. Sasha didn't know if it was because he feared her slipping in the dim light, but she loved the possessive way his hand clung to hers. When they reached their booth he stepped aside and allowed her to slide in.

He sat down next to her, and after glancing around the room gave her a questioning look.

Interpreting it correctly she shrugged her shoulders and said, "I don't know where they went."

The telephone in their booth rang and Sexton reached for it. "Hello? I don't think that she's interested, but I'll ask her." Holding the receiver out to her he said, "There's a man on the telephone who would like to speak to you. Are you interested?"

Sasha shook her head no. "I think that I have all the man that I can handle sitting here already."

Sexton gave her a sexy smile before he said, "She's not interested." He hung up the telephone, then took it off the receiver and let it hang so that they would not be interrupted again.

"Tell me what Sasha Diamond likes to do for fun." Sexton slid his arm around her shoulders and let it rest on the back of the booth.

As she reached for her half empty glass of champagne, Sexton stilled her hand and reached for the bottle in order to refill her glass. Then he reached into his pocket and withdrew his cellphone. He frowned as he read the text message. He reread it, frowned again and looked at Sasha. "They left. Calvin said that something came up and he would call me in the morning."

"What on earth happened?" Sasha asked.

"I don't know. He didn't say, but it can't be too much or I think he would have called instead of text messaging me."

"I guess so. Tiara and I were supposed to catch a cab downtown."

"I'll see you home. You're too beautiful to be running around at this time of night alone. New York City can be a dangerous place."

"Danger comes in many forms," Sasha responded flirtatiously from under her eyelashes.

"I got that," he said. "You have nothing to fear from me, Miss Diamond. I have only good things in mind for you."

"Is that so?" Sasha queried. The sexual undercurrent of their conversation was so obvious that Sasha decided to be upfront about what she was thinking. "How much longer do you want to stay here?"

Sexton looked down at his watch. The gold band glistened in the lighting. "Oh, about thirty seconds."

Sasha grinned. "Suits me just fine. I'm ready to leave if you are."

Once outside Sexton handed the valet a slip and waited for his car to be brought around.

"We've had more than a few drinks. Are you okay to drive?" Sasha asked.

"Thank you for caring. I guess that's the nurse in you. Because of my size I can have a little more than the average person. Even with three glasses of champagne I'm not over the legal limit."

"Good thing," Sasha said with relief. "I would hate to see you, or us for that matter in the arrested column tomorrow. I can't think of anything more humiliating."

When the valet stopped in front of them, Sasha was thrilled to see that Sexton was driving her dream car. His black Chrysler Hemi 300 sparkled and for the second time that night, she compared herself to Cinderella the night of the ball when she met her Prince Charming. She mentally chided herself. *Sexton is fine and nicer than you expected a pro basketball player to be, but do not lose your grip on reality. See this for what it probably is, a bootie call. Don't read anything long term into it.*

Once seated inside the sumptuous interior of the sedan, Sasha leaned back. "I live on 119th Street on the east side of Manhattan."

Neither spoke during the drive, content to listen to Marvin Gaye's greatest hits. It was usually about a thirty-minute ride to her apartment, but because the night traffic wasn't as thick, they were able to make it in about twenty.

Sexton parked in front of her building but left the engine running. In the darkness of the car, he reached for her.

The minute she felt his touch the butterflies in her stomach fluttered throughout her whole being. Sasha closed her eyes when she felt the palm of his hand at the back of her head pulling her to him. At first, his lips lightly touched hers, but then he kissed her more firmly, opening his mouth against hers. Abruptly he stopped.

Sasha opened her eyes and looked at him questioningly. "What's wrong?"

Her voice was so low he had to lean in to hear her.

"Nothing," he said. "I just want to know if you know what you're doing." He stared deeply into her eyes.

"What do you mean?"

"How much did you have to drink today?"

"Just enough," she replied.

"Enough for what?" He examined her closely in the dark interior of the car.

"Enough for me to forget my three date rule." She reached over to the ignition, shut the engine off and removed the keys. Then she unbuckled her seat belt to get out.

Sexton unbuckled his seat belt and walked around to Sasha's side of the car. He opened the door and held out his hand to help her. Once her car door was shut, she handed him his keys and deliberately strutted in front of him, swaying her hips more than usual, towards the entrance of her apartment. The only sound she heard as she as walked towards the entrance was the beep of Sexton's remote as he activated the alarm.

Once they were inside her apartment, she turned to bolt the door behind them. Though the lighting from the nightlight in the hall was dim, she could make out Sexton's facial features. His eyes seemed to glow in the dark like those of a mountain lion. She took Sexton's hand and led him down the hall to the bedroom.

Once inside, Sasha clapped her palms together, and immediately a soft glow of light illuminated the bedroom. She began to undress. Slowly she unbuttoned her shirt and let it drop to the floor. Next, she unbuckled her jeans. Sasha watched Sexton's eyes follow her movements as she peeled them down and let them gather at her feet. As she stepped away from the pile of clothes on the floor, that movement brought her one step closer to Sexton. Standing only in her undergarments and heels she reached for him.

Sexton remained motionless, but he looked ready to pounce as he let Sasha take total control of the situation. She unbuckled his pants and pulled his shirt free. He instinctively lifted his hands and bent forward as she pulled his shirt over his head. She gently tapped him on his chest and after he sat down on the edge of her bed, she dropped to her knees and picked up his foot. Without speaking, she took off one of his shoes, then his sock. Now for the first time since they'd entered the bedroom, Sasha spoke, "I never let a man make love to me with his socks on."

Sexton's only response was to nod his head in understanding. Then she repeated the same process for the other foot. Sasha lightly slid her hands across his torso.

His pecs felt smooth, soft, and hard all at the same time. Touching him, Sasha felt solid muscle. He was hairless, as if he had recently had his body waxed.

Reaching to his pants, she unbuckled them, paused, and drew a deep breath. "Do you want this?" Her voice was so husky with desire she barely recognized it.

"I wouldn't be here if I didn't." At that moment, Sexton took charge of the situation. He pulled back the comforter and lifted her onto the bed. Sexton gently positioned her on her back and then pulled down her panties.

She heard a slight rustling as Sexton rid himself of the rest of his clothes. Then he stood naked in front of her. "Now that I see what those cheerleaders were fighting about, I can say it is definitely worth the argument."

With a wry smile, Sexton stood there, unabashed in his nakedness, giving Sasha free rein to view him from head to toe.

"It's almost too good to be true," Sasha uttered as she stared at the long length of Sexton's throbbing penis. "I must say I'm quite impressed."

Then he joined her on the bed. Sexton reached out one hand and unsnapped the front closure of her bra. Once her breasts were freed, he kneaded them until they ached and she arched her body upwards, wanting more yet not knowing if she could stand any more.

Next, he leaned over and softly kissed her on the mouth before he drew her within the circle of his arms. For what seemed like an eternity he simply held her close, and then his tongue began to lick every part of her from head to toe. When Sasha could not wait any longer, she turned and opened the nightstand drawer next to her bed. She fumbled for a minute and then withdrew a small square packet, which she slid it into Sexton's hand.

Sexton quickly tore open the wrapper to the condom and sheathed his penis. In a voice husky with desire, he said, "I want to look in your face as I enter you." And then he did just that.

Even though Sexton was obviously the largest man she had ever been with, because she was so wet he slid easily into her. He paused for a second, staring down into her face, holding her eyes. She had to make a slight adjustment with her hips for them to have the perfect fit, and once she did, she sent him a message that she was tired of the appetizer and was ready for the full course meal.

Sexton stroked, and he stroked, and he stroked. Sasha clung to him and returned thrust for thrust, lifting her head, then letting it fall back on the pillow. Sasha had no idea how long they rocked together, but she did realize that when she reached her peak, so did he. They climaxed together and Sasha felt as if it was the first time in her life that she had ever really been made love to. If she'd had a trumpet, she would have blown it.

$$\sim$$

The next morning, Sasha turned her head to see a sleeping Sexton lying next to her. Very slowly she slid down the sheet that covered the bottom half of his torso until it gathered around his feet. Leisurely, she scrutinized every inch of him, especially what rested at the base of his abdomen. Sexton's shaft was nestled in a forest of curly black hair. Right above it was a jagged scar that ran horizontally across his groin. Sasha wondered about the scar since she knew that it was not the work of an appendix operation.

Sexton stirred.

Sasha felt her face grow hot when she realized that he was awake and had been watching her stare at his body.

In one swift movement, he lifted one arm and dragged Sasha under him. Leaning over her, he lifted his body slightly so that his full weight didn't overpower her. "Good morning, Miss Diamond."

"Good morning to you too, Mr. Sexton Johnson." There was a slight quiver in her voice because she was acutely aware by the stirrings of his body that Sexton could also take care of business early in the morning.

Sexton brushed Sasha's hair back from her face. "I had no idea yesterday morning that I would be waking up today with one of the most beautiful women in the world."

"I don't think that you have the authority to call me that. You haven't seen all of the women in the world, have you?" she murmured, conscious of the fact that she hadn't yet brushed her teeth.

"No, but I have seen quite a number of women because I have done a lot of traveling. There is definitely something about you that makes me feel a passion I've never felt before."

She dropped her eyes, feeling a little out of her depth. She was unused to a man being so up front about his desire for her. Abdul wasn't the kind of man who freely gave compliments, and the unfamiliarity of this new situation made her struggle for the right words. "I must admit I'm a little surprised by the chain of events also. When I went to the basketball game, I had no idea that we would end up like this," she admitted with a smile.

"No regrets?" he asked softly.

"No regrets," Sasha reassured him.

Sexton lifted her arm and turned it over. He planted a kiss on the inside of her arm right below her palm and Sasha again felt a warm stirring in her belly. "You caught me off guard. I usually like to wine and dine a woman before I make love to her, but I just couldn't pass up the invitation you so sexily delivered last night. I was just afraid that you were inebriated and didn't know what you were doing."

Sasha stared at Sexton and felt that she should explain. "I wanted to sleep with you without us going through the rituals. I haven't been dating for a while, but in the past I have always chosen to be intimate with a man before he spent any money on me. That way I didn't feel as if I owed him anything or that I was paying off some unspoken debt. Emulating the lifestyle of a hooker doesn't appeal to me."

"Oh," Sexton teased, "so you seduced me? You lured me up to your lair so that you could have your way with me. I'm just glad that you knew what you were doing, and that the alcohol wasn't doing your thinking for you."

"I have never slept with a man because I was too drunk to know what I was doing." She hesitated and then, because she wanted to be absolutely truthful to him added, "But there have been times when I slept with someone sooner than I planned. But this is different. I don't usually participate in one night stands."

Sexton looked down at her with quizzically. "What makes you think this is a one night stand?"

Sasha tried to explain what she meant. "I just don't want you to think that you have to call me or anything. We're adults and know that sometimes timing is everything. Someone can be at the right place at the right time, and people shouldn't ruin it by trying later to turn nothing into something."

"Are you trying to tell me that last night meant nothing?" Sexton moved from above Sasha and reached down for the sheet at the foot of the bed. He drew it up over their bodies. Then he moved further away from her to lie on his back.

"I'm saying no such thing." Sasha leaned over and looked deeply into Sexton's eyes. "You were more than I expected." She looked at him and saw his brow was still raised in question. "I mean that I have found in the past that fine men like you don't usually have a lot of conversation. Also, they're not that good in bed because they really haven't had to be. But I've been very pleasantly surprised by you."

Sexton stared at Sasha, digesting the information she had just given him. "So you think that I'm fine?"

"Umm hmm," she replied. "Believe me, I thoroughly enjoyed myself last night."

Sexton did not respond. It was obvious he was doing some hard thinking because he lay very still. His next words were enunciated very slowly and deliberately. "The time we shared last night was just the tip of the iceberg, Sasha Diamond, and the fact that you could say that it would be okay if I didn't try to see you again makes me know what I need to do in order to make you count the hours until you change your mind." He gave her a look of intense sexuality. And with single minded determination, Sexton went about the business of demonstrating to her just what he meant.

CHAPTER 5

A few hours later, Sexton and Sasha stood on the sidewalk next to his car. "Would you like to go out to dinner on Friday night?" he asked.

Sasha dropped her head in an effort to avoid the spell of Sexton's gaze. In the bright sunlight she felt shy as she thought of how passionate their lovemaking had been. Their bodies had moved in sync as if they had been lovers for a long time, and there had been none of the usual awkwardness that many couples experience their first time together.

She concentrated, thinking hard as she tried to remember what time her shift at work would end. "I don't know what time I will be getting off. Can I call you later and let you know?"

"That sounds like a plan," he answered, smiling down at her upturned face. Sexton patted the cell phone in his pocket. "If you don't call me then I'm going to call you." He took his finger and playfully touched the tip of her nose. At that moment, the harsh ringing of Sexton's cellphone broke their mood of intimacy. He looked down at the number and said, "It's Calvin." He clicked the Bluetooth in his ear and said, "Hey man, what's up?" Then he exclaimed, "You're kidding! When? I wondered what happened to you two last night." He was silent for a moment and Sasha could tell that he was shocked by whatever Calvin was telling him. "That's a damn shame. Of course, I'll come over."

"What's going on? What happened?" Sasha asked, worried by the expression on Sexton's face. "Is Tiara okay?"

"Yes, that's Sasha. What do you think? I'll tell her. Goodbye." Sexton clicked off his Bluetooth and stood looking at Sasha for a minute.

She became afraid when he remained silent. She could tell that he was trying to fathom what he had just been told. "Tiara's husband was caught soliciting a prostitute last night."

"What? There must be some mistake." Sasha took a step back, putting some space between herself and Sexton as if hoping that would shield her from the horrible news.

"The mistake was his. The hooker wasn't a hooker after all, but an undercover policewoman."

She was flabbergasted, and the look on her face showed it. "Is that what people do in Boise?" And then her words got louder when her brain really began to process what she'd heard. "Is that what Peter does when he goes away on business trips?"

Sexton replied sarcastically, "He wasn't still in Boise. Dude was right here in the city. He pretended he was out of town, but he wasn't."

"How's Tiara?" Tears welled in Sasha's eyes as she felt sympathy for the humiliation her best friend was living. "Why didn't she try to call me?"

Sexton reached over and his fingers were gentle as he wiped her tears off her cheeks. "I don't know. Calvin said that she's just staring into space, not talking," he responded quietly.

"Then why did he ask you to come over there?" Her tears had died down to sniffles.

"Peter's on his way to the house with his brothers to get his belongings. I think Calvin wants some back-up in case things get ugly."

"I don't see how things can get any uglier than they already are. I thought what Abdul did to me sucked, but I see there are many levels of disgust in this world." Sasha was too heated to notice the questioning look that came across Sexton's face at her words. "I'm going with you. Let me go and grab my purse. Tiara is my friend, and I'm going to go and be with her."

When they arrived at Tiara's house there was a small moving truck parked in the driveway. Sexton chose to park his car directly behind the rental truck, blocking the vehicle's exit. They gave each other a brief look. Sexton observed the scowl on Sasha's face as she got out and stalked towards the front of the house. He followed closely at her heels.

As they entered the foyer, they saw Calvin standing absently rubbing his bald head as he watched Peter and his brother Rufus take a mattress out of the spare bedroom. Peter's usual sallow complexion was red and blotchy from embarrassment, and he kept his head down, avoiding Calvin's angry gaze.

Even if Sasha hadn't recognized Rufus from the wedding, she would have known at once that he was Peter's brother. They each stood about five feet, six inches in height, and they appeared even shorter as they passed Calvin, who towered over them. As they passed by, Sasha tried to will Peter's eyes to meet hers, but they didn't.

Calvin beckoned them to follow him into the kitchen so that their conversation wouldn't be overheard.

"Where's Tiara?" Sasha demanded abruptly.

"She's in the master bedroom. She's almost catatonic. She says she won't come out until Peter and his brother leave," he added quietly.

"Why is Peter taking stuff out of here? He doesn't deserve anything after what he's done to her." Sasha whispered her words, but indignation was apparent by her tone and her body language as she stood with hands on her hips.

"He's taking only his clothes, the bedroom furniture out of the spare room and a loveseat out of the den. Everything else stays."

Sexton shook his head from side to side. "My God! What was he thinking? He's messed up his home life for sex with a hooker."

"Apparently before he got married that's what he did for his physical gratification, and he hasn't been able to break that habit."

"How did Tiara find out that Peter had been arrested?" Sasha asked.

"Once he got arrested, Peter called his brother Rufus to bail him out. Rufus came up short on the bail money and called their other brother Mike. Mike said that he had the money and was on the way to the jail to bond him out. He text messaged Peter, but Tiara and Peter had switched cellphones. Peter's phone had so many roaming charges from previous trips that he took Tiara's. She got the text message that Peter was locked up and that's why we left the club like that. When we showed up at the jail, that's when we found out why he was locked up."

"Damn!" Sasha spoke in a horrified whisper. "Can you imagine showing up at a jail to bail your husband out only to find out that he tried to pick up a hooker? Why didn't Tiara call me?"

"She's too embarrassed."

"She's not the one to feel ashamed. She doesn't share in the blame for this mess."

"I don't know if she's thinking straight. She's been hiding in the bedroom ever since she found out last night. When Peter and Rufus came she wouldn't come out of the room. I had to go in and get Peter's clothes and hand them out to him."

Sasha nodded her head. "I'm going in to talk to her."

When she entered the darkened bedroom she could barely see the Tiara. She was lying on top of the bed on her side, facing the wall. The drapes were drawn and the only light in the room was seeping in from the nightlight in the adjoining bathroom. Sasha gently sat down on the bed and lightly touched Tiara on the arm.

"Tiara," she whispered in a soothing voice, "it's Sasha." Then she hesitated, not quite knowing what to say. "Calvin told us what happened," she finally said.

Complete silence was Tiara's response.

Sasha cleared her throat. "Sexton and I are here, and we want to know if there's anything that we can do."

"Why is Sexton here? I don't want anyone to know about this." Tiara's tone was icy, and she turned over to face Sasha.

Sasha was unnerved by the puffiness of her friend's eyes and blotchiness of her face.

"We were together when he got a call from Calvin. Calvin asked him to come in case he needed some help in dealing with Peter and his brother."

"And who asked you to come?" Tiara glared at her.

Sasha was taken aback by the hostility of Tiara's words. "I just thought that maybe I could be of some comfort to you."

"I know that, Sasha. I don't mean to lash out at you. I know that you're just trying to help. It's just that I didn't have a clue that this was going on. I feel so stupid."

"There's no reason for you to feel that way. Peter said that he was on a business trip, and you had no reason to think otherwise."

"His brothers are so stupid. They ruined my marriage because they are so damn dumb. All they had to do was to come up with two hundred and fifty dollars to bond Peter out of jail and my marriage wouldn't be over. After the way Mike blew it, he was too much of a coward to come over here and face me."

Sasha was slow to answer Tiara making sure she chose her next words carefully. "Tiara, I agree that his brothers do seem kind of dumb, but they did not ruin your life. This is all Peter's fault. He's the one who has ruined your marriage; he's the cheat, and you need to acknowledge that. If your husband is going around soliciting prostitutes, that's a danger to you." She waited for Tiara the full impact of her words to sink in. "I think that you should come into the hospital this week and take an AIDS test."

There was a long silence in the room. Then Tiara began to talk so quietly Sasha could barely hear what she was saying. "You spend your whole adult life looking for a mate and you think that you've found him only to find out that it's all a sham."

"I know. That's how I felt when I caught Abdul doing the nasty with his piece on the side."

"That is nothing like this!" Tiara's voice rose to a high-pitched wail. "How can you equate that insignificant little episode in your life with this? The two of you weren't even married. You didn't stand in front of family and friends and pledge to be together body and soul for the rest of your lives. And you weren't humiliated for the whole world to see. My husband was caught picking up an undercover cop thinking she was a white prostitute. That she was white seems to make it all the worse."

Sasha couldn't help saying, "Does her color really matter?" Then she added as an afterthought, "Maybe she was the only one out there."

"Is that supposed to make me feel any better?" Tiara demanded. Animosity showed in the way she moved her head from side to side.

"No, I just want you to keep things in perspective," Sasha explained, attempting to place a Band-Aid on an open sore. "At least you found out now and not ten years down the road."

Tiara pointed to the empty side of the closet that had once held Peter's belongings. "Maybe you should keep things in perspective. You haven't been subjected to what I've been through since last night. Right now my husband is getting his things in order to move in with his brother."

Sasha mentally counted to ten, knowing that Tiara was under a lot of stress and didn't realize that she was venting her anger on the wrong person. "I know that your situation is different from mine, but that doesn't take away from the fact that I was still hurt by Abdul's shenanigans. The fact that we weren't married doesn't change that."

"I know." And with those words Tiara began to sob. They were deep, painful sobs that rocked her body and seemed to rise from her very soul. As she cried she mumbled the words, "Why me?" over and over again.

Sasha put her arms around her friend and held her and rocked her as if she were a baby. After what seemed an interminable time, Tiara's tears subsided and Sasha gently pushed her away. She gripped her by her shoulders, shook her slightly and promised, "You're going to get through this. I'm going to make sure of that."

Twenty minutes later, Calvin and Sasha stood at the top of the driveway as they watched Rufus slowly back the U-haul truck out, while Sexton stood at the bottom of the driveway directing him so that he didn't scrape the other cars.

After Rufus cleared the driveway, Peter inched his Cadillac STS out of the garage. With a look of longing he surveyed the house and all that he had lost. Then he backed out of the driveway and screeched off, the rear end of the car momentarily fishtailing. Sexton slowly walked up the driveway to where Sasha stood, searching her eyes for what she was thinking. Her expression was unfathomable, and he suddenly realized that after she had fixed Tiara a cup of herbal tea and left her alone in the bedroom, her conversation to him had been limited.

There was an uncomfortable silence as he drove her back to her loft. When Sexton heard the rumbling of her stomach he slid her a sidelong look. "Do you want to get something to eat?"

They had not eaten all day, yet she wasn't in the mood for a meal.

"I don't know," Sasha replied, avoiding his eyes. "Are you hungry?"

"Not really, but I know that I have to get something. I don't have any food at my house."

"Stop at Subway." She pointed to the small shop a little ways up the street.

There weren't any parking places in front, and she looked at Sexton. "What kind of sandwich do you want?" she queried.

"I'll have the meatball sub and a soda."

Sexton reached over to open the glove compartment, where she knew he kept his wallet, but she stilled his hand. "I got it." Before he could answer she quickly jumped out of the car and went into the shop.

While he waited for Sasha to return, Sexton sat thinking about her mood. He knew that she was upset for her friend, but her behavior towards him was almost hostile. There was more distance now than there had been when they'd met over a year ago at Tiara's party. It seemed as if they'd never made love. He didn't quite know what to make of the change in her.

Sasha returned with two separate bags, and Sexton leaned over to open her door. Once inside she said, "I got you the meal with the baked Lays. They're better for your heart."

Trying to regain the camaraderie that they had shared the night before he said, "So you're giving me orders already, are you?"

Sasha's voice was sharp. "I'm a nurse. If you don't like them, don't eat them."

Sexton's brow furrowed and he drew in a deep breath and demanded, "What's up with the attitude?"

"I don't have an attitude," Sasha denied.

"Yes you do. You've been behaving oddly ever since we got the call from Calvin this morning."

"You don't know me well enough to make that kind of judgment," Sasha replied. Then she added, "Just because we had sex last night doesn't mean that you know me."

Sexton looked at Sasha. "I know that you're upset about your friend, but don't take it out on me," he softly admonished her.

Though Sasha pointedly stared out the side window, she answered grudgingly, "I know this is not your fault, Sexton. It's just that I've come to realize how much of a hassle relationships are. I just got out of one and now my best friend has been devastated because of what her husband did. If I believed in reincarnation I'd come back as a man because it seems that if there's ever a problem in the relationship, the guy is able to get his clothes, a few sticks of furniture, and drive off without a backward glance."

"That's not the way it appeared to me. Didn't you notice him hesitating in the driveway before he left? He was hoping that Tiara would give him some sign that later on he could come back to talk to her without other people around."

"He must be crazy. Tiara needs to be afraid to go within five miles of him. People say that you can forgive anything with time, but I say that some things are unforgivable."

"I don't think that you're as hard as you pretend to be, Sasha. At least I certainly hope not."

Sasha dropped her eyes. "I'm not hard, but I'm done. In the last couple of weeks any faith that I may have had in relationships, or marriage for that matter, has gone down the tubes. I never want to get married."

The only response Sexton gave her was to say, "Never say never."

Sasha hadn't realized that Sexton had parked the car and they were once again in front of her building. In a matter of about twelve hours things had changed from anticipation of a relationship with a man other than Abdul to resignation that sooner or later she would be disappointed in love.

"So where does that leave us?"

Sexton stared at her so hard she felt that he could see into the deep recesses of her mind.

Sasha shrugged her shoulders in an awkward attempt to appear nonchalant. "I don't know. I can't think about anything right now. I'm exhausted mentally and physically and I have to go to work in about six hours."

"All right, Sasha. You take some time to think about things. But not too long," he cautioned.

Inside the close quarters of the sedan, she searched Sexton's face, as if hoping to find the answer to a question that she was afraid to ask.

He remained quiet, sensing that something was on her mind.

Sasha's eyes met his, and after intently scrutinizing him, she drew in a deep breath and said, "I want to ask you something."

"Go ahead."

In spite of the enormity of the events that had occurred since they had awakened that morning, Sasha still felt an intense sexual yearning for Sexton. "With all the beautiful women in the world who would die at the chance to spend time with you, why me?"

"Why not you?" He took his finger, tilted her chin, and gave her a warm, passionate but brief kiss which made her long for more.

The simplicity of his words, as much as his gesture, made her choke up. She turned and pretended to find something interesting to look at on the empty street.

"I'll call you later this week about going to dinner Friday night." Then he picked up Sasha's hand and turned it over. For the second time, he pressed his lips on the inside of her forearm, just beneath her palm.

She felt an immediate quivering sensation in her gut and all she could say was, "Okay," before she bolted from the car.

As she stood on the sidewalk, she felt forlorn watching Sexton drive away. She walked to the garbage can on the side of her building and threw away the food she had just purchased.

CHAPTER 6

A few days later, Sasha sat at the side of Mr. Ramirez's bed and tapped her foot with mock impatience as she waited for him to play a card. "Any day now," she teased. "You might as well put that ace in your hand down. You have it and you know that I want it."

"Don't be hurrying me," he answered. "That's what's wrong with young people today. They're always in a hurry."

"You're just stalling because you know that with this hand I'll reach five hundred and you'll lose again."

Mr. Ramirez drew a card out of his hand and with a thump, placed it down on the bed table. He reached over and drank from his cup of apple juice before he said with a pout, "I let you win because you've been down all week. I just wanted to get that sour look off your face."

Sasha was amazed by his astuteness. He was suffering from brain cancer and never knew which day would be his last, but he had easily read her. She made a big production of picking the ace up and placed it with the other two in her hands before she said "Gin. I win."

"Now that you think you've distracted me, what's the matter? You've looked worried all week."

"I am worried. My best friend and her husband broke up and I haven't heard from her since."

Mr. Ramirez looked concerned. "Did you call her?"

"Yes, but she hasn't answered the telephone. I would go out to her house but she lives on Long Island and I've been getting off too late after work to take the ferry out there."

"Did you try to reach her at work? I saw a report on MSNBC that people spend more time at work than they do at home."

"Her job was being a wife, and now she doesn't have that."

"Now I see why you're so worried. She'll probably turn up. Just give her a chance to regroup."

Just then the cellphone that Sasha kept on at work vibrated. "Maybe that's her." She looked hopefully at the phone and when she recognized the number, she placed it back into the pocket of her uniform and said with a grimace, "Nope, not her."

Mr. Ramirez watched her carefully and wagged a finger at her. "Are you still dodging that good-for-nothing Abdul?"

"No, now I'm dodging another guy. But I don't think that he's a good-for-nothing," Sasha said, thinking out loud.

"Then why are you not answering his calls? I heard that there's a man shortage out there."

"I don't necessarily think that there's a man shortage, but I will say that I think that there's a shortage of good men." Her tone was abrupt as Abdul's and Peter's faces rose to her mind.

Mr. Ramirez protested, "But you just said that he's not a good-for-nothing. Why aren't you answering his calls?"

Sasha didn't reply.

Mr. Ramirez watched the gamut of emotions that crossed her face, giving insight to the conflicting feelings she had regarding Sexton.

"Well, he's rich, handsome, sexy, and I think I that he's out of my league."

"I can't believe that you lack confidence when it comes to men."

"I have nothing to offer this guy," she protested.

"You have yourself. You are absolutely beautiful and possess a heart of gold," he stated. "Look at you sitting here with an old, sick man because he doesn't have any family. That's worth at least a million bucks."

Sasha exclaimed, "I just think that I'm out of my depth when it comes to him. There are women throwing themselves at him all of the time. How can I compete with that?"

"What makes you think that you have to compete at all?"

Sasha didn't have an answer for that so she just sat there. She heard herself being paged over the intercom and, giving Mr. Ramirez a look that spoke volumes, she said, "I guess I have to go. We'll talk later."

"I'm looking forward to it. In the meantime, call him. Don't write this guy off without giving him a chance."

Sasha walked over to the nurses' station and was surprised to see Tiara standing there. As she approached her she immediately became worried by Tiara's appearance. Her face looked drawn, as if she hadn't slept in days, and was devoid of makeup. Her hair needed a trim and her body was noticeably thinner.

Trying to mask her surprise at Tiara's disheveled appearance, she put on a happy face. "Hey, girl, how are you doing?"

Tiara's response was to give her a silent look.

"I've been calling you but I couldn't get an answer."

"I got rid of my cellphone," Tiara replied dully.

"Oh. Well then, what are you doing here?"

Tiara muttered, "I'm here for the AIDS test that you suggested."

Sasha paused. "Since you're here, why don't you also have a complete physical? Dr. Phillips is on staff. I think you'll feel comfortable with her because she's a woman and her specialty is gynecology. She'll take good care of you."

Tiara merely hunched her shoulders and stuck her hands in the pockets of her shorts.

Sasha smiled at her encouragingly. "I can hang around and wait for your results. I'll have the lab put a rush on them. There's no need for you to wait for days. We'll just cut through the middleman."

Tiara replied softly, "Thank you, Sasha. You're a good friend."

As she sat in the hospital cafeteria and waited for Tiara to complete her battery of tests, Sasha thought about Sexton. He had been a thorough lover, exploring every inch of her body. She had been pleased with the fact that he had seemed to know what she wanted. On his own, he had put his head down between her legs and licked her as if she were his favorite ice cream. Her thoughts were interrupted when Tiara plopped down in the seat at the table.

"I detest pap smears," Tiara complained. "They need to come up with another method."

"Girl, I know what you mean. I'm a nurse and I know how important it is to have your annual checkups, but I always dread it. Afterwards I always treat myself by going shopping and buying myself a fantastic dress or a piece of jewelry."

Tiara grimaced. "Well, I won't be doing that because I can't afford it. I can't even afford to have a cellphone."

"What are you going to do about your finances?" Sasha didn't want to pry, but she knew that Tiara's money situation had changed drastically because of her separation.

"I start substituting on Monday. I'm trying to get my teacher's certificate reinstated but that takes time, and I have no money coming in." Tears formed in her eyes but she blinked them away. "Sasha, even with a teacher's paycheck I can't afford that house. Calvin said that he would pay the mortgage for the next six months, but I feel terrible letting him do it because I know that he just purchased his apartment and he's cash poor."

"Calvin is a good brother to you."

Tiara nodded her head in agreement. "He's the best. I should have never quit my job. I feel so helpless."

"Don't blame yourself too much." Sasha placed her hand consolingly over Tiara's. "Hindsight is always better than foresight. How about Peter? He should help pay those bills. He talked you into quitting your job in the first place and he's the sole reason why you two aren't together."

"That's what I told him but his answer was that he left me with just about everything. He's conveniently forgotten that we financed all of the furniture with no interest for a two-year period and finance charges will accrue from the very beginning date of purchase in about six months if I don't pay if off. Peter left me our SUV, but he won't give me any money for the payments. I could take him to court but that takes time, and without children I don't know if the judge would give me anything."

"Is there any way I can help? I don't have a lot of money left over at the end of the month, but I do have a nest egg because I was saving to go on the Tom Joyner cruise."

"That would be a drop in the bucket for what I need. It takes me about four thousand dollars a month just to break even. Do you have that?" Tiara raised an eyebrow and looked at Sasha.

"No," Sasha replied regretfully.

"So you see, the only thing that would happen if you gave me your money would be that I would still be broke you wouldn't be able to go on your cruise."

There was long silence and then Tiara said, avoiding Sasha's eyes, "Peter wants to work things out."

"Of course he does. By not giving you any money he's putting you in the position of financial dependency. Peter is dangling money in front of you hoping that you're so strapped financially you'll turn a blind eye to his betrayal."

"He feels that we can get through this," she mumbled.

"He doesn't have anything to get through. I bet he wouldn't be so forgiving if it was the other way around."

"He made a mistake."

Sasha was flabbergasted, and her expression showed it. "Tell me that you're not considering taking him back. What excuse does he have for what he did?"

"He says that it's an addiction and he's willing to go to counseling."

"Give me a break. He's been reading the tabloids too much." Then she softened her tone, "I can't tell you what to do about your marriage, but you have people in your life who love you and want you to be around strong and healthy for many years to come. Your health is in danger because of his so-called addiction. If he was a real man and sincerely willing to change, he would help you with no strings attached."

Tiara responded quietly, "I know you're right." Then Tiara asked out of the blue, "How did you and Sexton end up arriving at my house at the exact same time?"

Sasha was thrown by the abrupt change of conversation. "We spent the night together. I was with Sexton when Calvin called him."

"I kind of thought something like that." Tiara paused and then asked, "Well, how was it?"

Sasha chuckled. "Leave it to you to come right out and ask me something like that. Let's just say that it was pretty damn good."

"But I thought that you weren't interested. What changed your mind?" Tiara studied Sasha's face.

"I got caught up in the moment."

"I hope that you don't think that anything meaningful is going to come out of a one night stand. If you want to marry a man you hold off on the sex for at least a month or so or he won't respect you. Make him work for it. In the end he'll want you all the more for it."

"I'm not trying to hurt your feelings or anything, but how long did you make Peter wait before you slept with him?" Sasha's tone was dry.

"A month or so." Tiara dropped her head.

Sasha made no reply because it was obvious what each of them was thinking.

"In any case, who said that I want to marry him?" Sasha continued. "I'm not looking for a husband and lately I haven't been real impressed by the institution of marriage."

Sasha's spectra link buzzed and she picked it up, saying to Tiara, "It's probably Dr. Phillips with your test results." As she held the phone to her ear she smiled at Tiara and gave her a thumbs up signal. "Everything turned up fine. Your blood test came back negative and your pap smear is normal."

Tiara responded defensively, "I knew that I didn't have anything. Peter said that was his first time and I believe him."

Sasha's only response was to give her a measured look.

"I know you don't believe that, but I do," Tiara said defensively.

Sasha gave her another measured look. They were quiet as Sasha walked Tiara to the parking garage connected to the hospital. As Sasha waved goodbye to her friend, she prayed for Tiara to have the strength to make the right decisions regarding her future.

CHAPTER 7

On the bus ride home, Mr. Ramirez's advice resounded in Sasha's ears. Throwing her pocketbook on the couch, Sasha reached for the phone and pulled up her caller I. D. list. She pressed the redial button, and feeling a little nervous, she waited.

"Hello." Sexton's voice was slurred from sleep, and Sasha fleetingly wondered if he was naked.

"Sexton, it's me, Sasha. How are you?" Now that she was talking to Sexton her voice sound breathless, and she knew it.

"So you finally decided to return my calls," Sexton responded.

"I'm sorry that I'm just getting back to you. I've been really busy." Sasha knew her excuse was lame.

"Liar," he said mildly. "You decided after the stunt Tiara's husband pulled that you were off men."

Sasha was chagrined that he had figured her out so easily. "I have to say that I was thrown for a loop. They've only been married for nine months. What could he have been thinking?"

Sexton yawned into the receiver. "A man will pick up a prostitute for one of two reasons. Either he doesn't have a steady woman or he's insecure about his sexual prowess. With a hooker you don't have worry about performance.

She'll tell you what you want to hear because her job is to make you feel like you're the man."

"Have you ever been with a prostitute?"

"Do I have any reason to feel insecure about my love-making abilities?" Sexton countered smoothly.

"No, you do not," Sasha answered emphatically.

"I didn't think so."

"So then you're telling me that you have a steady girl-friend," Sasha replied.

"Sasha, if I had a girlfriend I would not have gone home with you and I would not have called you three times this week." He paused to let his words sink in. "I'm a very busy man and don't have time to play games. Listen, I'm not again going to try to convince you to go out with me and I'm not going to keep reassuring you that I'm a good man. I'm feelin' you, and I know you're feelin' me."

"Why have you been so persistent?"

"Anything worth having is worth working for," he answered promptly. "Sasha, is there some dark secret about you that makes you question the fact that a man could want you from the moment he saw you?"

"No."

"Are you so unlovable that it's impossible to meet a man who may just want to get to know and maybe love you?"

"I hope not," she responded softly.

"Then let's see where the road can lead us."

There was a long silence and the air hung heavy between them before he said, "Why are you putting up these barriers between us?"

"I want to spend time with you, Sexton." She still sounded unsure. "I guess that it's because I don't want to get hurt like Tiara."

"Tiara's husband is insane. I am not."

At Sexton's words, Sasha started laughing. "His ass *is* crazy."

Sexton also chuckled. Once the laughter died down, there was an obvious lighter atmosphere between them.

"What are you doing tomorrow night?"

"I'm not working and I have no plans," Sasha answered.

"Good. I'll pick you up around seven-thirty and we'll go out to eat. Sunday morning the team is leaving town for a road trip and I would like to see you before I leave."

"All right, Sexton." Sasha tied to hide the fact that she was a little disappointed that she would not be able to see him that night because from the moment Sexton answered the telephone and she'd realized that he was in bed, her libido had gone into overdrive.

"Sasha," Sexton drawled.

"Yes, Sexton?"

"Dress casually," he ordered before he hung up.

When Sasha opened her door the next evening she felt desire curl inside her at the sight of Sexton Johnson. He wore a pair of blue plaid shorts with a matching light blue shirt. A baseball cap was pulled down so she couldn't read his expression, but she could tell by the flash of his smile that he was pleased by what he saw.

Sasha had done as she was told to do and had dressed in a light blue baby doll dress. She had finished off her ensemble with a pair of matching blue sandals.

She was tired of wearing her hair pinned up all the time, so she had brushed it back from her face and fashioned it into a ponytail looped casually to one side. Her makeup was lightly applied, but she had darkened her lashes and eyebrows. Her bright red lipstick was dramatic. Sasha had a passion for large earrings, and whenever she wasn't at work it was customary for her to wear three pairs of large hoops in her ears with the largest in the hole in her lobe and the other two running a train up her ear.

Sexton leaned over and gave her a peck on the cheek. She felt herself blushing because she had leaned forward, expecting him to him to kiss her on her mouth.

Sexton's smile widened and he said teasingly, "Sasha, if you want me to kiss you I will."

"I don't want you to kiss me," she denied, half-embarrassed.

"Liar," he said laughingly. Then he enveloped her in his arms.

She closed her eyes in anticipation.

When Sexton's mouth touched hers it was firm and insistent. He opened her mouth with his and then she felt tongue. Electric shocks coursed throughout her as his tongue explored her mouth.

She put her arms around his neck and curled her whole body into his. Sasha felt the hardness of Sexton's body before he slowly withdrew his lips from hers and gently pushed her away.

His voice husky with desire he said, "If we keep this up we'll never get to dinner, and I intend to sit down and have a date with you before I go on the road."

"Okay." Sasha dropped her eyes and reached for her purse and keys.

When she walked with him out of her building, she was surprised that he led her to a white Escalade. He opened the door for her to get in.

"What happened to my dream car?" she asked, once comfortably seated inside the car.

"Do you mean my Chrysler 300?" He glanced at her quickly before he pulled out into traffic.

"Yes."

"It's in my garage, along with my Benz. I only drive that Chrysler when I'm pressed for time and trying to navigate a lot of traffic. It's much easier in that situation than this Escalade."

"So you're living the dream, right?" she said, smiling at him.

"Not yet." Sexton momentarily took his eyes off the road to give her a direct stare. "You didn't tell me that the Chrysler is your favorite car. They look more expensive than they actually are. That dream of yours shouldn't be an unreachable one."

"It really isn't. My sisters offered to buy me one, but I turned them down."

"Why on earth would you do that?"

"Because it costs about five hundred and fifty dollars a month to rent a space in the parking garage near my loft and I didn't feel that I could afford the expense."

"If your sisters offered to buy you one, didn't they take that into account?"

"Of course they did, but I don't like to be dependent on other people for money." A vision of Tiara's worried face flashed before her. "Gifts are one thing, but needing someone to help you pay a monthly bill is another."

"Still, your sisters must be pretty cool to offer."

"My sisters are great. Dominique is the oldest and she's married to Benjamin, who's a doctor. We argue all the time, but usually I start it just to aggravate her and get her going. It's mad funny when I get the best of her in an argument. They have a set of twins who I'm just crazy about. And you met Desiree at Tiara's party."

"I remember her. She spent a lot of time talking to Calvin. I kind of thought that they were going to hook up, but I guess nothing ever kicked off."

"It doesn't matter. Now she's married to Tyler and I adore him. He's very good to my sister and has made her very happy. He's helping her to realize her dream of going to law school."

Suddenly Sasha started laughing and Sexton looked at her inquiringly. "What's so funny?"

"I have to tell you. That night at the party, Desiree and I were making fun of your name. Sexton Johnson. Talk about labeling a kid."

Sexton flashed a smile at her. "I'm not surprised." He gave her a tell-me-something-I-don't-know look. "I've heard it all before. So it's all girls in your family?"

"No, I have a brother, Marcus Junior. He's the oldest. He got a promotion at the post office not too long ago, and with last year's Christmas bonus he bought me that LCD television you saw at my loft. He's an avid sports fan and said that I need a decent television if I expect him to ever come and visit me."

"So you don't hate men after all? You have seen some good male role models?"

"Of course I have. My parents are happy and they've been married forever."

"So," he drawled, "you have seen some marriages that seem to be happy."

"Obviously I have, but unfortunately more times than not I've seen the drama that Tiara is going through. She's in total denial about Peter. You know, I think that she was considering taking him back for financial reasons."

"Don't give her any advice," Sexton cautioned. "In the end she's going to do what she wants to anyhow, and if you let her know that you think she would be a fool to take him back you'll lose a good friend if they do reconcile. She'll tell him what you said and he'll get angry and try to sabotage your relationship. Also, she'll resent you because she'll think that you're passing judgment on the choice she made." Sexton gave Sasha a knowing look. "That's why she didn't call you when she found out what the deal was. She was trying to keep Peter's betrayal a secret from you and everyone else."

Sexton parked the car. Looking around, she realized that they were on Lenox Avenue and that the purplish building was Sylvia's restaurant in Harlem.

"You brought me to eat at Sylvia's!" Sasha exclaimed.

"I sure did," he said with a smile. "I eat here at least once a week. It's the home away from home for every hungry bachelor in New York City."

"I just love their peach cobbler. It's to die for."

"Then let's go get some."

Sasha remained seated because she knew that Sexton expected her to wait until he walked around and opened her car door. As they started down the sidewalk, Sexton suddenly crossed behind her in order to position himself on the outside of her body.

Sasha looked at Sexton with a quizzical expression. "Why did you switch positions like that?"

"The man is supposed to walk closest to the curb when with a woman," he replied smoothly.

"And why is that?" Sasha slid Sexton a sly look.

"Back in the day, before there were inside toilets, people used to throw the contents of their spittoons and slop buckets out of the window. When you throw something the contents will form an arc. If the man is on the outside the contents will land on him and not the woman. He's sort of a shield for her."

Sasha's mouth fell open. "I can't believe that you know the reason. Some men know where they're supposed to walk, but I've never known anyone able to give the reason."

"So do I get an *A* on your little pop quiz?" Sexton asked with a smug look on his face.

"Absolutely." She smiled back at him.

When they entered, the restaurant was overflowing with people. The interior was reminiscent of the movie set for *Harlem Nights,* and at the tables people sat around laughing and telling stories. The minute Sexton entered the restaurant, he took off his cap and Sasha noticed that almost every female in the restaurant started staring at him. She had to curb her desire to stand in the middle of the room and shout, "I KNOW!"

She saw one lone table in the corner of the restaurant and tugged on Sexton's arm, pointing it out to him. He immediately made a beeline for it, motioning for Sasha to follow.

As she followed him across the room she realized that the women who had been staring so hard at Sexton were now sizing her up.

Sexton stepped aside to allow Sasha to slide in the booth and then slid his body into the other side, stretching out his long legs so that he could be comfortable.

A waitress placed a check on the table to their right and then walked over to them. She smiled and said to Sasha, who was reading the menu she found placed on the table, "Do you need more time before you order?"

"No," Sasha replied, "I already know what I want, I'll have Sylvia's World Famous Talked About Bar-B-Que Ribs, oven baked macaroni and cheese, collard greens, yellow rice, and peach cobbler for dessert."

"What would you like to drink?" the waitress asked as she quickly made notations on her pad.

"I'll have a Bedelia's Tropical Pina Colada."

"Got it," she answered. Then she looked at Sexton and smiled. "Do you want the usual?"

"Did you even need to ask? But instead of my usual Long Island Iced Tea I'll try the Devil in a Blue Dress." He looked at Sasha and lifted his eyebrow.

"Got it," She smiled again and walked off in the direction of the kitchen.

"I got that." Sasha smiled and touched the collar of her dress. "Good grief, Sexton, you eat here so much that the waitress knows what you're going to order?" She shook her head as if to say that was not a good thing.

"I know, I need a wife."

Sasha looked at Sexton, but his expression was unfathomable.

"Having a wife doesn't mean that you would be eating home all of the time. A lot of women can't cook," she said, wrinkling her nose at the memories of some of the dishes she had tasted by women who had boasted that they could cook.

"Can you?" he asked.

"Of course I can," she paused, "and I'm pretty good at it. My mother made sure of that."

The waitress returned with their drinks. He reached for his drink and took a long sip. "Uhmm, this stuff is good," he said suggestively to Sasha.

"I got that, too." She openly grinned at the sexual undercurrents of Sexton's banter. Then her attention was drawn to a couple of high school girls looking at Sexton and giggling. "I think that you have a mini fan club over there."

One of the teenage girls tore a piece of notebook paper out of a tablet and headed over in their direction.

The girl was inordinately pretty in her school uniform and she approached their table with pen and paper in hand. "May I have your autograph?" she spoke softly.

Sasha heard the nervous tremor as the girl shifted from one foot to the other.

"Of course you can. It's always nice to meet a fan. Is this for you or maybe your brother?"

"It's for me. Would you please write 'To Jasmine from Tyrese on her birthday?' That way everyone will know for sure that I met you."

Sasha had been in the process of taking a sip of her drink and began to sputter when she realized who the girl thought Sexton was.

She saw Sexton's hand grow still and then he quickly recovered and said, "Sure, young lady. Is it okay if I just sign it T. Gibson instead of the whole name?"

"That would be great," she shyly responded.

Sasha watched Sexton as he wrote on the sheet of notebook paper and handed it to her with a smile. "There you go, young lady. Enjoy your birthday."

"Thank you so much," she said excitedly. "This is the best birthday ever!" She sped back over to her friends.

Once she left, Sasha couldn't contain herself any longer. She laughed until tears formed in her eyes, and Sexton watched her with a wry expression. Once she stopped laughing she gulped out, "Why didn't you tell her who you really are?"

"And ruin her birthday?" Sexton said, raising one eyebrow. "I didn't want to disappoint her."

"But you're a star, too," Sasha replied.

"Not to her," he said mildly sarcastic. "I should be offended, but I'm not. She's young. One day she'll recognize me. Just you wait and see." He finished his statement with a confidence that made Sasha feel even more attracted to him.

Just then their waitress arrived with their food. "Good Lord!" Sasha exclaimed when she saw what Sexton's usual was. The waitress placed a plate of stewed turkey wings on homemade cornbread dressing, green beans, dirty rice, and a whole sweet potato pie. "It's a good thing you run up and down the court for a living. Otherwise you would have a weight problem."

"I don't think you did too badly yourself," he teased, "I'm glad that you have a healthy appetite because I hate to take a woman out to eat who just picks at her food."

"You never have to worry about that with me. I don't eat all of the time, but when I do, I can really get down."

"Sasha, I like you. I think that you're real."

Sasha blushed and smiled at him, "Thank God for Mr. Ramirez."

"Who's Mr. Ramirez?" He gave her a quizzical look. Sexton had a mouthful of turkey wing and some of the juice dribbled.

Smiling, Sasha picked up her napkin and dabbed at his mouth. "He's a patient of mine, and he's always quizzing me about my love life."

"Really? I'm a little surprised that you would get so close to a patient."

"I usually don't. But no one ever visits Mr. Ramirez. Because he doesn't have any family, I began to spend time with him."

"What's wrong with him?"

"Brain cancer, and it's terminal. I don't know how much longer he has." Obvious sadness was etched in her voice. "Some days he's in so much excruciating pain that all the pain reliever that we can legally give him doesn't help, and other days he's pain free. That's when we play cards. He told me months ago to break up with Abdul and then he advised me to call you. I'm happy that I did," she ended quietly.

Sexton asked abruptly, "Why did you finally break up with him?"

"I caught him doing his secretary," Sasha responded without feeling. That part of her life seemed light years ago, and she was glad.

"That's a classic." Sexton shrugged his shoulders as if to say that he wasn't surprised.

"As his secretary, she's not even getting paid minimum wage and she was doing him on the side."

"Well, then she got taken twice, didn't she?" Sexton replied, eyes twinkling.

Sasha started to chuckle and Sexton said, "See, you can find humor in every situation if you try."

As they walked out of the restaurant, Sasha could feel Sexton's eyes on her bottom. Looking back at him she said teasingly, "You know, you do kind of look like Tyrese."

Sexton's answer was to swat her butt as she slid into the seat of the car.

The next morning, she awoke with her head on top of Sexton's chest. He had one arm behind his head and the other around her waist. Sasha took her forefinger and began to trace the scar that stood out prominently on Sexton's stomach.

At her touch, Sexton opened his eyes, stared at her and then closed them again. "I see you noticed my battle scar," he murmured, his voice groggy from sleep.

"Is that what you call it?" Sasha asked softly.

Sexton hesitated and then replied softly, "I really think of it as the beginning of my life."

"What do you mean?" she said, looking up at him, willing him to reopen his eyes.

"I was knifed by my brother Sammy when I was in foster care." Sexton's voice sounded matter of fact, as if this had been an everyday occurrence for him.

"You've got to be kidding! You said that you had wonderful foster parents."

"No," he denied. "I said that I had a wonderful experience with my adoptive parents. Before that I was in foster care. It was an experience, but not wonderful."

Sasha was quiet for a minute, not wanting to be too nosy, but she found herself wanting to know everything that had happened to Sexton Johnson before he'd breezed into her life. She pressed him to explain by lightly by nudging his body with hers.

"I was in foster care until I was in the fourth grade. There were three of us boys. It wasn't until I started school that I even realized that they really weren't my blood brothers. I found out then because we were all in the same grade and the same class. When we were being taught to sign our names, my pre-K teacher pointed out the differences."

"So your name was Johnson and the other kids' names were something else?" Sasha asked.

"No, everyone's last name was Davenport because that was our foster parents' last name and no one ever questioned it. My first name was Sexton. My adopted parents' name, I mean my mom and dad, their last name was Johnson. After they adopted me they changed my name to theirs and my new life began." Anytime Sexton spoke of his mom and dad his voice softened and his expression took on a look of love and respect.

"They sound wonderful. Maybe one day I'll get to meet them."

"They're both gone. They were in their fifties when they adopted me. Dad went first. He died of lung cancer and then Mom died six months later. I think that she just didn't want to go on after that. They had been together since junior high school and she was at a loss as to how to spend her time without him or any children to look after."

"How did they end up adopting you?"

"My brother told them about me."

"You have a brother?"

"Yes, I have a brother. Teddy was their natural son and a lot older than me. He was a coach at the Boys and Girls Club and I used to go down there to play basketball to escape my home life. He looked after me, and when he found out that I had been stabbed by one of my foster care brothers in an argument over five dollars he asked his parents to adopt me. He wanted me out of that situation. They already knew me because I was also their neighborhood paper boy."

"Do you know anything about your real parents?" Sasha asked gently.

"No."

"Aren't you curious to know who they are or why they gave you up?"

"I may not know who they are, but I do know why they gave me up. Obviously they didn't want me."

"That's not always the case. At the hospital there have been young single mothers who give up their children because they think that's the best thing for them because they can't provide a loving home."

"That may be the case for some, but I was in foster care for years and to my knowledge, no one ever came to look for me. I'm not really interested in knowing anything else. Mom and Dad made me feel so loved and secure that I kind of feel like it would be a slap in the face now that they have passed for me to start looking for some mythical parents. When they were alive they offered to try to get some information through the foster care system, but I declined. Lillie and Henry Johnson had already taught me that family is made up of experiences and memories, not necessarily blood."

"So I gather that you had a really hard time during your formative years?"

He looked at her. "You certainly are loquacious when you wake up. My situation didn't seem so bad while I was living it. Life is like that. You accept that what you have is as good as it gets, and then something else comes along that is better and only then do you realize how bad things really are."

"I hate that you had to go through that terrible time. But you don't seem at all bitter."

"I wasn't always the person that you now see." He hesitated for a minute but obviously felt compelled to finish his thought. "For a while I was a little hellion, but my parents continued to love and pray for me and through their guidance I was able to put my demons behind me."

Gratitude was evident in his tone, and Sasha looked at Sexton admiringly.

Seeing this he said abruptly, "I was arrested."

"For what?" Sasha lightly rubbed his chest in an effort to ease the look on his face. Then gently, "I think every child has stolen a pack of gum or a candy bar before."

"It was more serious than that. I helped my foster brothers boost some stereo equipment from my neighbor's house."

She tried to mollify him. "I'm not surprised by that. Look at the environment that you were being raised in."

"That's not what happened." Sexton began to talk as if he were experiencing a catharsis that was long overdue. "I had already been adopted and was doing pretty well. My grades had gone up and Mom and Dad had enrolled me in an after school basketball program. It was a mentoring program, and some of the older high school kids would come and give us tips on how to be better athletes.

"One day Sammy talked me into skipping practice and being the lookout for him and Kendall as they ransacked a neighbor's house. Sammy had seen them bringing in boxes of equipment the day before. They wanted me to stand outside and warn them if anyone was coming. I agreed, even though I knew it was wrong. Ever since being adopted I had gone out of my way to prove to them that I didn't think that I was better than them, and that I was still one of the boys."

"So you got caught," Sasha guessed.

"Of course we did. The owner was in the bedroom asleep and she woke, grabbed her cordless phone, and hid in fear for her life. From the closet she called the cops and they caught us red-handed. We tried to drop the equipment and run, but when we rounded the corner there were two other cops waiting for us. They took us all downtown.

"In the back of the cop car, Kendall and I started to cry, and I can remember Sammy telling us not to let them see us cry."

Sexton's voice trailed off and Sasha could tell he was momentarily lost in memories.

"I don't think in all the years we were together I ever saw him cry." His brow was furrowed and Sasha reached up and smoothed it out with her finger.

"Then what happened?" she asked gently.

"They took us to the detention center. I was still in middle school and I could have been released that night in my parents' care but they left me there."

"They left you?" Sasha's eyes opened wide and she leaned up on one elbow and stared at Sexton.

"Yep," he said, "they left me there for three whole nights. When they finally came to get me, I knew the minute I saw my mother's face that if it had been her decision I wouldn't have spent one night locked up, but Mom and Dad always showed a united front when it came to me. Mom stood there looking at the raggedy cot, the bare gray walls, with fear written all over her face. Dad looked more stoic. He sat down at the end of the cot and stared me straight in the eyes and said, 'Can you imagine how your mother and I felt when the police called?'

"I didn't answer him. I heard Sammy's words over and over again telling me not to let anyone see me cry.

"When I didn't say anything, for the first time since I had been with them Dad spoke harshly to me. 'I told them that it was a mistake,' he said. 'My son wouldn't do such a thing.'

"After all this time, I can remember that even though I knew that I was in a lot of trouble, I felt happiness that he had called me his son without hesitation. And then I felt a sickening feeling in my gut because I had let them down. I looked at Mom's teary eyes and right then and there I decided that I would never be the cause of her tears again.

"Dad asked me whether I thought I would have been able to look our neighbors in the face if I'd gotten away with the robbery. Then he said, 'I won't have my son shaming me, so I let you stew in here for a couple of nights. If you choose to be a criminal you need to get used to being in a dingy dump like this.'

"That was when I hung my head and began to cry. Dad said that he was going to take the money that I had been saving from my paper route to buy a bicycle and give the money to the people we had stolen the stereo equipment from. It had been damaged when we dropped it while we were trying to flee from the police."

"What happened to Kendall and Sammy?"

"Kendall stayed for about a month in juvenile and then they let him out for time served."

"And Sammy?"

"Sammy ended up staying in jail for three months because he had a few priors. They were petty crimes, but he was a teenager. My foster parents didn't show up at his court date so that didn't help. When he got out he was harder than when he went in."

"What happened to you?"

"The judge let me off with a warning. He pointed his finger at me and said that he better not ever see me in his court again. After that I kept my distance, especially from Sammy. I had a moment of clarity about him when I was locked up waiting for Dad to come and bail me out. Sometimes it's hard to see people for what they really are and to realize that there are people in this world who want to do you harm because of jealousy or because they think that you have the chance of something wonderful happening in your life."

"So you never hear from them? I mean your foster brothers?"

"I occasionally hear from Kendall. He's a construction worker in Brooklyn and married with two kids."

"Where is Sammy?" Sasha asked, even though she was fearful of his answer.

Sexton said flatly, "He was killed over five years ago in a gang fight. He was protecting his turf."

"That's very sad." Sasha put her arm protectively around Sexton's waist.

"I have never told anyone that story before," he said quietly.

"Don't worry," Sasha promised, "I won't tell anyone."

"That's not it," Sexton shrugged. "It's just that I've never talked about it. I don't even think about that time of my life anymore. My parents made me feel wanted from the very first day I went to live with them. They sat me down and we had a family meeting. It was the first of many. They told me that they chose to make me a part of their family because they saw something special in me. Dad said that where you are born is by chance, but where you end up is by choice."

CHAPTER 8

Sexton swaggered down the street after leaving Sasha's loft, taking no notice of the numerous women trying to catch his eye. As he stopped in front of a newspaper stand to buy a paper, he suddenly felt a finger tapping him on his shoulder. Turning around, he was surprised to see Tiara.

Her body looked gaunt and there were dark circles under her eyes. Trying to mask his surprise, he gave her a small hug. "What are you doing in the city?"

"Oh, I had to go down to the school board and drop off my references. In order to teach, I have to start from scratch on all of my paperwork. It's so frustrating."

Sexton felt a tug of sympathy for her and said encouragingly, "In the end, you'll be okay, Tiara. You know what they say, it's always darkest before the dawn."

"When is the dawn?" she asked softly.

Sexton was silent for a moment and then said, "It comes when you least expect it."

Tiara said, abruptly, "Where are you coming from?"

He replied without hesitation, "Sasha's. We went out to dinner last night."

Sexton was unaware that when he spoke her name there was a twinkle in his eye that Stevie Wonder could have seen.

"The look you have on your face is the one that my husband used to have when he talked about me, and look what he did."

Sexton hesitated, thinking about how to address her remark. "It's a bad thing that he did to you, Tiara. But try not to let it color the way that you feel about all men. The right one is out there for you, just be patient."

"I know you're right." She pointed to the café across the street. "Would you like to sit for a while? I'm feeling kind of lonely."

Sexton hesitated for a second and glanced at his watch, but noticing the despondent droop of Tiara's mouth he agreed. "Okay, just for a minute or so."

Sexton cupped her elbow as he guided her across the busy street. Once they were seated Tiara eyed Sexton and said, "So I guess you and my girl Sasha are really hooking up now?"

"Sure, Sasha's tight," he finished with a smile.

Then Tiara said in a warning tone, "You don't know how high maintenance she can be."

"I'm not worried about that," he responded.

"But the man is supposed to be in charge." Tiara gave Sexton a flirtatious look from under her eyelashes.

Sexton gave Tiara a sharp look. "I've had enough sim-pering women to last me a lifetime. Anyhow, it's not about being in charge. A good man doesn't have to strong-arm his woman." Feeling the need to change the conversation, Sexton picked up the newspaper he had purchased. "I need to check the stock market and see if I made or lost money last night."

Tiara grimaced and said, "At least you have money to lose. Since my split, I'm pretty much destitute."

Sexton cleared his throat. "Calvin sort of mentioned that to me. I thought that he was going to cover your mortgage for a while."

"He is, and I appreciate that. But it's still not enough." One lone tear fell from her eye and she brushed it away with the back of her hand. "The school board said that because I didn't give enough notice when I quit to get married that my former principal gave me a bad end-of-the-year evaluation. It's on my permanent record, and I'm going to have to substitute teach for a whole year in order to clear up my bad performance review." Suddenly she said, "Damn!" She angrily banged her fist on the table. "This is all Peter's fault." Then her anger turned into a flood of tears. "I'm going to lose my SUV and my lights will be shut off in a couple of days if I don't pay the bill."

Sexton waited calmly for the deluge to stop. "Tiara, let me help out until you can get on your feet."

"I can't let you do that. It's too embarrassing." She sniffled, looking down at some invisible object on their table.

Sexton attempted to comfort her and tightly gripped her hand. "No one needs to know. I won't even tell Calvin."

"I can't," she said, averting her eyes from his. "We don't know each other like that."

"I don't have a way to fix your broken heart, but I can ease your money situation until you can get on your feet. Don't let pride get in the way of common sense, Tiara. How much money do you need a month to cover your bills?"

Tiara didn't say anything for a minute and Sexton could tell that she was calculating bills in her head.

"About five thousand a month." Her voice was low and she avoided his eyes.

Sexton reached in his pocket and pulled out his checkbook. He wrote a check out and signed it with a flourish. Handing it to her he said, "This should cover you for six months. Hopefully you will have resolved things by then."

Tiara slowly took the check. "Sexton, I don't know how I will ever repay you," she stammered.

"You don't have to repay me. It's a gift. Now I need to go before I'm late for practice."

With a satisfied smile, Tiara watched him cross the street and jump into his Escalade.

Sexton parked his car in the Madison Square Garden parking lot and walked past the many vendors selling their wares out of small booths. His eye was caught by a display of stuffed animals. A plush gorilla held a bright yellow banana in its hand. As he halted his steps to study it the vendor smiled at him, and eager to make a sale said, "It talks." He pressed the middle of the gorilla's stomach. 'I'm bananas about you' was repeated several times before the gorilla began to gurgle with laughter.

"How much?" Sexton asked, smiling.

"Twenty dollars."

Sexton handed him a twenty dollar bill and watched as the salesman placed the gorilla in a large bag.

He was standing at the receptionist's desk in the front lobby scribbling a note on New York Knicks stationary when Stefan strode through the doors. Sexton beckoned him over and said, "What are you getting ready to do?"

"Not too much, just passing time."

"Do you remember where Calvin's sister had you pick her friend up?"

"Sure, it was 119th Street."

"Do you mind delivering this to her? She should be at home."

"Not at all."

"Thanks, bud," Sexton said handing him a folded bill. "For your troubles."

⌁

Sasha walked out of the bathroom to stand in front of the dresser mirror with a towel wrapped around her body. She let the towel drop and examined her image. She had a blue mark on the side of her neck and one just below her collarbone.

Last night Sexton had explored every inch of her body. Never before had she felt so sexy or desired by a man. Sexton was a thorough lover, and they had fallen asleep exhausted, their bodies intertwined.

Just then she heard her doorbell ring. Annoyed at having her walk down memory lane interrupted, she went to her closet and pulled out a silk bathrobe. Padding barefoot down the hallway she shouted, "Who is it?"

"It's Tiara."

Sasha sucked her teeth with irritation, but masked it before she opened the door and beckoned Tiara in with a smile.

"Hi, Tiara. You're lucky you caught me at home. What are you doing on this side of town?"

"I had some business to take care of," Tiara answered.

"Take a seat. I put a pot of coffee on a little while ago and it should be ready by now."

"Sounds great." They sat at the breakfast table and Sasha grimaced as she turned in her seat.

"What's the matter with you?"

"I'm a little sore from my nocturnal activities."

"What do you mean by that?"

"Sexton was over last night."

Tiara said teasingly, "When your man leaves, you're not supposed to be feeling all bruised. You're supposed to feel all limbered up."

"It's a good kind of bruising, if you know what I mean." Sasha moved her eyebrows up and down at Tiara meaningfully.

"Is that a hickey on your neck? Don't you think that's a little tacky?"

"It's not as if he was gnawing on it. My skin is easy to mark."

"If a man really has it going on in bed, he doesn't need to bother with all that nonsense."

Sasha shot Tiara a look of annoyance. "You've developed quite the acidic tongue. Don't let your experience with Peter change you."

"My experience hasn't changed me," Tiara denied. "I just think that hickeys are juvenile."

"For your information, Sexton didn't spend all of his time on my neck. But you have heard of foreplay, haven't you? That was just the appetizer before he went in for the main course." Sasha didn't attempt to hide her irritation at Tiara's obvious cattiness.

Tiara continued to be argumentative. "Well it's been my experience that when a man takes the time to put a hickey on your neck, it ain't all that."

"Well, with Sexton it is all that. Sexton is so good it makes me want to holler. As a matter of fact, I do holler." Then Sasha was taken aback by the venomous look of envy that flashed across Tiara's face. "My goodness, Tiara! I do believe you're jealous."

Tiara didn't respond, and the silence in the breakfast nook was deafening. Then she said in a contrite voice, "I'm sorry, Sasha. I suppose what you're seeing is partly from frustration. As you can probably guess, I haven't had any since Peter decided to share himself."

Sasha sat quietly and the air hung heavy between them.

"I didn't expect my life to end up like this."

Sasha leaned towards her earnestly. "This is not the end of your life. You're barely thirty. There are other men out there, Tiara. Let me see if I can get Sexton to introduce you to someone."

Tiara shook her head. "It's too soon. Meeting new men is hard and I'm not ready."

"I hope that you're not still thinking about Peter." The words shot out of her mouth before she stopped to think. Too late she remembered the advice Sexton had given her.

"I know that's not possible. Even if in time I could forgive him for what he did, the way he left me in the lurch with our finances was like driving two stakes through my heart."

"Have you figured out what you're going to do about that?" Sasha's concern showed in her expression.

Tiara stared Sasha straight in the eye. "Don't worry about that anymore. I think that I have all my bases covered."

The doorbell rang and, as Sasha got up to go answer it, Tiara also stood and followed her to the door saying, "That's my cue to leave. I have a list of things to take care of before I start subbing on Monday."

When Tiara opened the door and saw the Knicks chauffer standing on the threshold she said in astonishment, "Stefan, how are you doing?"

He replied, "Very well." Smiling at the two women he handed the bag to her dramatically.

After Sasha took it, Stefan gave a courtly bow and said, "From your not-so-secret admirer." With that he turned and left.

Sasha reached into the bag and pulled out the gorilla and exclaimed, "Oh my goodness, he's so cute." She pressed the tag in the middle of its stomach that smiled as she listened to its speech.

Tiara reached into the bag and handed Sasha the note. "I can guess who it's from."

Sasha read the note silently and, unbeknownst to her, a dreamy smile settled on her lips.

"What does the note say?" Tiara demanded with narrowed eyes.

Sasha carefully tucked the note in the side pocket of her robe. After examining Tiara's face she decided to say only, "He'll see me in a couple of days."

After Tiara left, Sasha sat on side of the bed that Sexton had lain on the night before, and as she gently moved the palm of her hand across the sheets, she reread the words: "Seizing the moment can lead to true happiness if you let it. See you in a couple of days, Sexton."

As she cleaned her apartment that day, every time she walked past the gorilla she pressed its stomach.

Sasha's desk at work was cluttered with the usual end of the month stuff. There was the monthly budget book for her unit, notes with requests for days off from her staff members, and messages from doctors with complaints ranging from A to Z.

Out of frustration she took off her nurse's cap and sat with her head sandwiched between the palms of her hands. The ringing of her cellphone prodded her into action. She opened up the bottom drawer and pulled it out. Looking at the number displayed on the panel, she tried to sound nonchalant as she said, "This is Sasha."

Sexton's voice was its usual huskiness, and he sounded as if he was standing in front of her instead of on the West Coast. "Hello. This is Sexton. How are you doing?"

"I'm good. I saw the game last night. You were great!"

"So you think I did the best that I could with ten minutes, do you?"

"I was riveted," she replied teasingly.

"I would have called you last night after the game, but I was afraid that I would wake you up."

"Never worry about that. I'm used working different shifts here at the hospital. If you did wake me up I could drift back to sleep in a New York minute."

Sexton chuckled and said, "I'll remember that for future reference."

"Thank you for the gorilla. I absolutely love it. Whatever made you think of doing that?"

"I remember whenever my dad would surprise my mother with stuff like that it made her day." Then he laughed. "It would make Teddy's and my day, too. Mom would make him an extra good dinner. When I was a kid I loved smothered pork chops and succotash with rice and biscuits. Dad would be whistling as he headed to the shower before we sat down to eat."

Sexton sounded nostalgic as he reminisced. "Mom didn't really like us to spend the night over at our friends' houses because she didn't want us to make a nuisance of ourselves, but if she was ever going to say yes, that was the time to ask. She would want to get rid of us so she could thank Dad without us hearing them," he laughed. "Teddy and I knew to watch for certain signs, and we learned when to ask for stuff."

Sasha chuckled, "So in other words, you're trying to get me to cook for you?"

"You don't have to cook. Just be in a good mood when I return."

"When are you going to be home?" She eagerly anticipated another sexual encounter with Sexton.

"In a couple of days," he replied. "I'll plan something for us to do."

"I look forward to it." Then she said before he hung up, "Take care."

"I will, and you do the same."

There was a tentative knock on her office door and Sasha said, "Now I really have to go. Someone's at the door."

"Yeah, me too. Calvin's waving me over."

Sasha looked up and Susie stood in the doorway with an apologetic look on her face. "I'm sorry to interrupt, but I need to talk to you about something."

Sasha replied, "Actually, I'm glad you stopped by because I need to talk to you also. But you first. What can I do for you?"

Susie hesitated, then looked Sasha directly in the eye. "I need a raise. My son's daycare went up fifty dollars a week, and I just don't have the extra money to cover it."

She gave Susie a look of sympathy. "I'm sorry to hear that. I know that daycare is expensive. Some women don't even find it worthwhile to work until the children go to school."

"Well, I can't afford to stay home," Susie countered stiffly. "My husband Paul has been laid off his job and we can barely make ends meet with just one paycheck."

"I feel for you, but I can't give you a raise. You had your annual review just three months ago, and I feel the raise that came with that was quite generous. Most employees only got three percent, which is the average, but you got four because you were making around that when you were working third shift."

"I know, Sasha," Susie agreed. "It's just that I need more money."

"I don't know whether you are going to like my solution. The reason why I needed to talk to you is because, as you know, you came to this department to work second shift and occasional weekends for which you would get time and a half. That was supposed to start after your trial period, which ended four months ago."

Sasha tapped the desk calendar and said, "Starting next week your new shift will begin."

Susie stuck her lips out her lips in anger. "I have a child. I don't know how you could spring this on me at the last minute and expect me to make accommodations."

Sasha replied firmly, "I'm not springing anything on you. When you chose to switch to this department, I stipulated from the very beginning that I would work your shift for only a short period of time in order for you to learn your new position."

Susie replied sulkily, "But you never complained or said that you wanted to switch."

"I don't have to explain it to you, but it is not convenient for me to work nights or weekends anymore." Sasha said strongly, "I'm the head nurse. No other one in the hospital works that shift."

"But I don't have anyone to keep Dylan."

Sasha replied gently, "How about his father? You said that he's not working."

"He isn't, but he thinks that they are going to call him back to work in a month or so."

"Well, until they do, I don't think that it's unreasonable for you to expect him to watch his son." Sasha queried, "Do you?"

"No, not really," she answered dully.

The next afternoon, Sasha had just completed the finishing touches of the schedule when her office phone rang. Picking up the receiver she said, "This is Ms. Diamond."

"Miss Diamond."

Sasha recognized the voice of the new intern, Lolita, who was performing the duties of a candy striper in order to fulfill the obligations of community service hours for a college scholarship. "There's a gentleman here to see you."

"Is it the family member of a patient?"

"No, ma'am." And then she whispered, "He said that he's a friend of yours." Lolita lowered her voice even more, "He's fine."

Sasha smothered a laugh. *It must be Sexton.* I'm getting ready to leave for the day anyhow, so tell him I'll be out in a minute."

She grabbed her handbag from the file cabinet, snatched up her keys, hurriedly locked her office door, and walked down the hall to the nurses' station. As she approached the desk, her steps faltered when she realized that it was Abdul who stood there waiting for her.

Pursing her lips in displeasure, Sasha walked up to him and said sharply, "Why are you here?"

When Abdul looked at her, Sasha could tell by the tightness of his lips that he didn't appreciate her manner. "I need to talk to you," he replied tightly.

Sasha observed Lolita and the other nurses pretending to work, but knew that they were listening to their conversation. Motioning for him to follow her, Sasha led Abdul into a nearby empty room. Once inside, she turned around and said, "The patient who occupied this room died the other day. I think that this is an appropriate setting for a discussion between the two of us because it represents what happened to our relationship."

Abdul's eyes flashed fire, but his words were controlled. "You have the worst attitude, Sasha."

She didn't answer him but stood there with her hands on her hips, glaring at him.

"I'm sorry about what happened."

"Were you sorry when you were having sex with Pandora?"

"I wasn't having sex with her. She was having sex with me. There's a difference."

Sasha made an indelicate snort of disgust. "Not to me there isn't."

"I don't know why you're so angry. We never said that we were exclusive."

"If you felt that what you were doing wasn't wrong, why did you keep it a secret?" she demanded.

Abdul didn't respond. He just stared at her.

"You took the choice from me. If you had come to me like a man and said that you wanted to see women other than me, it would have been my decision as to whether or not I wanted to be with you under those circumstances. But you knew that I would have said no and not given you the time of day. So, you sneaked." Sasha's tone was derisive, "And you sneaked because you wanted me to only see you."

"It didn't happen that often."

"Once is more than enough," Sasha retorted. "I think that the way you're taking advantage of Pandora is the worst. You know that she's young, and dumb, and you're using her."

"She ain't that young. Pandora is over twenty-one and she went into our arrangement with her eyes wide open. She knew what she was doing. Young girls ain't what they used to be," he replied.

"Just because she's sexually active, it doesn't mean that she's mature."

"She's mature enough to know what to do in order to please a man. You don't know how to let a man be the leader!"

"If you knew how to lead, I might follow you!" she sneered. "But excuse the hell out of me because I don't want to follow you into the poor house. That's something I can do without! Why makes you think you deserve two women? You don't even deserve one."

Abdul's eyes glittered with a harshness that she had never seen before. "You drove me to do that. If you weren't so old fashioned in bed and could handle your business, I wouldn't have found the need to seek what I need elsewhere."

Sasha got white hot with anger and her reply was shrill. "Don't try to blame your cheating ways on me."

"Did you notice what Pandora was doing for me?" he paused, "You wouldn't! If a woman is really trying to please her man, that's what she does."

"You're disgusting, Abdul. First of all, I wasn't feeling it. Second of all, any sex that you got from me was far more than you deserved. It's not as if you made me feel like climbing a mountain."

Abdul continued trying to gloss over his behavior by blaming her. "You never were in our relationship for the long haul. You never really went out of your way for me, Sasha. When a woman goes out of her way for a man sexually, it means that she really loves him and is in it for keeps. When was the last time you even cooked a meal for me?"

There was a long silence in the room as Sasha digested his words. She deliberately let her eyes rest on the fly of his pants, and then she stated quietly, "You're right."

Abdul became even angrier with Sasha's casual acceptance of his words, but he tried to disguise it and do some damage control. "Having said that, I do miss you, and I came here today," he stopped at the incredulous look on Sasha's face and cleared his throat, "hoping that we could try to heal this breach between us. I'll fire Pandora and we can start fresh."

"No, thank you, Abdul. If I want a dog, I'll go to the pound," Sasha answered without hesitation.

Abdul sucked in a deep breath and said, "You're still angry. Let it go."

"I'm not really all that angry," Sasha denied. "Obviously I'm disappointed in you, but I'm just not interested in seeing you anymore. What drew me to you in the first place was respect, and I have none of that for you now."

"I know that I've complained about, let's just say about the lack of variety in our sexual relationship, but I really miss us, Sasha. You really are an expert in every other department. Can't we spend at least one more time together?" He paused, trying to sound cajoling, "How about tonight, for old times' sake?"

Sasha stared at Abdul, appalled that he could ever suggest such a thing. She made another indelicate snorting sound through her nose and replied brutally, "You sure think more highly of your dick than you ought to. No, thanks, I've been there and done that."

Anger and jealousy stole across his face and then he said heatedly, "You think that I don't know what's really going on with you? Pandora told me about seeing you at the basketball game with your rich friend, getting all out of a limo trying to shine." He stared at her and his nostrils flared with anger. "And I saw you going into Sylvia's with that basketball player, thinking you were all that. Nothing's going to come of it because he's just playing with you."

Sasha began to laugh. "So that's why you're here? And who are you to talk about a person's motives? You must be worried about something or you wouldn't be trying to slip in the back door." Sasha stared at his glowering expression and finished by saying, "You and Pandora are a match made in heaven. Go to her, Abdul. I don't ever want to see you again."

Abdul stood his ground and looked Sasha up and down. "I didn't want none no how," he sneered. "I was just trying you, to see what you were gonna say."

This made Sasha laugh even harder. "You know you're lying. You just trying to play it off and say you don't want none because you can't get none." She flung open the door for him to exit and it banged up against the wall with a loud thud.

Abdul slowly walked out the doorway. Then he stopped and turned. Just as he was about to say something Sasha kicked the door closed, and the decisive sound as it clicked shut ended their conversation once and for all.

Sasha was on the way to the grocery store and was still reeling from the scene with Abdul when she almost collided with Tiara. "Girl, what's your hurry? You almost knocked me down."

Flustered she said, "I'm sorry. I didn't see you."

Sasha eyed the bags Tiara carried and said mischievously, "Girlfriend looks like she's been doing some shopping."

"I don't need your permission to spend money, do I? It's not yours, is it?" Tiara gave Sasha a prickly look.

"I was just making an observation, Tiara. What the hell is wrong with you?"

There was a long, uncomfortable silence, and the next words Tiara spoke were considerably softer. "I know that I shouldn't be spending money, but I was feeling depressed. I just felt that I deserved something."

"Then go ahead and treat yourself. You've been through a lot lately."

Tiara searched Sasha's face. Satisfied with what she saw she said, "Are you on your way home?"

"Yes, but I have to pick up some grocery items first."

"Why aren't you at work?" Tiara asked.

"I'm just leaving, but I'm taking a few days off because my hours will be different when I return."

Tiara lifted her eyebrow. "Really?"

"Yeah, I'm tired of working nights and I've paid my dues. I want to work nine to five like normal people." In an attempt to make Tiara laugh she added, "That's why I went to college."

Tiara smiled her response and then she looked at her Gucci wristwatch and said, "I have to get going. I got a permanent sub job at the school, and that means that I'm getting paid as a sub but I do the work of a teacher. I have papers to grade for tomorrow."

Sasha stared at Tiara's retreating back and shook her head as she watched her throw her Bergdorfs and Bloomingdale bags in the back seat of her Lexus SUV and take off in a hurry.

There must be a full moon tonight because people are really getting on my nerves.

CHAPTER 9

Sasha was standing in front of the meat case at Wholesome Foods when her cell phone rang. She smiled when she saw Sexton's number and spoke into the mouthpiece, "Are you back?"

"Yes, ma'am. We got in about an hour or so ago. Do you want to get together tonight?"

He sounded so sexy that Sasha felt a sudden moistness in her groin area. "That sounds great."

"Why don't we grab a bite to eat?"

"Sounds like a winner to me," she readily agreed. "How about around seven?"

"See you then."

"Sexton?"

"Yes?"

"Dress casually," she ordered.

"Yes, ma'am," he replied.

~⌒~

Sasha hurriedly unpacked her groceries and placed them on the kitchen counter. Glancing up at the clock on the kitchen wall, she noted that she had only an hour and a half before she was expecting Sexton to arrive.

She walked over to the LCD television and pressed her TiVo list for *Oprah*. The topic of the show today was how to help children in Africa and where to send donations to help build schools. Sasha quickly scribbled on a pad the toll-free number that was on the bottom of the screen. Then she turned up the volume so she could hear the show while she cooked dinner.

After she prepared rice and succotash, she left the pork chops to simmer on low. She again glanced at the clock and realized that Sexton should be arriving within thirty minutes.

Hurriedly, she peeled off her clothes and stepped into the shower. She gave an involuntary shudder as the spray of cold water hit her body and then relaxed after the temperature adjusted and hot water sprayed her.

She gave her face a thorough cleansing with her facial bar while in the shower and completed her routine with astringent and moisturizer after she got out. The only makeup she applied was eyebrow liner and a coral lipstick for color.

Then she reached for a bottle of pure shea butter and applied it from her neck to her feet. She finished by spraying her favorite perfume, Insolence, in the air and walking through it.

Crossing into the bedroom she opened a drawer and pulled out thong underwear and bra. After quickly donning them, she reached into her jewelry box and put on a small pair of hoop earrings with matching necklace.

Sasha was standing in front of her closet, absently chewing her bottom lip in concentration, when she heard her doorbell ring. "Just a minute," she yelled. Grabbing a dress with a zipper down the front, she quickly put it on and hurried down the hall.

Sexton stared at the lovely vision Sasha made as she stood in the archway. She had pinned her hair in a top knot and several tendrils on each side had escaped and framed the delicate features of her face.

Sasha reached her hand out to him and he let himself be drawn into her charm.

"I smell something good in here, and it's not just you." He slapped her playfully on her behind.

"You sure do. I kind of figured that after your road trip and eating out for days you might like a home cooked meal."

Sexton followed Sasha into the kitchen. He towered over her as she lifted the lids off the pots to show him what she had prepared. "You like?" she added, pleased with the expression on his face.

"I like," Sexton replied softly and lifted her hand turned it over and kissed the area just below her wrist.

＝＝

Sasha watched Sexton as he ate his second helping of food. "I TiVoed your games while you were gone."

"You did?" he said.

"I sure did. You're moving up in the world. You played at least one quarter in each game," she said teasingly.

Sexton gave her a wry look. "Sasha got jokes."

She laughed. "I saw the first two games, but I had to work the night you played the third so I watched it later. In the second game, it seemed as if that rookie from the Suns was deliberately baiting you."

"Everyone does that. If the other team can make you lose your cool they have the advantage. Mind control can be the difference between winning and losing."

"It's kind of like that in medicine. We have some patients that we know aren't going to make it because they've given up hope, and then we have others that we don't think will live and they end up recovering and going on to live healthy lives for years."

Sexton said abruptly, "Calvin didn't travel back with the team. He caught an earlier flight. He wanted to get back to New York as soon as possible because Tiara is having such a hard time adjusting to the single life."

Sasha looked at Sexton for a minute and then said, "Tiara acts as if she's angry at the world. I'm getting a little tired of her attitude. She and I have been best friends forever, but I'm sick of bearing the brunt of her anger. She's not the first woman, and certainly not going to be the last, to have her man cheat on her. Maybe she should try to deal with the blow that has been dealt to her and move on."

"That's not easy for some people. Give her more time."

"I have no other choice. I'm certainly not going to cut her out of my life. That would be hard for me as well as for her." Sasha stood and picked up Sexton's empty plate. Putting it in the sink full of warm water, she motioned for him to follow her into the den. Sasha had muted the television while they ate. Now she handed the remote to Sexton, giving him a knowing look when he immediately changed the channel to ESPN.

"Are you scheduled to work the night of the twentieth?" Sasha had returned to the kitchen and he watched her through the pass-through window that divided the den and kitchen.

She quickly put leftovers into containers and placed them in the refrigerator, then stacked the dishwasher. "No," she responded. "I'm not scheduled to work any more Saturday nights. My shift has changed at the hospital and starting Monday, I'm a nine-to-five girl Monday through Friday."

"How did that end up happening?"

"I decided that I want to have a life," she murmured quietly.

Pleasure was written all over Sexton's face. "Coach's wife is having a birthday party for him at their house and I want us to go."

"What kind of attire?" She sank down on the couch and sat close enough to him that she got a whiff of his cologne.

"Usually their parties are dressy-casual. Everyone connected to the team will be there."

"That sounds interesting," she said musingly. "Now what shall I wear?"

"Of course that is the question of all questions."

"Well, I don't want to embarrass you in front of your friends at my coming out party."

"Honey, you couldn't embarrass me if you were dressed in a potato sack. You have a way about you that is truly mesmerizing. I noticed it the night we met. You were in a roomful of men, yet I didn't see you policing the area trying to figure out who would be the best catch. When I was a teenager, my mom told me what to look for in a woman."

"And you think I'm it?" Sasha asked.

He thought her eyes looked like liquid fire in the soft light. "I knew from the moment I saw you that you're the kind of woman that a man could leave behind on a road trip and not have to worry about another man sleeping in his bed while he was gone."

Sexton gently touched her cheek with his finger. "I just love the way you tilt your head when you're listening to what someone is saying, and your walk is one of the sexiest I've ever seen. It's not overdone like the models on the catwalk, but every person in your vicinity becomes focused on your movements. You carry yourself like a queen."

The ringing telephone shattered the sexual tension in the room and Sasha listened for the caller I.D. to identify who it was. When the automated voice said, "Cellular, Long Island," she looked at Sexton and said, "It's Tiara. She'll leave a message if it's important." There was silence and then the sound of the dial tone.

"I guess it's not," Sexton said.

Sasha repeated his words and stood. "I guess it's not." With her back to him she unzipped the front of her dress and stepped out of the pool it made around her feet.

Sasha bent over, and picked it up, then threw it to land in Sexton's lap. Clad only in her bra and thong, she turned and headed down the hallway with Sexton following on her heels. Her bedroom was lit with scented candles, seemingly waiting for them.

~

Sasha visited Mr. Ramirez during her morning break. "How about a game of cards?" She stood at the end of his bed reading his chart. Once she had entered his room and seen the pallor on his face she had become nervous; his condition had rapidly deteriorated during the weekend.

"I hope you don't mind if we skip it today. I'm feeling unusually tired."

Sasha attempted to mask her worry by smiling brightly. "I know that you're just tired of beating me, and I'm glad that you decided to give us a break. Before we duel again, I need to practice on someone else."

Mr. Ramirez made an effort and gave her a weak smile. "Sasha, don't end up alone like me."

There was a tense silence in the room. "You're not alone. You have me."

"But what if there is no one like you for yourself?" He leaned over to his nightstand and handed her a sealed envelope. "The chaplain was in to see me earlier today and I wrote a few things down. He has a copy of it because I wasn't sure that you would make it in today."

"I'm here all day now. That means when you're awake, I'm here."

"That's a good thing." Mr. Ramirez's voice became stronger and his face brightened. "How's that new man of yours?"

"Not too shabby, if I say so myself. We're going to a party at his coach's house Saturday night."

"Good. You're young. You need to be around life, not death." Sadness hung in the air after Mr. Ramirez's words.

Sasha's spectra link buzzed and she pressed the button. "Sasha Diamond."

Lolita spoke so low that Sasha could barely hear her. "You have a visitor at the front desk, and this one is even finer than the last."

Sasha knew that it had to be Sexton. "He is, isn't he?" she bragged. "Can you direct him to Mr. Ramirez's room?"

"I'll walk him myself," Lolita replied eagerly.

Sasha looked at Mr. Ramirez with a wry smile because of Lolita's words. "I want you to meet him," she said quietly.

Sasha became ever more amused when Lolita entered the room with Sexton in tow, because her expression spoke volumes.

"Thank you," Sasha smiled at her.

Lolita grinned at Sasha as she walked out, and from behind Sexton's back she mouthed the words, "Oh my goodness!"

"I came by to tell you that Coach wants me and Calvin to travel to Philadelphia, and we won't be back until Friday night."

"Why does he want you to go there?"

"To do public relations stuff for the team. There's a basketball camp for underprivileged kids this summer and he wants me to run a sort of mini-camp. Calvin is going to give a workshop on how to stretch and limber up before playing a sport."

"So I won't see you for the rest of the week?"

"No. That will give you a chance to miss me."

"I miss you already," Sasha said with a small pout on her lips.

Then, as if she suddenly remembered where they were and that they were not alone, she said, "I'm glad you stopped by because I want you to meet my favorite patient."

Sexton walked over to where Mr. Ramirez was sitting propped up in the bed and extended his hand, "Nice to meet you, sir. Sasha has told me a lot about you."

"Same here." He looked Sexton over and a look of acceptance crossed his face. "You have a gold mine in that one," he said, pointing at Sasha as she blushed.

"I know," Sexton agreed. "She's a keeper."

Once they were alone Mr. Ramirez eyed Sasha shrewdly. "I like your young man."

"I like him, too."

CHAPTER 10

"Where have you been and what have you been up to?"

Sasha laughed when she heard her sister Dominique's voice.

"Good morning to you too, sister dear."

"Don't 'sister dear' me. Mom is worried about you. She tried to call you at work the other day and no one seemed to know where you were."

Sasha yawned into the receiver and looked at the clock. "I switched shifts. I'll call her and let her know. Do you realize that it's only eight o'clock on a Saturday morning?"

"Of course I realize that. The twins have been up for hours."

"Well, I sure hate it for you," Sasha responded.

"Stop dodging my questions. I demand an answer. Hold on a minute. That's my call waiting, and it's Desiree. I'll put us on three-way call."

Sasha waited patiently and then heard the gentler voice of her sister Desiree.

"Sasha, where have you been and what have you been up to?"

Sasha laughed and replied, "My goodness, Desiree, you get more like Dominique every day. Those are the exact words that she said right before you beeped in."

"And she still hasn't answered my question. Come on now, young lady. Give an account of yourself."

"I'm grown. I don't report to the two of you," Sasha answered teasingly.

"Well, whatever you've been up to, you have to put it on hold," Dominique ordered.

"That's right. Benjamin got us front row tickets to go and see Tyler Perry's Broadway play *What's Done in the Dark.*"

"My brother-in-law is the bomb," Desiree chimed in.

"When is the play?" Sasha asked.

"Next Saturday night at eight. It's sold out, but we got lucky. One of Benjamin's patients works on the set, and he gave him front row tickets."

"Is the guy too sick to go? I don't want to go to the play because of someone else's bad luck," Sasha said.

"No, he's fine. That's why he gave Benjamin the tickets. He's very grateful."

"In that case, I'm surprised that you don't want to go with Benjamin. You know how you like to show him off all the time."

"Ha, ha, ha," Dominique replied without rancor because she knew it was the truth. "No, this time I'm taking my sisters. It's been a long time since we did something special that was just the three of us."

Desiree echoed Dominique's sentiments and Sasha smiled because it always amused her how much the two of them had in common even though their demeanors were totally opposite.

"It sounds like fun," Sasha acquiesced.

"What? No 'Let me check my schedule and get back to you'?"

"No. This is the perfect opportunity for us to catch up. I have some news for the two of you. You will find this very interesting, Dominique. You might even dance the Irish jig."

"Well, don't make me wait for two weeks. Tell me now," Dominique demanded.

"No," Sasha responded, "I have an appointment at the beauty parlor this morning so I don't have time to go into it. Besides, I want to see the look on your faces when I tell you."

"Is it good news or bad news?" Desiree asked.

"Its great news," Sasha replied.

"Let's meet at the theatre around seven fifteen sharp," Dominique instructed.

"Sounds good to me," Sasha said.

"Sounds good to me also," Desiree agreed.

Kitty's House of Beauty was located on Lee Boulevard in Brooklyn and it took Sasha three subway connections to get there. As she thumbed through the latest issue of *Cosmo* as she traveled, her eyes focused on an article that gave step-by-step instruction on diverse sexual tricks guaranteed to please your man.

Sasha was so engrossed in the article she looked up in surprise when the subway ground to a halt at her stop. Glancing down at her wristwatch, she realized that she would have to step on it to make her appointment. She stuffed her magazine in her bag, climbed to the street and hurriedly walked down the block to the salon.

The salon was one of three located on the block. It was always crowded with customers because it had the reputation of having the best hairdressers and the most up to date hair stylist techniques. If a customer saw an actress sporting a hairdo that she wanted to duplicate, all she had to do was to bring in a photo or cite the television program and the 'do' could be replicated immediately. Sasha rarely had to look in the style books because she always knew what she wanted before she reached the salon.

When Sasha opened the door to the salon she noted wryly that it was the typical Saturday with the radio blaring music and a television that was muted but playing videos that were featured on B.E.T.

Sasha was met with a chorus of hellos and smiles when she entered the parlor and as she walked past the barbers. "Hey everybody!" she said. "How are you guys doing?"

"I'm fine. What's new?" Candy asked as she looked Sasha up and down from head to toe. Candy had the chair closest to the barbers and she never had a curtain around her booth because she was so nosy she didn't want to be cut off from everyone else and miss the gossip.

"Not much," Sasha replied. She had been a patron at Kitty's House of Beauty for over a decade, and she usually had a good laugh or heard one or two rowdy discussions before someone got mad and told someone else off.

However, she was always careful not to discuss her personal life at the salon because she had witnessed patrons confiding information about themselves only to become the topic of conversation after they left.

Clarence and Chauncey were the only men who worked in the salon. They specialized in cutting men's hair and shaped up the edges of women who were wearing the stylish short hair cuts. Whenever there was a discussion about anything, they felt inclined to volunteer the man's point of view.

Sasha walked down the aisle that divided the store. When she reached her hairdresser's booth she saw that the chair was empty. She plopped down into the seat and asked, "Marjorie, where is your sister?"

In the opposite booth Marjorie was in the process of braiding a young girl's hair. "She said that she'll be right back. She went next door to get some chicken gizzards. You know how Kitty likes to eat."

Sasha laughed. "I hope that she's not planning on eating that mess and doing my hair at the same time."

Marjorie laughed. "She wouldn't do that. She'll just make you wait until she's finished every morsel."

"Not today she won't. I have to get out of here as soon as possible, and I want to get my hair crimped."

"What's going on? Do you have big plans tonight or something?" Marjorie gave her a quizzical look.

Sasha hesitated and then replied nonchalantly, "I'm going to a party and I need to look my best."

Marjorie looked at the pretty picture Sasha made in her plaid green shorts, matching skirt and Sketchers. She looked like a model in an Old Navy commercial. Marjorie said, "You should get the Halle Berry cut. Now that she's rockin' it longer, you won't look as if you're a wannabe."

"No, thanks," Sasha politely declined. "Short hair is harder to take care of than long hair. You have to use a curling iron every day."

"No you don't," Marjorie denied. "All you have to do is wrap it at night. You should think about it. You're so pretty you can get away with a real short hair cut. Not every woman can because they'd look too mannish."

Sasha turned as Kitty stomped towards them with an apologetic look on her face. "I'm sorry, girl. They told me that their gizzards would be done in a minute, and it took them ten."

"Well, where are they?" Sasha asked, looking at Kitty's empty hands.

"I ate them on the way over here."

She caught the look that passed between Sasha and Marjorie and said defensively, "I only ordered twenty." Neither of them said anything and then she said with a stronger tone, "You know they give you those little itty-bitty pieces."

Marjorie said in a mildly exasperated voice, "Do what you want. But if you're not careful you're gonna be as big as a house, and then you'll never get a man."

"I'm only a size sixteen. I heard on the news that seventy percent of the women in the United States wear from a size twelve to sixteen." Kitty made a derogatory snort. "Anyone smaller than that is on television."

"But you're only thirty-three, and the stats show that most people gain an average of ten pounds a year. If you keep eating like this you're going to weigh a ton when you hit forty."

Kitty was obviously upset by her sister's criticism and said, "Being skinny doesn't guarantee you a man. Ain't that right, Sasha?"

"Don't draw me into your argument," Sasha protested. And then she looked at Marjorie. "I don't appreciate you making your sister mad when she's getting ready to do my hair. I don't want to leave here looking like I had a Britney meltdown."

Marjorie stared at Sasha. "I'm not trying to hurt her feelings. I just want her to cut back on her food intake. That's the third trip she's made to the store today, and it's not even lunchtime."

"I like my size. I eat when I'm under stress, and believe me, I'm under a lot of it. Being the owner of a beauty parlor and dealing with all of these different personalities and their issues isn't all fun and games," Kitty said. "You've always been skinny. You eat a lot, too."

"But if I had to watch my weight, I would," Marjorie claimed.

"People always say that they can do something when they don't have to do it."

Sasha attempted to change the conversation when she saw the amused looks from the other people in the salon as they listened to the argument between the two sisters.

"I want my hair crimped." Sasha smiled cajolingly at Kitty.

Clarence always enjoyed a good argument, and not wanting the subject changed, he yelled down to them from where he stood cutting hair. "I like my women plump. There's more for me to love."

"You just like big women because you want people to think that you have a big one. You're trying to overcompensate." Chauncey laughed as he edged his customer's hair at the base of his neck.

"I ain't got nothin' to be ashamed of. I'm Gigantor's son," Clarence bragged.

"That's a lie. You ain't got nothin' going on there but the rent."

"How you know? You been checking me out in the bathroom, old man?"

"Ain't nobody looking at you. Your ex-wife told my girl." Laughter erupted in the salon.

"But your momma told me it's the biggest she ever had and she wished that I had been around before she met your daddy. Then maybe you wouldn't have to buy those toys so your woman can get satisfied."

Laughter in the salon erupted again and Clarence and Chauncey stopped cutting hair long enough to give each other a high five. Then Chauncey said in a serious tone, "If you talk about my momma again, they're gonna find you six feet under."

"I'm trembling," Clarence replied dryly.

Another hairdresser, Shaneka, was also not quite ready for the first conversation to be let go. "I agree with Kitty." She sat in her chair and was in the process of polishing off a can of Pringles that had on the label 'thirty percent reduced fat'. "Skinny women ain't always got it going on. Look at Sasha's girl, Tiara. She's skinny and running around thinking she's a big deal driving that Lexus SUV, and her husband was caught picking up a hooker."

An uncomfortable silence fell in the salon and several hairdressers studiously kept their heads down, focusing on their customers as they pretended that they didn't hear what had been said.

Kitty said, "That was uncalled for, Shaneka. Why did you have to go there?"

"What? We've been talking about it for weeks." She pointed at her. "You the one that told me that the guy was Tiara's husband."

Kitty cast Sasha an apologetic look. "We were all discussing it and I just said that the guy is Sasha's best friend's husband. You're the one," and now she pointed to Tawny, whose station was on the other side of hers, and said, "who said it was good enough for Tiara because whenever she came in here she thought that she was too good to talk to you because you have four kids and have never been married."

Tawny put her curling iron down and said, "I did say that because it's true. I notice she ain't been in here since that shit hit the paper. I heard that if your man cheats on you your stuff ain't no good!"

"Then your stuff must be real raggedy, Tawny, because your baby girl has two half-brothers that are around the same age she is." Clarence looked at Tawny, daring her to say that he was lying.

"I don't care what Joe did. Anyhow, we were on a break when that mess happened."

"As a former player, I can tell you that when men tell their woman that they need a break it's an excuse so they can try out some new stuff." Clarence couldn't stop himself from needling her.

"That ain't what happened. I left him. He didn't leave me. It's not as if we were married or anything. He ain't trying to go nowhere now, is he?"

Clarence couldn't let that pass. "That's because he can't afford his own place with all those kids."

"That's what you say. Joe pays all of my bills. Everything I make I get to keep for me and my daughter. He don't do nothing for those other kids." She stood with her hands on her hips as if she was daring anyone to dispute her story and glared at Clarence.

Sasha had been quiet throughout the pointing of fingers, but then she looked at Shaneka and said firmly, "Tiara is my best friend, and I'm not going to talk about her business with anyone." Next, she shot Tawny a dark look and then added, "I've been in here at the same time as Tiara and I've never noticed her snub you or anyone else. Maybe you have an inferiority complex." Another long silence hung in the air.

Chauncey bent his head, pretending to need deep concentration as he edged his customer's sideburns, while Clarence grinned at the ruckus he had helped create.

Tawny's eyes flashed angrily at Sasha and she opened her mouth to retaliate but instead closed it.

Obviously wanting to ease the tension in the room by changing the conversation, Kitty said to Sasha, "I have a new girl who's doing the waxes. She's Asian and doesn't understand English very well, but she's real good and she's cheap. She's in the back." Kitty bent her head and whispered to Sasha, "She never comes out and associates with anyone, and I don't blame her. I'm tired of these hoochies running their mouths."

Sasha was grateful as well for the change of topic and said, "Good. I'll have my eyebrows waxed." For the rest of the time as Kitty attended to Sasha's needs, neither of them looked in the direction of Shaneka or Tawny. While Sasha was getting her hair blow-dried, Marjorie walked over and said, "You would have been out of this hell-hole over an hour ago if you had shorter hair."

"As I already told you, that doesn't work for me. I'm a hard sleeper and whenever I wrap my hair, the scarf is hidden somewhere in the covers when I wake up in the morning. At least with long hair I can pull it back into a pony tail if all else fails." Exasperated, she finally exclaimed, "Why don't you cut yours if you like short hair so much?"

With an attitude, Marjorie stomped back to her chair and her customer who was staring at the ceiling, attempting to not notice the cattiness.

Once her hair was done, Sasha felt that all the hours that she had been in the salon were worth it. Looking in the mirror, Sasha said to Kitty, "Girl, you gave me the hook up. I love it."

Kitty had taken an extra long time and crimped her hair into small sections. The effect was to make Sasha look more sexy and adventurous than she usually did.

Sasha stood up and stretched. "I think I'm ready for that eyebrow wax now."

"Tawny!" Kitty called sharply. "You aren't doing anything. Go and tell Kym that she has an eyebrow wax coming up." Again she lowered her voice and whispered, "It's the least she can do."

They watched Tawny walk sulkily to the back of the salon where the waxes were done. Kitty then dropped her voice so she wouldn't be overheard. "I'm sorry about them. I can't do anything about it right now because they have leases on their booths. Once their leases are up we'll have a talk and decide whether or not they should continue to work here."

Tawny reentered the salon area and drawled, "Kym's waiting for you. I told her what you need." Then she walked over to the counter and pulled her pocketbook out of the bottom drawer and looked at Shaneka. "I'm going to lunch. My next appointment isn't until five o'clock." Then she looked Sasha up and down. "I hope you're gone when I get back," she said huffily, then made a quick exit.

Sasha turned angrily to Kitty and said, "If you don't get rid of her, you're going to have to change the name of your salon to Kitty's House of Cats!"

Kitty shook her head regretfully. "I can't get over her being so spiteful to you with you guys almost being kin and all."

Sasha was bowled over. "Whatever made you think something like that?"

Kitty said, "You go with Abdul."

"Go on." Sasha's eyes were narrowed into slits and her words were deceptively quiet.

"Well, Tawny and Pandora are first cousins. Pandora and Abdul are cousins also. So you're all kind of family, aren't you?"

Sasha's voice was harsh. "I'm not seeing Abdul anymore, and he and Pandora aren't blood cousins. They're play cousins, and the only playing is with each other. I caught Pandora giving him a blow job. And no, I didn't know those heifers even knew each other. What a bunch of sneaky women. Go figure. He's probably screwing Tawny, too."

CHAPTER 11

Sasha buzzed Sexton in, and not breaking his stride, he stretched out his arms and gave her a big hug. She expectantly lifted her face to his and he gave her the long, languishing kiss that she craved. It nearly took her breath away.

Once Sexton released her he held her at arm's length. His eyes widened in appreciation as they took in the black silk mini-dress she wore. It was a striking contrast to the gold French hook earrings that had square diamonds threaded on them and a matching necklace. They had been a present from Desiree the previous Christmas, and Sasha wore them only on special occasions.

This time her stilettos were made of black eel skin that matched her purse. Even in five-inch heels, she only came to just beneath his chin.

Sexton folded his arms across his chest and said, "I like."

He was dressed in a pair of black trousers and matching jacket. With every movement of his body, the fabric of his suit moved with him. Underneath the jacket he wore a beige shirt trimmed with black buttons. Sasha folded her arms across her chest and said, "I like." Then she reached for her keys to lock the door.

As they waited for the elevator the sexual tension was nearly overwhelming. When the elevator arrived, a neighbor exited and gave them a knowing look before he entered his apartment.

They reached the street and she saw that Sexton had driven his Mercedes. She looked at him teasingly and said, "Show off."

He only winked at her.

—⚡—

As Sexton drove to his coach's house in upstate New York, Teddy Pendergrass's music was playing softly in the background. Sasha placed her hand gently on Sexton's knee and squeezed it playfully. "Don't you have any current music? Every time I get into your car I feel as if I go into a musical time warp."

"I love old music. The lyrics have meaning, and it brings back memories of my parents. You can change it if you want something different," he offered.

"Not a chance," she replied. "I love it, too."

After about forty-five minutes, Sexton exited the interstate and veered to the right down a dark winding road. In the darkness of the car, Sasha studied his profile. "Don't you ever get angry, Sexton? You have the most accommodating personality that I've ever run across. I would think that your personality would be more aggressive. All I ever hear on the news is how out of control our NBA players are. You are the exact opposite."

"I have my days. You just haven't done anything to incur my wrath."

" 'Incur your wrath'?" She raised one eyebrow at him. "When you put it like that, I certainly don't want to. It sounds frightening."

"I never want you to be frightened of me, Sasha. Fear does not promote a healthy relationship." Before Sasha could answer, Sexton slowed the car down and pulled up alongside a booth with a guard. "How are you doing tonight, Clarke?"

"Everything's great, Mr. Johnson." He ducked his head down so he could get a good look at who Sexton had in the passenger's seat. Clarke gave Sexton a conspiratorial manly smile and pointed to the long driveway that led to a brightly lit mansion. "Almost everyone on the list is already here. Enjoy your evening."

After Sexton rolled his Mercedes to a smooth stop, Sasha understood what Clarke meant. There were countless makes and models of every expensive car on the market: Infinitis, Hummers, Range Rovers, Corvettes, and everything else that a person with money might want to view if car shopping was available in one spot.

Sasha pointed at the cars and said, "I'll take one of those, and those, but maybe I'll take that one in a different color." She laughed.

Sexton's only response was to smile, get out, and open her door.

She clung tightly to his hand, her heels clicking on the cobblestone walkway that led to the entrance of the house. Sexton pressed the doorbell and it was immediately opened by a woman in a very short, very revealing, knit dress. She was beautiful, with long black hair that was complemented by her skin. She looked as if she had just stepped out of a tanning salon.

"Why so formal, Sexton? No one else is ringing the bell. The gate guard is making sure none of the riff-raff gets in." She leaned forward and held her cheek out to Sexton, which he dutifully kissed.

"Shiloh, this is my girlfriend, Sasha." He stepped to the side so that the broad expanse of his body no longer blocked the woman's view of Sasha.

Sasha's body had stiffened and the tightening of her hand in his let him know that she'd been taken aback at hearing him call her his girlfriend.

Shiloh gave Sasha an open smile and held out her hand for a warm handshake. "It's nice to meet you," she said. "You know, he turned me down and I didn't like it so I threw a tantrum. Now I understand what's been the hold up. You are astonishingly beautiful, so if you ever get tired of Sexton, call me."

Sasha didn't quite know what to say, but the look on her face made Shiloh burst into a raucous laughter.

"I've surprised her. Don't you know that's the trend?"

"I can't say that I did." Sasha couldn't help sounding a little put out by the suggestion.

Shiloh gave Sexton a long look. "I didn't think that it was possible for you to find someone as old-fashioned as you are. Come on in. The food is laid out in the kitchen, and they're dancing on the porch and in the recreation room. Daddy's in his office talking business with some old guy. Others are just sort of milling around trying to look important."

After giving her assessment of the party, Shiloh turned around, motioning for them to follow her further in the house.

Still holding Sasha's hand, Sexton bent over and whispered in her ear, "Ignore Shiloh. She says and does things to get a rise out of people."

"She's quite good at it," Sasha retorted. "Did she really come on to you?"

Sexton laughed the throaty way he did when he was really amused. "She invited me to do a threesome in which I would be the only male. I politely declined. I know that she didn't mean it to be, but I considered it an insult."

As Shiloh had described, the party was in full swing. Sasha recognized a famous model and an up-and-coming actress leaning against a wall drinking what appeared to be champagne. A group of video vixens chattered a little too loudly, obviously trying to be seen by the ball players.

Immediately she recognized some of the greatest basketball stars and she gave herself a shake mentally, cautioning herself not to gawk at them. Dwight, James, Dwayne, and Penny were all gathered together in one circle talking. If the ceilings in the house weren't so high Sasha wondered if they would have been able to stand up. "Why are players other than the Knicks here?"

"Why wouldn't they be here? Besides a mutual respect for each other, we all love the game, and have a lot in common."

"I understand that, but I've seen some of these players go at it on the basketball court and sometimes their fights have caused them to be ejected from the game."

"That's on the court. Obviously emotions run high when money and ego are at stake. But at the end of the day, we all have the same goal in mind, to make basketball as interesting and competitive as possible." He gave her a look tinged with seriousness, "We're not animals."

"I know that." She squeezed his hand as he led her over to the group they had just been discussing.

"Fellows, this is Sasha." He gave her a look. "You know who they are."

They all smiled and replied in unison. "Hello." Just then Dwayne held out his empty glass to Sexton and said, "Man, I know since you're just getting here you want a drink. Will you go and get me a refill of a Long Island iced tea while you're over there?" He pointed to the waiters at the bar who were in the process of mixing drinks for guests.

"Nice way for you to try to get rid of me so that you can hit on my woman. Get it yourself, I'm no damn waiter."

All the guys in the group fell out laughing, and Penny slapped Dwayne on the back. "That's a good one. Too bad he didn't fall for it."

Sexton led Sasha away and gave the group a stern look over his shoulder at the men still laughing and making jokes. Smiling at Sasha, he said, "What do you want to drink?"

"With all of this testosterone in the air I think that I want to keep it light. A glass of white wine will do me just fine." She spied Calvin and was startled to see Tiara standing next to him.

"Calvin and Tiara are here," she said with surprise.

"I expected to see them here. He always brings her to these things."

"He does? She never told me that."

When they walked up to them a broad grin lit up Calvin's face. He was obviously glad to see them. "Girl, you look smokin'."

Sasha gave a small curtsy and said, "Thank you, Calvin. You look quite dapper yourself. And who is this model that you have at your side?" she asked, looking at Tiara, who was appraising her.

It was true. Tiara looked absolutely breathtaking in a sleeveless coral silk mini dress that buttoned down the front. She wore a string of pearls and matching pearl accessories. As usual, her heels were a perfect match. Sasha noticed that Tiara had had her hair trimmed since the last time they had seen each other.

Tiara dutifully leaned forward and Sasha made smooching sounds at each of Tiara's cheeks, careful not to actually touch her and ruin her makeup. "You look great, Tiara. Why didn't you call me and tell me that you were coming to this?"

From the look on her face, Tiara was obviously groping for an answer that didn't sound selfish. "I figured that Sexton was going to bring you so I felt that I didn't need to call you."

Sexton and Sasha's eyes locked momentarily before Calvin interjected, "Man, I was just going to get a drink for us when I spotted you. How about it?"

"Sounds good to me." For the first time since they had arrived at the party Sexton let go of Sasha's hand. "I'll be right back."

Sasha's eyes followed Sexton as he made his way through the crowd. Then her attention was brought back to Tiara.

"Girl, those two cheerleaders that were fighting over Sexton at the basketball game are here."

Sasha swung her head around and spied the two women that Tiara was speaking about. Rosemary and Monique were part of a group of women who were laughing and talking with some of the Knicks. "I guess they made up because they look like they're having a good time."

"Maybe they're going to form a little group or something and call it 'The Toss Away Club.'"

"That's not very nice, Tiara. Besides, Sexton said that he only dated one of those girls, and it was a while ago."

"I know," Tiara cautioned consolingly, "but take it from me, watch your back."

Sasha bit back a sharp reply and then said, "I'm not worried about Sexton going with some cheerleader. He's already been there and done that."

She turned and saw with relief that Sexton and Calvin were on their way back with their drinks. "Your brother is so handsome and personable."

"I know," Tiara grinned. "He thinks you're beautiful." Then, as if she were confiding some great secret, she whispered, "Calvin talks about you all of the time."

Sasha looked at Tiara in surprise. "He does?"

"He does. As a matter of fact, I think that he wants to go out with you."

Now Sasha felt even more surprised. "He does?" Sasha turned again to look at Calvin, and his eyes met hers. He and Sexton had been stopped by a group of teammates and Sexton was engaged in a heated discussion.

Tiara scrutinized Sasha's expression. "Are you interested?"

"No."

At Sasha's flat refusal Tiara bristled, "Why not? He's better than Abdul!"

Sasha felt her cheeks grow hot with anger, but she held her temper. "I agree with you on that, but as you know, I'm sleeping with Sexton and I don't do friends. I'm stunned that Calvin would even want to go behind Sexton. I thought that they were best friends."

"They are good friends, and that's why he has some reservations about it," Tiara admitted. "That's also the reason he's never approached you. As a matter of fact, he would kill me if he knew that I even mentioned it to you. It's just that I know that after Abdul you said that you weren't looking for anything serious with anyone, so I kind of figured before you took any more of Sexton's time or got into anything too deep with him that you might want to know that you have other options."

Sasha looked at Tiara and replied with mild sarcasm, "Thank you for looking out for me, but I'm quite content with Sexton. It's true that I wasn't looking for something permanent, but he's already worked his way into my heart. I don't want to mess up what we have going on. I want to see where our relationship is going to lead us."

She looked at Tiara's disappointed face and felt as if she needed to appease her. "If Calvin and Sexton weren't friends, and I wasn't in a relationship, I would have been more than happy to get to know him on a personal level. But now that I've been with Sexton, even if he and I were to break up, I could never go out with Calvin. My mom raised me better than that."

Sasha was relieved when Calvin and Sexton returned with their drinks and conversation turned to sports.

Because of what Tiara had confided to her, as Calvin talked Sasha paid a little more attention to him than she usually did, but whenever her eyes met his in conversation, she neither saw nor felt an undercurrent of sexual interest.

The music at the party was a mixture of salsa, rhythm and blues and light rock. Shiloh had invited a group of her friends, and when Nelly Furtado's music began to play, they stood and began to salsa. Sasha turned to Sexton and said, "Do you know how to salsa?"

"Baby, I can do it all." He led her to the dance floor. As they were doing the two step, Sasha had to practically yell over the music, "Who taught you how to dance like this?" Then a note of jealousy crept in her voice. "Your last girlfriend?"

"No, as a matter of fact I had to teach her," Sexton said with a teasing glint in his eyes. "After my brush with the law, Mom enrolled me in dance classes as part of my punishment. I can even ballroom dance."

"Really?" Sasha replied, somewhat surprised.

"After my stint in the hoosegow, I was grounded for a couple of weeks and at the end of my time, Mom came into the room and told me she'd signed me up for dance classes. I suppose she was trying to get some of the heathen out of me."

Sasha laughed at his description of himself, which she knew to be opposite to the kind of man he really was. "I should turn your name into *Dancing with the Stars*. You could be the next Emmitt Smith," she laughed.

"I try to be the best at whatever task is given to me," he replied with a touch of smugness.

They continued to dance, and on the third song Tiara and Calvin came onto the floor next to them.

The music changed and Calvin turned and held out his hand to Sasha.

Instinctively she looked at Sexton and saw a slight nod of permission. She let herself be drawn close to Calvin's body. As soon as they began to dance, the tempo of the music changed from salsa to a slow one by Levert.

She did not feel at all uncomfortable in Calvin's arms. He didn't hold her so close that she felt his sexual organ as she had when she danced with Sexton. Sasha peeked over Calvin's shoulders to find where Sexton and Tiara were dancing.

Sexton had his head bent at something Tiara was saying and he threw his head back and laughed.

A surge of jealousy coursed through her body at the sight, and then surprise at her reaction made her miss a step and she stumbled against Calvin's body.

He steadied her and she looked up into his face to apologize. Calvin stared down at Sasha, but when he realized that she was watching him, something that she couldn't quite fathom was replaced by an expression that she was familiar with.

"Focus on me for a minute, please," he teased. "I know that you're in love with my boy, but you have to pay attention to your dancing partner if you don't want to damage him with those lethal shoes you and Tiara insist on wearing all of the time."

Calvin's words startled her. *Was she in love or falling in love with Sexton?* In the past, whenever someone had asked her if she was in love with Abdul, she'd denied it forthwith. But she had no verbal response for Calvin's words.

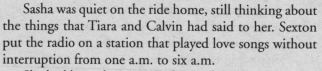

Sasha was quiet on the ride home, still thinking about the things that Tiara and Calvin had said to her. Sexton put the radio on a station that played love songs without interruption from one a.m. to six a.m.

She had been dozing in and out of sleep and was surprised when Sexton pulled into a parking garage in the village. Sitting up, she looked around drowsily and said, "Where are we?"

"At my place. Don't you think it's time for you to see where I live?"

Sasha was wide awake now. "You're right. I need to make sure that you don't have a mistress or a passel of kids in hiding," she quipped.

Sexton gave her a dark look. "That's not funny. What kind of men *have* you been used to?"

Sasha felt chastised. She knew that her words were wrong for an intimate moment, but she was still reeling from the recognition of the depth of feelings she'd developed for Sexton in the short time that they had been seeing each other. She didn't know how to describe what she felt. *Was it love? The sex was wonderful, but did sex alone make for everlasting love?*

Sexton had parked in an open reserved spot. On one side was his Escalade and on the other, his Chrysler 300. "Come on," he ordered. After exiting the door that he held open for her, she stopped in front of him and slid her hand in his. Looking down at her, Sexton silently nodded his head at the look of apology apparent on her face and pinched her backside.

They walked under a covered walkway to a set of steel doors with a key pad to the left. Sexton quickly punched in a combination of numbers and led Sasha down another long hallway. "We have a lot of security checkpoints in this building."

As Sexton led Sasha down the brightly lit hallways towards two sets of elevators that looked like cages, she was amused to see a guard dozing with his feet up on the desk. He roused only when he heard the sound of the elevator as it made its journey down to the first level.

He sat up and his expression showed that besides being embarrassed to be caught napping at his post, he was obviously surprised to see Sexton with a woman. He sheepishly tipped his hat at them and Sexton's only response was to nod his head. Once the elevator doors shut, Sasha whispered, "Thank goodness there are a lot of checkpoints that you have to go through to get upstairs."

"I know." Sexton explained, "Rudy works three jobs in order to help put his daughter through medical school."

"He's a good man then," Sasha said.

"He's a good man," Sexton agreed.

The elevator stopped at the fourteenth floor and Sasha exclaimed, "Wow. You're really up here, aren't you?"

"I'm a tall man, so I need a tall building."

"Well, you got it." Sasha looked around admiringly as she followed Sexton down the hallway to a large mahogany door with a brass knocker on the outside. She pointed to a door almost identical to the one that Sexton was in the process of opening. "Who lives there?" she whispered even though there was no need to since it was all the way down at the other end of the hall.

"A dancer with the Alvin Ailey Dance Theatre of Harlem."

"Wow. I didn't know that they make that kind of money."

"I guess they do okay, but I know that she lives with three other people. They are such a one-of-a-kind ballet troupe. People should include a yearly donation to them just as a matter of principle."

"Do you?"

"Maybe," he responded with a secretive smile. "As for the others, one of the girls is a writer, and the other two are actresses. None of them are ever there for long periods of time so I guess it makes sense for them to share."

Another surge of jealousy coursed throughout her body, and it was reflected in her voice. "You certainly know a lot about your neighbors. I can't even call my neighbors' last names."

"That's bad business," he chided. "It's only smart to have a certain amount of knowledge about the people surrounding you, if for no other reason than for them to look out for you when you're not home."

"So I take it that you don't have a roommate?"

"Obviously not. I wouldn't be bringing you here to stay the night if I did," he replied, and then added, looking her up and down, "for obvious reasons. Calvin is the closest thing I have to a roommate. He's the only other person who has a key to my place. He lives on the fifth floor."

"He does?" Sasha replied with surprise. "I knew from Tiara that he'd recently bought a place, but I didn't know where."

"He was lucky that there was an unexpected opening. People don't usually move out of this building, and there aren't any apartments left to buy. I bought two connecting apartments and had the walls between them knocked down."

At this, Sexton threw open the door. Sasha was immediately impressed by the large expanse of living area that was almost unobtainable in New York City. Then he hit a switch and the room was suddenly flooded by light. A window facing them took up three-quarters of the wall. The drapes were open and Sasha walked over to look at the moonlit view.

"So I take it that you're not afraid of heights," Sexton said.

"If I was, I certainly wouldn't be dating you."

Sexton chuckled and Sasha turned to him, waved her hand and queried, "Do you mind?"

"Not at all." He motioned for her to take a look around. "I'll check my messages." He walked over to his answering machine on the kitchen counter.

Sasha quickly went down the hall to the far end of the apartment and inspected his bedroom. She was amused by the fact that Sexton fit the bachelor stereotype. The bedroom had a king sized bed, dresser mirror and large television that took up the wall in front of the bed. There were no pictures. There was a bathroom off to the left, and in it was a double closet crowded with clothes. The inside of the bathroom had a double shower with a sunken tub that looked as if had never been used and an empty makeup counter with a sink.

Sasha took a tour from room to room, smiling as she spied a Jacuzzi and a weight room.

Turning around, she was startled to find Sexton close to her. He had walked to stand behind her and the thickness of the carpet had made his journey noiseless. "I could really have a good time decorating this place. Why are your walls so bare?"

"I don't know," he shrugged. "I thought about hiring an interior decorator to do it but I don't like impersonal houses."

Together they walked back into the kitchen. "This is a chef's dream," she exclaimed excitedly, seeing the state-of-the-art appliances and huge center island. "I could really make a meal a lot fancier than pork chops and succotash."

"What are you talking about, girl? That meal was fit for a king. It tasted better than caviar to me because it showed that you listen to me when I talk."

Sasha lightly nudged Sexton's leg with her foot. "Of course I listen to you."

He nudged her back. "I know."

"What was Tiara saying to you when you were on the dance floor?"

"I don't know," he replied dismissively. "Why?"

"No reason," Sasha lied, "I just wondered."

"You're jealous," he responded in disbelief.

"No, I'm not. It's just that you laughed so hard I wanted to be in on the joke, that's all," she replied.

"Let me think." Sexton absently rubbed the hair underneath his chin. "I think that she said that it looked like you were coming on to Calvin."

"That's what she said to you?" Her expression was indignant. "And you laughed at that?" she asked huffily. "Are you that secure about me?"

Suddenly the conversation had turned serious and, realizing that, Sexton's expression sobered. "I do feel secure about us because of the kind of woman you are. You wouldn't sleep with a friend of mine any more than I would sleep with a friend of yours. As I already told you mom told me what to look for in a woman," he placed his hand over his heart, "and I know that you're it." He started to say something more, and then paused at the

169

last minute to say with conviction, "Let's just say that I know that you're safe with Calvin. Now I'm tired and ready to go to bed." Having said that, Sexton took hold of Sasha's hand and led her to the bedroom.

The drapes in the room were drawn, and Sasha was grateful for the tight hold that she had on him so she didn't stumble into anything.

He quickly shed his clothes and threw them on the occasional chair beside the bed. Then he took Sasha's hand and closed it around his hard, taut member. Sasha felt the ooze of desire surface between her legs just by the feel of him. Her legs slightly buckled, so in fear of falling she hastily stepped out of her stilettos.

Then Sexton began to unzip her dress and Sasha lifted her arms and bent her head so he could easily remove it. She felt miniscule as she stood in front of Sexton wearing her crotchless panties, and lace bra. Sexton bent down and lifted her into his arms, turned and placed her gently on the bed. Then he lay beside her and gently undid the front clasp of her bra. Once her breasts were free they seemed to reach upwards towards Sexton's lips. He suckled one breast with his mouth and kneaded the other as if he were rolling dough for a pie crust. Instinctively, her body arched and she threw her head back. "Sexton, Sexton," she moaned.

Suddenly he stopped and taking her chin in his hand so that he could stare deeply in her eyes he asked, "What's my name?" Desire was threaded through his words and the look on his face was a mixture of amusement and urgency as he waited for her to answer.

"Sexton Johnson," she murmured and slid her arms around his shoulders.

"Do you still find it funny?"

"I don't find it funny at all, Mr. Sexton Johnson."

Her words were so low he could barely hear her and he leaned in even closer.

She could feel his breath on her face and it felt cool in contrast to the heat from their bodies.

"Say my name again," he ordered.

Sasha quickly obeyed, murmuring, "Sexton Johnson, Sexton Johnson, Sexton Johnson," before he stilled her words with his mouth.

Sexton searched Sasha's eyes. Satisfied with what he saw, he breathed a sigh of relief. He kissed her long and hard, pausing to let her breathe, and then he kissed her again.

Sasha welcomed his tongue with such eagerness he feared it would make him spill his desire and he struggled for control.

"I love you, Sasha," he whispered in her ear.

This was the first time Sexton had openly expressed these words to her and she was too choked up to respond. When the full enormity of what he had disclosed sank in, she her heart beat rapidly and for the first time in her life she felt she had it all.

That night, as Sexton made love to her, Sasha clenched his manhood with every thrust as he moved inside her. She satisfied him in a foreign way, and as she gripped him, he felt as if he was being pulled down into a whirlpool of pleasure. As Sexton climaxed, he called out her name over and over again.

The next morning as Sexton showered, she went into the kitchen to make a pot of coffee. The only coffee maker she found was one on a shelf still in its box. After reading the directions several times, she put it back in its box, frustrated. "It's too hard," she exclaimed in disgust.

"I heard that." Sexton as usual had padded noiselessly into the room. When Sasha looked up, he planted a brief kiss on her upturned mouth.

"Why don't you have this kitchen set up? You have this big expensive place and it's not even habitable," she complained.

"I haven't been here long enough to worry about it. Listen, I'm not going to be able to take you home because I have a morning meeting."

"Okay." Sasha tugged at the hem of Sexton's shirt that she was wearing. It fell to her knees and it made her feel small and petite. "I'll change out of your shirt and then I'll get going so that I don't make you late."

"There's no need for you to hurry, Sasha. It's not even ten o'clock yet. You can go back to bed if you want. I have something for you." He turned around and pulled the "something" out of a kitchen drawer and held it out to her. It was a key ring with several keys attached. "These are the keys to the lobby, my front door and the Chrysler 300. I want you to be able to come and go as you please and travel more easily."

Sasha mutely stared at the key ring, not attempting to take it from the palm of his outstretched hand.

"I don't know about the car, Sexton." She shook her head from side to side.

"Honey, I can't have you traveling the bus or subway all times of night. It's too dangerous."

"I've been using public transportation for years and never had a problem," she denied.

"But now you're my woman."

Hearing this, Sasha raised an eyebrow at him. "You know that you have never officially asked me to be your girlfriend."

"I didn't think I had to. We sleep together, we feed each other, and now I'm trying to protect you. If that doesn't make you my girlfriend, then you need to tell me what does. I have enough to do without having to worry about your safety," he said flatly and his tone made no room for argument. "And I've arranged for you to park it in the garage near your loft." Sexton leaned over to kiss her on the cheek. "Now I have to go before I'm late. Make sure you lock up before you leave."

As Sasha later navigated through the congested traffic, she tamped down the impulse to be childish and drive by A Dose of Reality in Harlem, stop the car in front of the store and beep the horn so Abdul and Pandora would look out the window.

CHAPTER 12

Sasha was standing in front of her closet trying to figure out what to wear to the play when the telephone rang. The I.D. said, Cellular, Long Island. Sasha cast her eyes towards the ceiling in annoyance but felt compelled to answer it.

"Hello," she said quietly.

"Hey, Sasha. It's me." Tiara sounded bubbly, and that gave Sasha hope that she'd want to hear what Tiara had to say.

"I know." Sasha sounded more disgruntled than she'd intended.

"Did I catch you in a bad mood or something? What happened, did you have an argument with Sexton?"

Sasha drew in a deep breath. "Actually no, Sexton and I have been doing great. I've seen him every night this week."

"He has the most free time that I have ever heard of for a pro ball player."

"I beg to differ. He's busy all of the time. Even though the team didn't make the play-offs he has other interests that take up a lot of his time."

"Girl, you're beginning to sound as if you have stars in your eyes. Has what started as a fling turned into something bigger?" Tiara teased.

"Why are you spending so much time thinking about us? I would think that you have enough to worry about." Sasha's sounded openly caustic, and now she didn't care.

"Why are you so snippy? You didn't even want him in the beginning."

"Well, I want him now," Sasha retorted sharply. "Why did you tell Sexton that it appeared that I was coming on to Calvin?"

There was a long silence from the other end. "I was just kidding around, Sasha," Tiara stuttered.

Sasha decided not to let Tiara off the hook with that lame excuse. "I don't think that you were."

"It seems to me that your boyfriend is a bit of an instigator," Tiara replied defensively.

"Sexton is not the instigator in this little scenario. It's you."

"I'm surprised at you, Sasha. You never used to turn on your friends over a little dick."

"It's not a little dick, Tiara. It's a big one," she retorted. "The problem is that ever since you separated from Peter you've changed. I can't handle it anymore."

"We've been friends forever. Now all of a sudden you're tired of me?" Tiara was obviously incensed by the fact that Sasha had drawn Peter's name into their fight.

"It's not all of a sudden, Tiara. I've been trying to work with you, but you've become hard to be a friend to. I know what Peter did was a blow to your ego, but you don't have to try to sabotage everyone else's relationship in order to lessen what your husband did." Then Sasha softened her voice. "I think that you should get some counseling," she suggested.

"I can't afford it," Tiara whined.

"That dress you had on at the party cost at least five hundred dollars. Get your priorities straight and try working on your inside as well as the outside."

Hearing Tiara began to sniffle, Sasha felt a pain in her heart.

"So you don't want to be my friend anymore? You think you're too good for me."

The sympathy that had begun to form again for Tiara quickly died. "That is so ridiculous I refuse to dignify it with an answer." Sasha paused, choosing her words carefully. "I'm just saying that I think we can use a break from our relationship. Sometimes friends need to take a hiatus to get perspective and to get back to what made them so close in the first place."

Tiara's answer was silence.

"I have to go now because I'm meeting my sisters for a Broadway play." Then she said with a solemn ring of decisiveness, "Take care, Tiara, and think about what I said." The sound of the dial tone in her ear was the only response that Tiara gave her.

~

As she walked down the street, Sasha craned her neck, trying to estimate how much farther the theatre was. The traffic had been heavy even for a Saturday night in New

York and she hadn't anticipated the extra thirty minutes it took her to find a parking spot. She knew that the play was being held at the Broadway Theatre and hoped that her sisters were waiting for her outside, or at least had left her ticket at the Will Call window.

The closer the time had drawn for their outing, the more she had anticipated it and she didn't want anything to mar their evening together.

She spied her sisters standing in front of the entrance looking around in every direction, obviously for her. Dominique had her hands on her hips, which spoke volumes, and Sasha knew without seeing it that she was tapping her foot impatiently. Desiree, the taller of the two, looked worried as she anxiously scanned the area. Sasha was breathless by the time she reached them and formed an apology that was shut down before it was spoken.

"You would be late, Sasha! The curtain is about to go up and we've been worried sick. Why don't you ever answer your telephone?"

"I love you too, Dominique," Sasha responded. "I really am sorry, though. The traffic took me off guard."

"You really should be more considerate, Sasha. When there's an event at hand it really is common sense to take an earlier train," Desiree added in a much milder tone.

Sasha reached over and gave her an air smooch on her cheek before she rolled her eyes at Dominique's exasperated expression.

"I didn't take the subway, ladies," Sasha drawled, "but I don't have time to explain right now."

"I didn't see you get out of a taxi," Desiree said, perplexed.

Sasha responded without explanation, "We're already running late, so I'll fill you in during intermission." With a flourish, Sasha snatched one of the tickets out of Dominique's hand, and with head held high, determinedly pushed through the crowd still waiting for other members of their party to show.

Halfway through the play, there was a twenty-minute intermission and the Diamond sisters managed to secure a small round table in the bar area. As they each sipped a glass of white wine, Dominique and Desiree looked at her over the rims of their glasses. "What gives? Why are you looking so smug?" Desiree demanded.

"I don't know what you're talking about," Sasha teased.

"You're looking kind of full of yourself, Sasha. What's going on?" She added sarcastically, "Has Abdul decided to drop the I-don't-care-that-I-ain't-got-nothing facade and actually gotten a real job?"

At these words, Desiree unsuccessfully tried to stifle her laughter.

Sasha looked at both of them, completely unruffled by their teasing. "Say what you want to about him. You ladies can't hurt my feelings anymore with those remarks, not that you ever did. I got rid of that zero and got myself a hero." She shrugged her shoulders nonchalantly.

Dominique and Desiree put their glasses down, both stunned by Sasha's statement.

Dominique asked. They gave each other a questioning look before returning their attention to Sasha. "Whatever are you talking about?"

At that moment, the lights blinked three times and a bell began to sound. "Intermission is over, so you cats have to wait until the end of the play to find out. It kind of serves you right," she ended flippantly and stalked out of the bar.

At the end of the play, the Diamond sisters stood with the crowd and gave the cast a standing ovation. "I love Tyler Perry's plays," Sasha said admiringly to her sisters. "They always have a message. He's right, black men don't go to the doctor enough. They're always trying to cure their illnesses after the fact." She spoke directly to Dominique and said, "Make sure you tell Benjamin how great the play was and how much I appreciate him for hooking us up."

"I will," Dominique answered.

Desiree glanced at her wristwatch. "It's only eleven o'clock. Let's go to the coffee shop around the corner. It's not that far a walk."

"Sounds good to me. I know that my feet are happy to hear that." Sasha looked down at her shoes and said, "I'll be able to kick these bad boys off under the table and probably nobody will even notice."

Minutes later, they sat at the table and Sasha deliberately took her time telling them her news. "*What's Done in the Dark* is the perfect lead in for what I'm getting ready to tell you. Abdul and I are finished."

Neither of them spoke for a minute, and then Dominique said in a mildly sarcastic voice, "Sure you are. I thought that you had something interesting to share."

Desiree agreed. "That isn't anything new, Sasha. You tell us at least every couple of months that you're going to get rid of him, but you don't."

Sasha was a little disappointed that her announcement didn't have the dramatic response from her sisters that she'd hoped.

"I caught his cousin giving him a blow job," she said dramatically.

Both of her sisters' jaws dropped and Sasha said smugly, "Now you're getting it."

"His cousin? Yuck! Someone should call the law!" Dominique said in disgust.

"Well, it turns out that Pandora's not really his blood cousin. They just always call each other that. In fact she's his 'play' cousin. But all the same this has been going on behind my back for who knows how long. I probably would never have known had I not gone to his shop and caught them. Talk about what's done in the dark."

"Are you okay?" Desiree searched Sasha's face. "I mean, you've been seeing him for more than a minute. How are you taking the breakup?"

"Quite well, actually. When I realized that the person that I cared about didn't really exist, it didn't feel so much like the end to a relationship. It was more like ripping a

Band-Aid from a wound that wasn't all that serious in the first place."

Dominique breathed a sigh of relief. "The Lord rains blessings from above. I've been on pins and needles for years, afraid that you were going to marry that nut and end up living on Loserville Boulevard."

"Talk about getting caught with your pants down," Desiree said with distaste.

Dominique snickered and pointed at Desiree across the table. "That's a good one," she said.

As they snickered, Sasha tried to shush them by saying, "I'm not through with my news."

"You mean there's more drama? I think that last bit will be hard to top."

Sasha looked Dominique straight in the eye. "I think you more than anyone else in the family will find this interesting. I have another man." She paused for an added effect. "He's black and rich."

Dominique's mouth fell open in surprise.

Sasha grinned, "I knew you'd like that."

Desiree looked doubtful. "Don't you think this is pretty sudden, Sasha? It's not like you to go straight from one relationship to another."

"I know." She didn't realize it, but she had a faraway look on her face as if she were somewhere else with someone else and not sitting in a coffee shop with her sisters. "But I really like him. This has caught me completely by surprise. It's not every day you meet single, rich, famous, good-looking black men in New York. But it's not that. He's different. There's just something about him that has already cemented him in my heart." Sasha decided to make that comment the last when it came to discussing how much love she already had for Sexton because she didn't want to ruin their evening by giving either one of them a heart attack.

Now she deliberately raised one eyebrow at Desiree in their typical Diamond family mannerism. "And this is your little surprise, Desiree. You have already met him. It's Sexton Johnson."

Desiree's mouth gaped open. "The basketball player?" Desiree demanded.

"That's him," she ended, relishing the fact that she had managed to stun both of her sisters in one evening.

Sasha leaned back in her chair and continued to enjoy the look of astonishment on both her sisters' faces she leaned towards them and whispered, "And believe me, ladies, he does have one sexy Johnson." Then she reenacted Meg Ryan's scene in the movie, *When Harry Met Sally.*

Desiree shook her head in admonishment at Sasha's antics when she realized that couples at the tables surrounding them were eavesdropping.

Dominique scoffed, "You can't build a relationship on that! After a time, sex can wane even between couples who love each other dearly. You better make sure you have more in common than what's between the sheets so that you have reasons to stay together."

"What do you like about this guy?" Desiree asked.

"I don't have to tell him what makes me happy. I like the way he treats me in and out of bed." Sasha's answer was frank and without deception. It came out automatically.

Dominique replied in a voice which was tinged with awe, "I'm impressed, Sasha. I didn't think you had it in you," she quipped.

"Those are very important ingredients to a happy relationship," Desiree acknowledged. "Obviously, I don't care for Abdul. He came to my wedding and tried to snoot his nose up about the fact that I was marrying a white man. If he felt that strongly about it he should have stayed home."

Dominique couldn't resist taking another snipe at Abdul's expense. "And miss a free meal? Surely you jest."

Desiree ignored that, not wanting to be distracted from making her point. "But the main problem that I had with Abdul was that he also seemed to take some of your spontaneity from you. I have always admired how vivacious you are, but the longer you were with him the less happy you appeared to be. Sometimes you were downright morose." She advised, "Have fun with Sexton. Be the Sasha that I have always known you to be. Be a friend and lover to him and if he is the one, everything else will fall into place. That's how I ended up falling in love with Tyler," Desiree ended with satisfaction.

"Abdul was too serious," Dominique affirmed. "He walked around brooding all the time. I don't find that sexy at all."

Sasha laughed. "Well, Sexton isn't like that." Her tone changed to one of a more serious nature. "We have so many of the same likes and dislikes it's scary."

"Have you met his family?" Dominique asked.

"Sexton was adopted."

Both her sisters were quiet as they digested this information. Sasha added, "But the people who raised him sound as if they were clones of our parents. They died a while go and he has a brother, but as yet I haven't met him."

"When am I going to meet Sexton?" Dominique demanded.

"Never!" Sasha responded emphatically.

"Oh, come on, Sasha!" Desiree said cajolingly. "Bring him around. I liked him the time I met him at Tiara's party."

At the sound of Tiara's name a look of annoyance crossed Sasha's face and Dominique said, "Why did you look like that the minute Tiara's name was mentioned? I thought Tiara was your girl."

"*Was* my girl is the correct term. She has too many issues. Ever since she and her husband separated, she's been a different person."

"They're separated already! I guess it's true. Marry in haste, repent in leisure," Dominique said.

"She didn't really know him. He tried to pick up a police officer in that undercover prostitute sting operation."

"My God!" Desiree said. "How humiliating!"

"Oh," Dominique drawled the word, "she's probably suffering from self-esteem issues just like that girl in the play who was going with that married man. I know I would be if I were in her shoes."

"She's acting like she has something to prove. She's become needy and sort of demanding, as well as a bit of a troublemaker. I've decided to distance myself from her until she can regroup." Then even more noticeable irritation crept into Sasha's voice. "Tiara gets angry over little or nothing. When I told her that I wasn't interested in dating her brother Calvin she copped the worst attitude."

"Clearly she has issues," Dominique said with understanding, "But under the circumstances, I think that's to be expected."

Desiree gave Sasha a long, probing look. "Tiara is trying to get you to go out with her brother?"

"Yes. Calvin's fine and all that, but he's Sexton's best friend. How tacky is that!" It was a statement and not a question.

Dominique held her hand out for emphasis. "I know. Never do relatives or associates. Men always tell at least one friend if he's having good sex with his woman."

Desiree was quietly mulling over what she had heard and said, "You're right to distance yourself from Tiara. You need to drop her like she's a bad habit. She doesn't have your best interests at heart."

Sasha and Dominique stared at Desiree because it was so unlike her to be so adamant when giving advice to someone, but before Sasha could question her further

Dominique demanded, "When am I going to meet this stud?"

"Never!"

Desiree chimed in. "Come on, Sasha. You brought Abdul to meet us after seeing him for only a couple of weeks."

Sasha cocked her head in Dominique's direction. "I was just trying to aggravate her. I don't feel that way about Sexton."

Just then, Sasha's cell phone rang as if on cue. She looked at the number and said to her sisters, "Saved by Ma Bell."

"Hey baby." Sasha's voice became a lot sexier than it had been before.

Dominique muttered to Desiree, making sure that Sasha could hear her, "She'll answer for him, but when we were trying to call her before the play, her phone went straight to voice mail."

Desiree smiled and nodded in agreement.

"We're having late night coffee. Not too much longer. That's okay. I'll drive over to your place when I'm done."

Dominique leaned across the table and snatched the cell phone out of Sasha's hand.

"This is Sasha's oldest sister, Dominique," she spoke with authority.

"What the hell?" Sasha exclaimed as she held her hands out helplessly and looked at Desiree, whose answer was to simply shrug her shoulders and give her a look that said, 'What do you want me to do?'

"I'm inviting you and Sasha over to lunch at my place next Sunday. Good! So you're free! How about one o'clock? Great! I look forward to meeting you." Dominique closed the cell phone, handed it to Sasha and said in a conspiratorial whisper to Desiree, totally ignoring Sasha's presence, "He said he can't wait."

Sasha shook her head with resignation and signaled to the waitress that she was ready for the check. "Did you ever stop to think that I might already have plans?"

"Do you?" Dominique asked teasingly.

"Yes, with Sexton." Sasha stressed each word.

"Fantastic. That means my luncheon will fit right in with your plans since you'll be bringing him." She turned to Desiree, "You and Tyler come also. I'll have the twins go to my mother-in-law's. That way it'll be a grown up thing with no distractions."

"How about Mom, Dad, and Marcus Junior? Are we going to make it a family affair?" Desiree asked.

"Not yet. I need to screen this guy first. I don't want to get their hopes up unless Sasha's finally managed to find marriage material."

Sasha waved her hand in front of their faces. "I am sitting here, ladies, and I can hear you."

"Do you mean to tell us that you're not going to start giving your speech about how you don't ever want to get married?" Desiree's eyes were round with speculation.

Sasha remained mute and avoided her sisters' eyes.

"My, my, my," Dominique murmured with satisfaction. "I think the cat finally has her tongue."

As they stood on the corner in front of Dominique's car, Desiree looked around doubtfully. "It's after midnight, and I don't want you on the subway. I'll give you a ride where you're going."

"I don't need it." She leaned over and planted a smacking kiss on each of her sister's cheeks. "Sexton gave me his Chrysler 300. I parked in there." She pointed across the street to a brightly lit parking garage. "See you guys next weekend."

As Dominique and Desiree stood watching Sasha trot happily across the street, their faces were filled with hope.

CHAPTER 13

A few days later, Mr. Ramirez plopped his last card down on the tray and said, "I won again. We really need to come up with another game because you haven't been able to beat me once the last six times we played."

"Instead of complaining you need to be glad that I'm such a good sport."

"I am glad," Mr. Ramirez agreed. "But part of the fun in winning is if you barely do. Something on your mind?" he asked, watching her closely.

"Not really." Sasha didn't bother to explain that she had been distracted because she was thinking about Sexton and wondering what he was doing.

"How's your young man?" he asked perceptively.

"Sexton is great!" Sasha was unaware that her tone was almost gushing.

"When's the wedding?" Mr. Ramirez asked.

"It's too soon to even think about something like that," she protested.

"Why? How long does it take?"

"I would guess longer than eight weeks."

"Whose rule is that?" He admonished her, "I hope that you're not reading one of those self help books that are so popular."

"Not at all," she denied. "But my friend Tiara's husband was hiding a dark secret about his character and they dated for almost a year before they got married."

"That's them and not you, and certainly not that man you introduced to me. What you see is what you get when it comes to him," he declared with forcefulness.

Sasha was happy that Mr. Ramirez had been so impressed by Sexton because she valued his opinion. "I always figured that I would first live with my future husband in order to really get to know him."

"Don't do that," he cautioned. "You don't want to be a rent-to-own bride."

Sasha laughed. "You really have a way with words. You don't really believe that 'men don't buy the cow when they can get the milk for free' adage, do you? We're practically living together anyhow. We each have our own place but we spend every night together when he's in town. Are you saying that we shouldn't spend so much time together?"

"All men are different. Practically living together and actually living together are different. Just make sure you continue to maintain different residences. Statistics show that people who live together first end up in divorce court quicker than people that don't."

"You see, I don't get that. Why does that happen? It would seem that they should know what they were getting into."

"I don't know. I guess that someone in the relationship was pretending to be something they weren't so they could get married. Then after they got what they wanted and the real person came out, the one that was fooled is so angry at the change, he or she wants out."

"My goodness. You're a fountain of information on this," Sasha said with a smile.

"I have a lot of time on my hands. Dr. Phil has become a staple of my life." Mr. Ramirez asked abruptly, "When am I getting out of here?"

"They're going to release you at the end of the week." She looked at her friend's downcast expression and said gently, "That's a good thing. It means that they think that you'll be okay."

"Or it means that they've done all that they can and have decided that the state should stop footing the bill on a lost cause."

Sasha reached over and gently covered his hand with hers. "Where will you go?"

"I'm going back to Mexico. I still know some people there. I've been gone so long maybe my ex-wife won't have a problem running into me at the market."

"The weather would be beneficial for you," Sasha said encouragingly. "New York winters can be hard on the bones." She patted his hand consolingly. "Now I need to go and check on some of my other patients that don't have such a good bedside manner."

~

It was Friday night, and it had been a long and tedious week at the hospital.

"What do you want to do tonight?" Sexton sat on the side of the bed, sliding his feet into the bedroom slippers that were a part of the wardrobe he left at her place.

"I don't know. Do you have anything special in mind?" There wasn't a doubt that they would be spending the evening together. Spending all of their free time together had become a habit. Sasha loved the fact that she didn't have to wait by the phone wondering if they were going to do anything fun.

"How about bowling? There's a new bowling alley that I pass on the way to your loft called Boardwalk Bowl. It looks as if it's real nice on the inside."

"Good Lord, bowling. Can't we do something else?" she whined.

"What's the matter? Don't you know how to bowl?

"Actually I used to like to bowl a lot in college, but now," she held out her hands to show off her perfectly manicured fingernails, "it's not as one would say, financially rewarding."

"Stop being such a spoilsport," he said cajolingly. "If you break one, just go and buy yourself some more." He grinned at her.

"Ha, ha, ha, very funny, Mr. Johnson."

"I never realized that you were such a hothouse plant," he added. "And I must say I'm kind of surprised."

Not wanting Sexton to think that she was superficial, she agreed to go.

Boardwalk Bowl was not the kind of bowling alley that she and her friends had gone to in the past. It had a bar with huge plasma televisions showing different sporting events and a dozen or so pool tables occupied by some serious-looking people playing as if their lives depended on it.

Sasha followed Sexton to the counter. A teenager with spiked red hair smiled and spoke to them. "How are you guys doing tonight?"

Sexton answered, "Fine. We would like to pay for three games and rent two pairs of shoes."

"Sure, what size do you guys need?"

"I wear a size thirteen. How about you, honey?"

Sasha didn't answer at first. She wore a size ten and had always hated the fact that her feet were so large. Sexton repeated his question. "Sasha, what size do you need?"

"Size ten," she muttered.

The teenager turned around and yelled to his coworker who was in the process of arranging shoes that had just been returned. "I need a size ten shoe in women's and a thirteen in men's."

Sasha could have slid to the floor from embarrassment. Glancing at the couple standing behind them in line, she became even more chagrined when she realized that the couple was Asian and the woman looked as if her shoe size was about a size five.

"You guys are on lane seven."

"Thanks." Sasha grabbed her bowling shoes off the counter, hastily switched them with her sneakers, and stomped off, leaving Sexton to pay their bill. When Sexton joined her, he wore a huge grin and gave her a knowing look. "Gee, darling, what big feet you have."

Sasha glared at him, seriously annoyed.

"What's the matter with you? Why so peeved, young lady?"

"Don't even try it. I don't think it's funny that you're making fun of the fact that my feet are so huge."

"I don't get it. What's the big deal about wearing a size ten shoe? Your legs are so long, you'd look funny if they were small." He smiled gently at her. "My feet are bigger than yours."

"They're supposed to be. You're a man, so that's a sign of machismo."

"Then should I be angry because my feet don't do me justice?" he asked teasingly.

Sasha, calmer now said, "I guess not."

They were fierce competitors. Sasha lagged behind in the first game, but by the second she had found her rhythm and gave Sexton a run for his money. Between the first and second game, Sexton ordered a pitcher of beer and an order of wings. Afterword, Sasha felt bloated from the food and was relieved when the last game was finally over.

She looked at Sexton and said good naturedly, "You ought to feel satisfied, Mr. Man. You won all three games. How did you get to be such a good bowler?" she asked, swallowing the last of her beer.

"During summer camp they used to take us bowling every Friday."

She stood up and stretched. "You owe me a massage for agreeing to this."

"All that means is that I win twice in one day, right?" he quipped.

At home Sasha got in the shower and let the hot water pelt her. She made the temperature as hot as she could stand because her knees were already sore.

Closing her eyes, she immersed her face under the showerhead. When she opened them again, she was surprised to find the bathroom completely dark. Sexton had turned the light off and noiselessly slipped into the shower behind her. In the darkness, she could barely discern him. Like a blind woman, Sasha reached out to him and slid her hands down his body, stopping her journey to clench his manhood and pull him closer.

Sexton was holding in his hand a soft sponge and, without speaking, he poured shower gel on it. Turning her around, he began to gently massage the back of her neck with it, moving in slow, circular motions. With the other hand he fondled her. Finally he turned her around to face him and he gently entered her with his finger. She eagerly spread her legs to give him full access.

Sasha was on fire, and it wasn't from the heat of the shower. She started to move towards the showerhead to rinse herself off and hurry Sexton to bed, but he pulled her close. Now he began to suck her nipples and she ached in frustration, wanting to feel him inside her. She threw her head back and moaned.

Slowly, Sexton got on his knees and began to tease her with his tongue. Something started building in her and she tried to stamp it down but she couldn't. When Sasha felt her release coming, she braced herself against the shower wall, afraid that the force of her climax would make her slip and fall.

Sensing this, Sexton stood and pulled her to him. His arms enveloped her in a way that made her feel as if he were shielding her from all future worries and pain. He squeezed her body tightly, held her close to him for a minute, and then kissed her on the side of her neck.

Sasha broke free of the kiss and began to use her lips to lick every inch of Sexton's body. His nipples were as hard as rocks. She feathered kisses all over his body and her hands, wet with lather, followed the path of her lips. Then she slowly bathed him. Pressing Sexton forward under the spray, she rinsed him and when she was through, he stepped aside for her to rinse herself before she followed him out of the shower. They dried themselves quickly and went into the bedroom.

Sasha was wet with desire. When he entered her, she returned thrust for thrust. The tempo of their lovemaking was furious and after what seemed to be an eternity, they fell asleep facing each other with their arms around each other's waist.

The next morning Sasha drowsily walked into the kitchen expecting to see Sexton sitting at the table reading the morning paper, as was his habit. Surprised to find an empty apartment, she looked around and saw an envelope propped up against the coffee pot. She picked it up and opened it. She looked at the familiar scrawl and read, "I've made an appointment for you at Francine's. Go get yourself a manicure and pedicure for those unusually large feet of yours." Shaking her head in amusement, Sasha said aloud, "I'm going to get him."

Later that week, Sasha and Sexton were standing in front of the bathroom mirror at her apartment, getting ready to go to bed. Sasha stood at the sink in her bra and panties with Sexton towering behind her in the boxers that he had pulled on after his shower. They were brushing their teeth like two people comfortable with each other after being happily married for years.

As Sasha bent her head to spit out her toothpaste, her telephone rang. As she listened for the caller I.D. voice to identify the caller, her eyes automatically looked at the clock, noting the lateness of the hour.

When she heard St. Mary's Hospital being identified, she hurriedly crossed the room and picked up the telephone. "Hello."

"Sasha, this is Anita from social services."

"What's going on, Anita?" Sasha knew that it had to be important for her to get a call at home.

"It's Mr. Ramirez. We lost him about an hour ago."

Sasha clutched her stomach and braced her hand against the headboard.

Sexton had followed Sasha out of the bathroom and stood watching her with a questioning look on his face.

"Oh no." Tears began to slide down her face. Sexton walked into the bathroom and came out with a handful of tissues, which he handed to her.

She sat slowly down on the side of the bed. "I was just with him today."

"We knew that he could go at any time," Anita responded gently. "Be thankful that he went peacefully in his sleep. I knew that you had a special relationship with him and I didn't want you to come to work tomorrow morning to find his room empty. He left you a letter, but it's sealed."

"I'll be right down," Sasha replied dully.

"There's nothing that you can do, Sasha. His body has already been taken down to the morgue." There was a slight hint of hesitation before she said, "I'll put the letter on your desk." Anita advised gently, "Stay at home and get some rest. Tomorrow will be a difficult enough time for you as it is."

Sexton sat close to Sasha as she dried her tears. He watched her grieve, feeling it best to say nothing.

That night marked the first time that Sasha and Sexton slept together without making love. Sasha clung tightly to him, so tightly he felt her fingernails digging into the skin on his shoulders. He regretted he couldn't do more for her.

The next morning when Sasha emerged from the bedroom dressed for work, Sexton pointed to a chair at the breakfast table and said, "Sit."

Sasha obediently sat down at the table, looked at the bowl of cereal and glass of orange juice Sexton had prepared for her and said with a grimace, "I don't know why you're always trying to feed me. I could stand to lose a few pounds. Since I started seeing you my uniform is a lot tighter than it used to be."

"I like thick women," he said with a smile. "When I was a little boy I was fascinated by women's breasts. I couldn't figure out why there were so many different sizes and shapes. Then when I was a teenager I changed into a butt man, the rounder the better." He looked her up and down. "Now that I'm full grown, I want the mixed bucket of chicken. I like butt and breasts. Besides, no one but a dog wants a bone."

Sasha knew that he was trying to lighten her mood. The weak smile she gave him let him know that she appreciated his efforts.

Sexton cleared his throat. "Are you going to the hospital morgue to see your friend?"

Sasha made a face. "If he's still there. County may have him because he was pretty much destitute. They'll give him a five or six hundred dollar funeral."

"That's sad," Sexton replied gently. "I text messaged Calvin and Coach to let them know that I wouldn't be in for conditioning until this afternoon. I know that you have to leave for work now, but I'll be right behind you."

"Thanks," Sasha replied gratefully.

"Don't go and see him until I get there," Sexton instructed gently.

Sasha stood up and walked over to where Sexton sat. She gave Sexton a kiss that held more gratitude than sexual desire.

—

As she sat at her desk in her office and stared at the envelope, she blinked back tears. Mr. Ramirez had scrawled in large letters, *To my daughter, Sasha Diamond.* She heard a rapping on her door and looked up.

Lolita pushed open the door and said with eyes as big as saucers, "He's here."

Sexton walked into the room and asked Sasha gently, "Are you ready to go and say goodbye to your friend?"

"He's gone. I was waiting for you before I opened this."

Sexton didn't answer, he just sat down in the chair across from her desk.

Sasha carefully slit it open and withdrew the letter. It had three pages. She quickly scanned the contents, then carefully read it three times before placing it back in the envelope. Sasha tried to reseal it and, when the flap wouldn't stick, she pounded the back of the envelope with her fist.

Sexton leaned forward and took the envelope. Then he pulled a long piece of tape from the desk dispenser, calmly sealed the envelope, and then handed it back to her.

For a minute there was silence in the room. Then Sasha said, and her voice sounded far away. "He wants to be cremated. He left a separate letter for Anita with his wishes."

Sexton looked surprised. "Does the hospital do that?"

"No, because it costs between two and three thousand dollars," she responded quietly. "But he wouldn't have known that."

"If your friend wanted to be cremated, we'll cremate him," Sexton stated with authority.

The rest of the day, Sexton stayed by her side as she made the arrangements. They went to the crematorium that the hospital recommended and arranged to have Mr. Ramirez's remains delivered to her afterward.

~

Friday morning, Sasha and Sexton managed to find a place of solitude on the Long Island Ferry. She stood inside the circle of Sexton's arms and following the instructions of Miguel Ramirez, bending over the rail and letting his ashes float into the water.

After they arrived home from scattering the ashes, Sexton asked her to play a game of cards with him. Sensing the denial that was forming on her lips, he held the deck out to her and said quietly, "For your friend."

As they sat at the table and began to play, Sasha soon saw that Sexton was not going to allow her to have a pity party and take it easy on her.

Hand after hand, he kept his edge, and before long his total reached five hundred, "Game," he announced, "Mr. Ramirez would have enjoyed his send-off," he finished quietly.

The accuracy of those words made her realize how in tune he was to her feelings and how much she'd come to rely on him for support and comfort when she needed it.

That night, as her body lay tangled with Sexton's, she felt overwhelmed with thankfulness that he had come into her life. In no other relationship had she felt such intimacy. But instead of being afraid of her feelings for him, she relished them.

She looked over at Sexton's sleeping body. He slept on his stomach, and the sight of his buttocks as they rose and fell with his breathing ignited a curling sensation in her gut.

She reached over and softly slid the palm of her hand from his shoulder blade to the top of his thigh. Feeling her touch in his sleep, Sexton rolled over onto his back. She stared at amusement at his penis standing at attention and ready for inspection.

Sasha began to gently fondle him as if she were using Braille and was trying to understand every thought and feeling that he'd ever had.

She was suddenly aware that her touch had awakened him. He was watching her through hooded eyes as he gave her full access to his body.

Smiling in the darkness at his open invitation, Sasha began to play with him. She took the palms of her hand and massaged his chest with circular motions. Then she pulled her body up and half covered his so that she could feather kisses along the area that she had just touched. Sexton closed his eyes and let his head sink back into the pillow.

She took her forefinger and drew an imaginary line down the center of his body, from the top of his chest to his navel. Then she followed the path with her tongue, all the while keeping the firm yet soft hold she had on the power between his thighs.

He began to moan, and he hardened even more inside her hand as she gripped him, slightly eased the pressure, and then gripped him again.

Feeling a power she had never felt before, Sasha slid her body down until her face was positioned just below his navel. She cocked her head to the side and reached for him.

Sasha felt Sexton's body flinch from surprise. First, she took her tongue and leisurely licked the tip of his penis. Then she let her tongue trail up and down the sides.

Sexton's body jerked upwards and his feet moved in excitement. Then she took him completely into her mouth. Several times, Sexton convulsed, and when it felt as if he were going to pull away from her, she stilled his movements, flattening the palm of her hand against his body.

For what seemed to be a time without end, Sasha pleasured Sexton and only when she felt he was on the brink of losing control did she pull away from him.

Immediately, he pulled Sasha up to him and after gently easing her onto her stomach he lifted her buttocks and then slid easily into her.

Her body was moist from the pleasure that had built inside her while she had pleasured him and they climaxed together.

Sasha awoke a few hours later and saw Sexton was sleeping in a position that he never had before. He was turned onto his side in the fetal position and appeared to be sleeping as soundly as a baby. Peering over at him, she smothered a laugh at the smile plastered on his lips. As Sasha watched Sexton sleep she spoke softly, "I love you, and I'm glad that I do."

Because she was so intent on not disturbing him, she didn't see Sexton's eyes flutter open at the sound of her words. Then, with a smile, he closed them again.

———

Sexton looked at his wristwatch as he drove the turnpike to Ridgefield. "We're going to be a little late getting to your sister's house."

"Anytime from one o'clock until two will be good for her."

"I couldn't get you out of bed."

"We couldn't get each other out of bed," she corrected him in an affable tone. "You should feel special. She has never invited any of my other boyfriends to her house."

Sexton shot Sasha a look. "Why do you think that is?"

"Obviously she didn't think that they were worthy." Sasha decided to leave out the fact that she had always told them not to bother because she didn't think the relationship was going anywhere. "I hope that she doesn't like you too much. I don't know what I would do if she actually liked someone that I want."

Sexton looked at her teasingly. "So you want me?"

"Obviously." Sasha let her hand drop between Sexton's legs and she cupped him.

"What are you trying to do? Incite me to make a quick pit stop at a hotel on the way? Then we would really be late for your sister's affair."

Sexton's voice was laced with desire and the throatiness made her squirm in the seat of the Escalade. "We could do that. So what if we're two hours late? At least we would be putting our time to good use," she replied flippantly.

Sexton looked at the exit they were approaching and slowed the SUV down, pretending to exit. Sasha laughed and said, "I was only kidding."

"I know." Sexton straightened the wheel. "I was just calling your bluff."

"How did you know that I didn't mean what I said?"

"You wouldn't be that inconsiderate of your family when you know that they're waiting for us. That's one of the many things that I love about you."

Sasha looked at Sexton from the corner of her eye and, clearing her voice, she said, "You know, that was a virgin act I performed on you the other night in bed."

"I know," Sexton said, grinning at her with satisfaction.

The smug look on his face made Sasha want to be contrary. "You don't really know that. You just hope."

"No," he responded with certainty. "I knew that was your first time. A man can always tell."

Sasha was put out. "Are you trying to say that it wasn't good?"

"I would never say something like that. It's just that I felt teeth."

"What?"

"I felt teeth. I knew that you were a novice because I felt teeth. If a woman tells a guy that she's never done that sort of thing before and you don't feel her teeth you know that she's lying. Seasoned women know how to grip with their mouth so you don't feel them."

Feeling mortified Sasha muttered, "And I thought that I was really doing something."

"You *were* really doing something. As long as you didn't gnaw my boy off. I was so overjoyed that you made the effort it made me want to touch the ceiling." Sexton placed his hand on Sasha's bare thigh. "I'll show you what I like. And I have a feeling that you're a quick study."

There was silence for a while and then Sasha said, not knowing what else to say, "Two hours is a long way to drive for a meal."

Allowing her to change the subject, Sexton looked at Sasha and said, "The purpose of this visit is not to eat. It's so your sisters can smoke me over."

She giggled. "I know, but don't blame me. Dominique invited you and you readily agreed. This is your doing."

"I don't have a problem meeting your family. There are no skeletons in my closet." The GPS began to beep and Sexton said, "I see we're not too far from your sister's house."

"No, we're not. Their house is on the outskirts of town. They wanted enough land for the twins to have horses to ride."

"Sounds like a plan." His eyes were enigmatic as they met hers.

Sexton pulled off the interstate. Soon they turned down a small country lane and he had to slow his SUV for a family of ducks crossing the road to a small pond. "Would you ever like to live in an area this rural?" he asked, watching her carefully.

"I don't think so. I like the hustle and bustle of the city. There's an energy in New York that no other city in the world can compete with. There's always something to do."

"Would you like to raise kids in the city?"

"I don't know. Obviously people's priorities change with time. I know that a person's mind can change at the drop of a hat and things that you thought that you would never want can become something that you want very much." She avoided his eyes because they always seem to see into her very soul. She spotted the long, winding driveway that was the entrance to her sister's estate. "We're here."

The house was a large stone front Tudor style. Two large marble lions flanked the double doors. The minute Sexton shut off the engine, the front door opened and Dominique and Desiree appeared.

Sexton looked at Sasha. "Are you sure you guys aren't triplets?" he teased.

"You knew from the pictures at my loft that we look very similar."

"I can't wait to meet your parents. They're to be commended for gracing the world with such beauties."

Dominique and Desiree stood at the top of the steps waiting for them to get out. As Sasha sat and waited for Sexton to open her car door she intercepted the look that passed between her sisters.

Sexton followed Sasha up the steps and the sisters converged into a group hug. Once they broke their embrace, Sasha turned and introduced him with pride. "This is Sexton Johnson." Sasha pointed to Dominique. "This is my sister Dominique and," pointing at Desiree, "you remember meeting Desiree."

"Nice to meet you." Sexton nodded at Dominique.

Sasha felt a wave of satisfaction at the look on Dominique's face. She was trying not to stare, but Sasha realized that would be a hard thing to avoid. Television didn't do Sexton justice. Today he was a real hunk in his carpenter style denim shorts, white polo shirt and white sneakers.

She, too, was casually dressed. Her hair was tied back with a yellow ribbon and she wore white shorts with a yellow and white striped polo shirt. Yellow espadrilles crisscrossed halfway up her leg.

Sexton turned and smiled at Desiree. "Nice to see you again. It's been too long."

"You're telling me." Desiree pointed her finger at him. "You know, the night I met you I had a feeling that I would be seeing you again. However, it did take a little longer than I expected."

Sexton gave Desiree a look. "It took a little convincing to get Sasha to believe that I have only her best interests at heart."

Dominique finally found her voice. "Well, it looks like she's on board now."

Desiree began to laugh and Sasha shot her a quelling look. "Where are my brothers-in-law?"

Dominique pointed to an area where there was a small stable. "They're down there tending to the horses. It's the twins' responsibility to feed them, but since they're at his mother's house, Benjamin is doing it. Here they come now."

Sasha found herself carefully examining the look on Sexton's face. She had deliberately left out the detail that

Desiree's husband was white. If Sexton was taken by surprise he hid it well.

Benjamin wiped his hands off with a cloth and held his hand out to Sexton. "Nice to meet you. I've seen you play ball on television. You have a good hustle."

"Thanks, man," Sexton said.

Desiree walked over to Tyler and slid her arm around his waist. "This is my husband, Tyler."

Tyler reached out his hand and shook Sexton's saying, "Nice to meet you."

"Same here," Sexton replied affably. "Man, where are you from? West Virginia?"

"I sure am. Born and bred."

"I picked up on the accent right away. My college roommate was from there."

"No matter how old I get or how many bowls of New England clam chowder I eat, I can't seem to lose my accent."

"Why try at all? The twang that people from West Virginia have can't be duplicated by anyone else. There's nothing wrong with standing out in a crowd."

"You're right," Tyler answered with a chuckle.

"Let's go inside. I'm starving because I didn't want to spoil my meal by snacking," Dominique declared.

Inside, Dominique had produced quite a spread for lunch. Honey baked ham, potato salad, cole slaw, chicken fingers and rolls were only a part of the sumptuous repast.

Conversation went smoothly from one topic to another as Sasha sat back and let her sisters grille Sexton.

"How old are you?" Dominique asked in her straight-forward manner.

"Old enough," Sexton replied smoothly.

Benjamin and Tyler laughed out loud and Benjamin gave his wife an indulgent look before he said, "Serves you right."

She clicked her tongue in mock irritation. "You look like a baby."

"I'm everything but," Sexton answered.

Tyler stopped laughing long enough to tell Sexton, "You wouldn't believe the hard time she gave me when Desiree and I announced our engagement."

"Why did she give you such a hard time?"

"Because I'm white," Tyler answered without rancor.

"You're white?" Sexton responded in mock surprise. "I assumed you were an albino like Larry Bird."

Everyone at the table broke into laughter.

Dominique explained, "That's not why I gave you a hard time. It was because Desiree kept your relationship a secret for so long."

Desiree gave Dominique a stern look. "You know why I did that. I didn't want you in my business. And I certainly didn't want you to scare him off."

"Like I could," she replied dryly as she intercepted the look of love that passed between Desiree and her husband. "Well, I was wrong. I can admit when I've made a mistake. Tyler is the best thing that has ever happened to you," Dominique declared with satisfaction. Then she turned a strict eye on Sasha and nodded in her and

Sexton's general direction. "Now if I can get Sasha settled, my sisterly duties will be finished."

Sasha declared emphatically, "Sasha doesn't need you to get her settled. She's doing quite nicely on her own. Isn't that right, babe?" Sasha eyed Sexton.

"That's right." He reached over and clasped her hand with his.

Benjamin and Tyler gave each other man looks that spoke volumes.

⌇

On the way home, Sasha looked at Sexton in the dark interior of the car. "They like you. You did well."

"So did they," he responded quietly.

Sasha gave him an inquiring look. "What do you mean by that?"

"I was also checking them out. My mom told me if you marry a woman who connects well with her family you'll get yourself a good wife and mother."

When Sasha heard the word wife, she turned her head and looked out the window to conceal her expression of hopefulness.

CHAPTER 14

Sexton walked over to the intercom system on the wall by the double front doors. "Yes, Rudy?"

"Good morning, Mr. Johnson. You have a visitor."

"Who is it?" he asked, glancing at the clock on the wall.

"He said that he's your brother, Kendall." Sexton knew the doubtful tone in Rudy's voice was because Kendall had never visited him there.

"Okay, send him on up." Sexton glanced at Sasha as she sat at the breakfast bar. She was dressed, as usual, in one of Sexton's shirts.

Correctly interpreting his look she said, "I'll go and put something on." She slid off the bar stool. When she returned she was dressed in a pair of khaki shorts and a navy tee shirt. She watched Sexton open the door and shake the man's hand. He beckoned him inside.

Turning towards Sasha he said, "Kendall, this is my girl, Sasha. Sasha, this is my brother Kendall."

Kendall gave her a brief nod, "Nice to meet you."

To which Sasha responded with a smile, "Same here."

Sexton had told Sasha that Kendall was only three years older than him, but he had lines of worry on his forehead that could not be erased by a good night's sleep. He was tall, and except for a small beer gut, thin.

Kendall was holding a grey fireproof box in his hands and Sexton eyed it with a questioning look. Kendall said, "I need to talk to you, Sexton." He shot Sasha a look of apology and said hesitantly, "Privately." His voice was gruff but his eyes were gentle and Sasha felt warmth from him despite his words.

Immediately Sasha turned to mutter her excuses and leave, but Sexton stopped her. "I have no secrets from her. She can hear whatever it is that you have to tell me."

Sexton motioned for him and Sasha to follow him into the den. Sexton sat on the couch with Sasha close to him.

Kendall sat in the leather recliner in front of them and began to talk without the preliminary niceties of catching up on each other's everyday life. "I bought our old house," he said in a solemn tone. "You know, the one we lived in while in foster care."

Surprise immediately registered on Sexton's face and noting this, Kendall said flatly, "I know. It's not as if we had so many good times there that I cherished the place. After our foster mom died the other year, some distant relative of hers inherited it. The girl who inherited it didn't keep up the taxes and I saw it on a list of foreclosures. I bought it because I needed a bigger house for my wife and kids and I thought that even though the place hadn't been kept up, it would still be a pretty good fixer-upper. It was being sold below market value and it has a good floor plan with enough room for us to grow."

"Helen," he looked at Sasha, "my wife, wanted a large playroom for the kids so we were knocking down one of the walls and found what appeared to be a opening. This was inside." Kendall tapped the lid of the box that now lay on his lap. Watching Sexton closely he said, "It's adoption papers."

Sexton's jaw clenched and he just stared hard at the box. For what seemed like a long time, no one said anything and Sasha slid even closer to Sexton, as if her proximity could ward off any bad news.

"At first I was shocked, and then I went through them. Do you want me to tell you what they say or just let you read them for yourself?"

Sexton bent his head and stared at the carpet as if he was looking for something.

Sasha knew that he was doing this in order to hide his thoughts.

"They said that they didn't have any information about us," Sexton said.

"They lied," Kendall stated flatly.

"I kind of wish that you hadn't found that stuff. I closed the door on the idea of ever finding my parents a long time ago."

Sasha was fearful of the tone in Sexton's voice. Gone was the strong and confident sounding man that she was so used to and, even though she knew he was trying to maintain his composure, his body language gave away his nervousness.

"I know what you mean." Kendall stared off into space before his eyes were drawn back to Sexton. He looked at him as if he had never seen him before. "There's good and bad news, depending on how you look at it."

Sexton laughed harshly. "Give me the good news first."

Kendall opened the box and withdrew some papers. "Here are our birth certificates. We were born in New Jersey."

"Were we born in the same hospital?"

Kendall handed him one of the papers in his hand. "The last name on my birth certificate is Sexton. They even have my baby footprints."

Sexton's body jerked in shock. There was an indecipherable look on Kendall's face and he shrugged his shoulders. "It appears that we have the same mother, but no dads are listed. I'm guessing because of our appearance that we are only half-brothers." He rubbed the palm of his hand across his forehead in a frustrated gesture. "I have no idea why the Davenports did what they did."

Finally, Sexton said tersely, "They could have told us. I can't believe they left this earth without telling us." Raw emotion clouded his words and he looked at Kendall. "What's my first name on my birth certificate?"

"There isn't one. It just lists Sexton as a last name." Kendall waited for Sexton to digest this information before he dropped the next bomb. "But what your birth certificate does list is that you have a twin." Kendall extended the other paper in his hand out toward Sexton, who slowly took it.

Sexton said nothing, but sat shaking his head as he read the birth certificate over and over again. "Shit. How the hell am I ever going to find him?"

"Do you want to find him?" Kendall asked.

A series of emotions crossed Sexton's face. "I don't know," he mumbled.

Sasha sat dumbfounded. She felt if she should not interrupt this emotional scene with questions because she knew that the two men in front of her were at a loss as to how they really felt now that they knew they were blood and not just foster brothers.

Sasha remained on the couch in order to let Kendall and Sexton say their good-byes in private. She heard them talking quietly before the door was shut with a decisive click.

After Kendall left, Sexton returned to the den, grabbed the remote control and surfed the channels. Sasha knew that he wasn't really looking for a show to watch, was instead just trying to process what he had learned.

She went into the kitchen and began washing dishes and busying herself with other tasks. When she couldn't stand it anymore she walked back into the den. Without saying a word, she took the remote from him and shut off the television. "Now you have a blood brother. That can be a good thing."

"Long ago I accepted that I would never find my roots. I tried to view it as a clean slate that would let me map out my destiny. All this does is dredge up things that I'd put behind me."

Sasha sat down on the couch and gently said, "But you said that you always liked Kendall. He seems like a nice enough guy."

Sexton stated flatly, "He's done reasonably well for himself, considering the circumstances, but this opens up

a whole lot of questions that I don't want to deal with."
Sexton's voice was uneasy. "I mean, is our birth mother
still alive? How about our fathers? Did they even know
about us? And my God, I have a twin brother! Why did
they separate us? Does the twin know, or even care to
know, about me?" The eyes that Sexton turned towards
Sasha were filled with anger and uncertainty. He stood
and said abruptly, "I'm going to go and see Teddy."

Sasha stood and smoothed down the front of her
shorts in a nervous gesture. "I'm coming, too."

The car ride to Brooklyn lacked the typical camaraderie that they usually shared when they went places.
Sexton's countenance was somber, and she respected his
unspoken wish that he didn't want to talk.

When he pulled to a stop in front of a large brick
building that had a sign identifying it as The Boys and
Girls Club Youth Center, Sasha got out before Sexton
had the chance to walk around to her side of the car. For
the first time in hours, he gave her a small smile. She slid
her hand into his and clung to him as he climbed the
stairs to the club entrance.

The inside of the youth center was brimming with
activity. Summer leagues of basketball teams were playing
and on the far side of the gym were ping-pong tables.
Sexton surveyed the gym, obviously looking for his
brother.

A short, rather balding man who was wearing a white
shirt and navy blue gym shorts emerged from the office
carrying a clipboard. Sexton pointed him out to Sasha
and said, "That's my brother Teddy."

Teddy saw himself being pointed at and a huge grin spread across his face. He began to cross the gym to where they stood, only momentarily stopping to give instructions to a group of teenagers who were sitting on top of a ping pong table.

"Sexton, it's great to see you! And who is this beauty?" he asked, smiling at Sasha.

"This is my girl, Sasha." Sexton's words were clipped. "Is there somewhere we can talk?"

Teddy took in the agitated look on Sexton's face and said, "Sure, we'll go into my office." Teddy turned around and led them back to the office he had just vacated.

Sexton motioned for Sasha to sit on the chair across from the desk while he stood next to it. "Did Mom and Dad ever tell you anything about my real parents?"

The harshness of Sexton's voice made Teddy ease back in the desk chair he had sat in once entering the room. "I don't think they ever knew anything about them. What's going on?"

Sexton recounted what had transpired that morning. When he was finished, Teddy stared at Sexton with a stunned look on his face.

"I never knew any of this, or even heard any gossip in the neighborhood. We just thought that you and Kendall were foster brothers."

"That makes three of us," Sexton replied dully.

"If Mom and Dad knew anything about this, they would've at least told me so that I would be able to tell you when the time was right." He paused, "I don't know what to say, Sexton. Are you going to try and find your family?" Teddy's expression was anxious as he worried about what Sexton would find out.

"You are my family." There was no emotion in Sexton's voice and his expression was unfathomable.

Teddy chided him gently. "You're not taking anything from our parents' memory if you choose to pursue this. Everyone deserves to know where they came from."

"I just don't know if I feel like looking for people who didn't want me."

"But how about your twin? I mean, he might be in the same boat you are."

Sexton's answer was not to respond.

Teddy stood up. "Follow me out to my car for a minute."

They walked in silence out the back door to a small parking lot. Teddy walked over to a silver Camry and, using the key ring in his hand, unlocked the door and opened it. He began turning the pages of a leather planner. Then he pulled a small business card out of its side pocket. Handing it to Sexton he said gently, "This is the name of a private investigator. The center has used him in the past. He's pretty damn good and he knows how to be discreet. If you decide that you want some information on this, call him."

Silently Sexton took the card. "Thanks a lot, Teddy." He held his fist out to his brother and their knuckles braised each other in an informal goodbye handshake. "I'll talk to you later. Sasha and I have to go."

Teddy avowed decisively, "If you don't call me, I'll call you." Then he said, "nice to have met you, Sasha."

"Same here." Her expression showed him that she obviously wished that they had met under different circumstances.

On the ride home, Sasha shot a look at Sexton's profile, which was still uncompromising, to say the least. Once they arrived back at his place, Sexton again picked up the remote and again started surfing the channels. She looked inquiringly at Sexton's morose countenance. "Are you going to call the private investigator?"

Sexton looked doubtful. "I don't know. I'm not ready for this to be shared with anyone other than family."

Sasha cleared her throat, "Sexton, hospitals have archives. I can use my contacts to try to find some of the answers to these questions."

Sexton didn't answer her. He just sat there, and the next time he turned his eyes towards her he spoke without emotion. "Leave it alone. Maybe I'll try to find out something later on, but right now I just want to let sleeping dogs lie."

CHAPTER 15

"Uh-oh!" Sasha spoke to the television after she saw the Knicks walk off the court with downcast expressions. Her heart went out in sympathy for them.

She walked over to the intercom system and hit the buzzer.

"Yes, Ms. Sasha?"

"Rudy, I need a favor. Mr. Sexton should be home in a couple of hours. Can you call me when he reaches the garage? I want to plan a surprise for him."

"Not a problem, Ms. Sasha."

She went over to the pantry, withdrew a bottle of champagne and put it in the refrigerator to chill. Then she went into the bedroom and grabbed Sexton's slippers and robe and took them to the game room with the Jacuzzi. Returning to the master bedroom, she took a long, leisurely bath, oiled her body, and stretched out on the bed.

The intercom buzzer startled her awake.

Sleepily, she pressed the button, "Yes?"

"He's here," Rudy whispered.

Now wide awake Sasha said gratefully, "Thanks, Rudy."

When Sexton opened the door, Sasha stood there clad in her terrycloth robe.

Looking at the gloomy expression on his face, she calmly took the duffel bag from his hand, placed it on the floor, and without speaking crooked her finger at him.

Sasha slowly backed down the hallway, her eyes never wavering from Sexton's as he obediently followed her down the hall to the game room.

She dropped her robe and stood naked in front of him. The she tested the temperature of the warm, swirling water with one toe. Nodding appreciatively and with much exaggeration, she immersed her whole body into the water, beckoning him with her eyes to join her.

Giving her a look, he quickly stripped and sank into her outstretched arms.

Neither talked at first, content to enjoy the closeness, and after awhile Sasha whispered as she massaged his shoulders, "I saw the game tonight."

"That certainly was a waste of a few hours." His voice had a bitter quality to it.

"You need to be rejoicing instead of looking so sad," she said, trying to cajole him out of his somber mood. She reached over the side of the tub and poured him a glass of champagne from the chilled bucket.

"Why would you say that?"

"You guys were blown out. I heard the sportscaster say so," she said as an attempt at humor.

Sexton responded somewhat miffed, "You do know that's a bad thing?"

"It depends on how you look at it. The coach didn't let you play at all, so there's no blight on your record."

"I guess if you want to look at it like that," he retorted.

"Also, now more than ever, he should know that he needs to change things around and give you more playing time."

Now Sexton's tone brightened up. "Do you think that will happen?"

"Absolutely," she said. "And to top it all off, you have one more thing.

You have a woman who loves you more than words can say." She kissed him on his forehead.

For the first time since he had gotten into the Jacuzzi, she felt his body totally relax.

When the elevators doors opened, they were surprised to see Calvin standing there.

"Man, I was just coming to talk to you."

"I'm on the way to practice. Aren't you going?

"Sure. Coach called me and told me to see if you were home. He's been trying to get in touch with you since last night."

"I hooked my cell up last night because the battery is low. Why didn't he call my home phone?"

"All I know is he wants you to call him right away." Calvin homed in on Sasha and smiled. "How are you doing? I haven't seen you around lately."

Sasha was dressed in her uniform, and no patient looking at her would know that she had been up half the night talking and making love with Sexton. "I'm fine, Calvin. How about yourself?"

"I'm hanging in there. When's the last time that you talked to Tiara?"

Sasha looked carefully at Calvin and tried unsuccessfully to read his expression. If Tiara had told him anything about their argument, she couldn't tell because his eyes were as friendly as they always were when he looked at her.

"I don't know," she answered, shifting her guilty eyes away from him. "Is she okay?"

"As well as can be expected. Peter filed for divorce, and it should be final soon. Tiara signed the papers because she doesn't want to drag things out, either." He gave her a long look. "Maybe you could call her when you get a chance."

Sasha's response was evasive. "Maybe I'll do that." They had stepped into the elevator, and when it reached the lobby she gave Sexton a quick kiss, smiled at Calvin and said, "I've got to hurry, I'm late enough at it is."

Sasha sat at her computer surfing the net for records of local adoption agencies. Frustrated, she sat back in her chair and reached for the phone.

"Anita?"

"Yes, Sasha. What can I do for you?"

"I have a personal matter. I need to find out information for a person who knows he was adopted. He has a twin but doesn't know who or where this person is."

"Do you know where he was born?"

"Yes, in New Jersey."

"What else do you know about him?" Anita sounded businesslike and decisive. Sasha visualized her jotting down things on a notepad.

Sasha gave Anita all the information that she had and then she said, "This is a personal matter so I really need you to be discreet. I've been trying to find out something and I can't get any information."

"Those records would be sealed unless the mother left information so that she could be found at a later time in case her children wanted to locate her." She added musingly, "I have some contacts. Let me see if I can find out anything."

"Thanks, Anita. You don't know how much I appreciate this."

"It's all in a day's work," she answered before she hung up.

When Sasha let herself into Sexton's apartment, he emerged from the weight room and bounded towards her. She turned her face up for his usual kiss of greeting but instead, he lifted her and swung her around in a circle.

When he finally set her feet on the floor, she was almost breathless. "What's got you so excited?"

"Sasha, guess what Coach wanted?"

"I don't know, but whatever it is it's made you happy." She was thrilled by the look of animation on his face. She hadn't seen him look so happy since he had gotten that earthshaking news from Kendall.

"He wants me to go to Las Vegas and play on the East Coast Conference team. It's almost unheard of for a player with as little game time as I have to get invited to play, but since Sylvester is having reconstructive surgery for his knees Coach wants me to represent the team."

Sexton was so excited that Sasha could barely understand what he was saying.

"I'm so proud of you. This is so great, Sexton. I told you just to be patient and your time would come.'" She beamed. "So my boy is going to Vegas?"

"We're going to Vegas," Sexton corrected her.

"We?" Sasha responded, shocked yet excited by the prospect.

"Of course. I can't go to Las Vegas without my Shorty. Can you take a whole week off?"

"I sure can! I have to get someone to cover me, but I have the vacation time, so they can't really say no." She was already making plans. "I need to e-mail my administrator and give him the dates." She stopped suddenly and gave him a look filled with love. "I'm so proud of you," she ended softly.

"Why thank you, ma'am." He paused for a minute, mentally making plans. "We'll see some of the shows while we're out there."

"I've always wanted to do that." Her eyes widened in anticipation.

"Then I'll make sure that it happens." He lifted her hand in his usual manner, turned it over, and kissed the area just beneath her palm.

A few days later, Sasha rolled over to find Sexton staring at her. "I told you that you would get the hang of it," he whispered and then closed his eyes. He wore a teasing grin and Sasha made a playful jab at him.

They were naked. The sheet that had covered them the previous night lay at the foot of the bed. Sexton moved his body onto hers and stared deeply into the soulfulness of her eyes. "Sasha, I—" he began. Just then the ringing of the telephone broke the intimate moment.

Exasperated, Sasha reached over and picked up the receiver.

"Yes," she barked into the mouthpiece. The voice on the other line was so faint that she could barely make out the words.

"Sasha, I know that you don't want to be my friend anymore, but I need you."

Startled, Sasha held her finger out to Sexton, motioning for him to hold on a minute. "Tiara, it's not that I don't want to be your friend anymore." She stammered out of guilt because she hardly thought about her. "It's because things got to be too hard."

"I know, Sasha."

Tiara sounded so forlorn that Sasha felt a tug of sympathy for her.

"My divorce became final today."

Sasha looked over her shoulder and saw Sexton heading towards the bathroom. He mouthed, "I'm going to take a shower." The bathroom door shut with a decisive thud. Sasha couldn't help thinking that before the telephone had rung, something momentous had been about to happen. Now it might be lost forever.

Dragging her attention back to the situation at hand she said, "I ran into Calvin and he told me it was in the works." She felt genuine sadness for what Tiara was going through, and it showed in the inflection of her voice.

"I think that I'm going to kill myself."

Her words were so faint Sasha didn't think that she'd heard her correctly.

"Repeat what you said," Sasha ordered.

"I don't know if I can go on," Tiara mumbled. "I don't know that I want to."

"Tiara," Sasha said sharply, "you are a beautiful, educated, intelligent woman. You don't want to end your life over something that was never real in the first place." She hesitated and then spoke the words she felt Tiara needed to hear. "He's not worth it. If you want another loser I'll take you out to the club Friday night and you can have your pick of those at happy hour."

Sasha was relieved to hear a small chuckle from Tiara.

"Will you come over?" she said. "I'm just so lonely."

"Of course I will," she agreed at once. "I'll bring lunch."

Tiara's voice noticeably perked up, and she eagerly asked, "What time will you get here?"

"I don't know. With traffic, probably one o'clock."

"That long?" Tiara complained.

"I'll be there as soon as I can."

"Thank you, Sasha," Tiara said humbly. "You're a good friend."

Sasha hung up the phone and looked at Sexton, who had just emerged from the bathroom. A towel was draped around his waist and Sasha's eyes met his in the mirror he was in front of.

"I guess you heard," Sasha said.

"Not all of it, but enough to know that your drama queen friend is at it again." He was rubbing lotion on his arms.

Sasha didn't correct him because he only spoke the truth. "Her divorce is final."

"What is she mourning? She was living in a fool's paradise and she found out while she's still young enough to get on with her life. She ought to throw a block party."

"I think she's still remembering Peter as the man he showed her when they were dating. That's her feeling of loss."

"But he never was that person."

"I know." Sasha propped her head up with her arm. Sexton sat down on the side of the bed.

"I think I should go and see her."

"I thought that we were going shopping for our Las Vegas trip today. You said that you wanted to buy some things."

"I know, but we still have time. The trip is a few weeks away."

"But what am I going to do today?" Now Sexton sounded plaintive.

Sasha's expression was indulgent as she looked at him. "Since I'm going to be with Tiara, why don't you call her brother and you two can play together."

"Funny!" he answered. "I think that I'll go down to the gym and get some practice in."

———

Dressed in green and white Bermuda shorts, white tee shirt, and flip flops, Sasha rang the doorbell at Tiara's house. Immediately the door was flung open. Sasha gasped at the sight of Tiara. Her body was almost waif-like and there were dark circles under her eyes.

Sasha plastered on a smile as Tiara reached for the food. Only half jokingly, Sasha said, "Dive in right away. You don't have a minute to waste."

Without answering, Tiara led Sasha into the kitchen and placed the packages from Quizno's on the counter. She stared at Sasha and said, "You look good."

"So do you. You're too thin, but still beautiful."

"I've always been the kind of person to eat with company and I don't have that anymore."

Sasha felt remorseful. "We went through a rough patch. Friends do that sometimes. Look at Paris and Nicole. If they could work things out, I know that we can."

"If only I had their money," Tiara said wistfully.

"Money is not the end all or be all of happiness."

"Spoken by a person who has it."

"I don't have any money," Sasha denied.

"Maybe not, but you have access to it."

"Sexton does things for me, but I'm not on his pay-roll. I've learned how to budget for the things that I want."

"Calvin said he would continue to pay my mortgage for another six months, but I've decided to sell the house."

"I think that might be best. You can make a fresh start with the money you make from the sale."

"I can't keep draining his finances." Tiara averted her eyes from Sasha's.

Sasha nodded her head in understanding. "Where are you going to move once you sell the house?"

"I'm seriously thinking about moving to Atlanta. Everyone that I have ever known to move there doesn't come back, so it must be okay. All three of my sisters are now living there."

"Really?" Sasha responded surprised. "I thought that Penelope was in Las Vegas."

"She was, but her job relocated her. She still has her place in Vegas but mostly she's in Atlanta."

"You come from a close-knit family, as do I. They can help you through this, and the money from the sale of the house will make you financially independent until you decide what you want to do." Sasha decided to change the subject to a topic that wasn't so taxing on the nerves. "I didn't know what you wanted to eat so I brought you broccoli and cheese soup with Caesar salad and bread. That's what I always get." She started taking their lunch out of the bags.

"Thanks, Sasha. That sounds delicious."

Sasha looked at Tiara as she sipped her soup. "Is there anything that I can do to help you through this?" She felt another tinge of conscience caused by her long absence.

"Sasha, you just being here has lifted my day." And when she smiled at her Sasha saw behind the sadness of her eyes a glimpse of her old friend.

That afternoon Sexton was bent over tying his sneaker laces when he heard his name being called. "I'm in here." He straightened just as Calvin walked towards him, smiling. "I saw your Benz in the parking lot. What are you doing here? I thought that Saturdays are your 'All About Sasha' days."

Sexton held back what he was about to say to Calvin about Tiara's demands, which had infringed once again on his time with Sasha. "She and Tiara are having lunch together so I had the opportunity to get some practice in."

"They are?" Calvin seemed surprised. "I'm glad to hear that. She hasn't said it, but I know that Tiara's been missing not having her around as much as she used to."

Sexton didn't want to get into that discussion. "Are you going to the All Star game?"

"I sure am. I'm going to be on the team of trainers for the East Coast." Then he gave Sexton a knowing look. "I bet you can't wait to get to Vegas. This is your turn to shine." He sat down on the bench and started stretching his calf muscles.

"In more ways than one," Sexton spoke without thinking.

"What do you mean by that?"

He mentally weighed his answer before he admitted, "I'm going to ask Sasha to marry me while we're out there."

"Oh, my God! That's great news. Dude, you really are sprung!" Calvin slapped Sexton on the back in congratulation. "I mean, I didn't think that you would ever get married. You used to be so wild."

"Those days are over. That gets real boring after awhile. I want a woman who I can trust when I am in and out of town and someone to be there for me when I need it."

"I think Sasha is fantastic. I told Tiara if I was ever going to marry, it would be someone like Sasha. She's so beautiful and vivacious." Calvin halted when he caught Sexton staring at him with narrowed eyes and amended his words. "I mean, if I ever get married again. The last marriage that I had will probably last me a lifetime."

Taking what he said at face value Sexton said, "Instead of eyeing my woman, maybe you should start shopping around for yourself. Jump back into the game."

"Maybe I will," Calvin said, passing off Sexton's suggestion.

When Sasha let herself into her loft she found him asleep on the couch. She tiptoed over to him and began to tickle the bottom of his feet. He moved them restlessly in response to her touch.

Immediately his eyes opened and they were completely unguarded. For one very long minute they held each other's gaze.

"Do you want to do anything tonight?"

"Yes," she stated, brutally honest. "I want to spoil you in and out of bed."

She held a bag in her hand and Sexton sat up in an effort to try to see what she had.

"I thought that we were going together to go shopping for clothes for the trip."

"We are," she said giving him a coquettish look. "But I saw this on a mannequin in a window and couldn't pass it up. Sit back and watch a DVD while I freshen up before I cook dinner."

Sexton settled back, eagerly anticipating the evening.

When Sasha sashayed out of the bedroom thirty minutes later she was wearing a black and white French maid outfit.

As she walked, Sexton glimpsed a black ruffled garter belt at the middle of her thigh. On her feet were black heels with fur across the top. Sexton sat up straight to get the full effect.

Sasha positioned herself in front of him. Her outfit was black satin with a lace cap. Sexton was enthralled.

"Monsieur Sexton, may I interest you in a glass of wine?" Sasha had her accent down to a tee.

Sexton's words were throaty with desire. "*Si, senorita.*"

Sasha grinned, "That's not French, silly, that's Spanish."

"I know. I took Spanish, not French in high school," he replied, not at all put out.

"Well, I took them both," she bragged. "I'm what you might call your international flavor of the month."

"Not a flavor of the month," Sexton corrected her, "but the flavor of a lifetime."

Sasha blushed at his words and then reiterated her question. "Wine, Monsieur Johnson?"

"*Oui*," he answered. "I know that word."

When Sasha turned around to go into the kitchen, Sexton let out a loud snicker. The back part of her maid's uniform left her buttocks exposed. A satin thong disappeared between her cheeks.

"Sasha," Sexton called out as she poured him a glass of wine.

"*Oui*, Monsieur?"

"I thank God that I met you."

She sauntered over to him and handed him a glass of wine. She sipped from her wineglass and after swallowing softly replied, "So do I. Every day and every night."

Sasha prepared spaghetti and meatballs with garlic bread. After three helpings he said with feeling, "That was fantastic," and patted his full stomach.

"Thank you." She bowed her head in acknowledgement. "In order to keep the theme of the evening consistent, maybe I should have cooked something French, but I don't know how to begin."

Sexton replied devilishly, "You can French kiss me later and that will suffice."

Sasha began to clear the dishes and when Sexton started to get up to help she instructed him to sit back down. "I told you that I'm going to spoil you tonight, so that means no dishes for you."

"What did I do to deserve this?"

"You understood about me canceling on you today," she answered as she rinsed the dishes and stacked them in the dishwasher. "How long were you at the gym?"

"For a couple of hours. Calvin was also there. He said that he's going to Vegas with the East Coast team of doctors."

"Cool," she replied. The telephone rang and they looked at each other.

"Let the machine pick it up," he ordered.

Cellular Long Island.

Sexton rolled his eyes dramatically, then looked at Sasha and said, "I'm allowed to do that, aren't I?"

Sasha admitted grudgingly, "She does have a knack for picking the wrong time. I'll call her tomorrow."

Later that night they were in bed when the phone rang again. Next to her Sexton stirred in his sleep. Sasha lay there with her eyes cast towards the ceiling. She heard the automated voice identify the call as coming from a pay phone. Startled, Sasha looked at the clock and when she saw that it was after three o'clock in the morning, she nervously grabbed the receiver. "Hello?"

The voice on the other line slurred her words. Sasha slid out of bed and took the phone into the bathroom.

"Sasha, it's me, Tiara."

"Where are you, and why are you calling me from a pay phone?" she demanded.

"I called you earlier and I guess you weren't at home so I came into the city to have a drink or two. Because I have lost so much weight I can't hold my liquor like I used to. Girl, I'm totally smashed and there's a guy here that says that he can take me home so I'm just letting you know if something happens to me his name is Rick and he drives a beige Charger."

Sasha was incensed. "Tiara, you are a pain in the ass. This guy could be a murderer or rapist."

"You told me go to happy hour and meet another guy, so I'm following your advice."

"Don't hang this on me. I was being facetious and you know it." Her words were clipped from fury.

Tiara began to whimper and Sasha demanded, "Where are you?"

"I'm on East Sixty-eighth at a place called Shooters."

"Sit tight and don't you move," she ordered. "Sexton and I will be there as soon as possible."

"Don't bring him!" Tiara wailed. "I'm humiliated enough as it is."

Sasha whispered, but the biting anger that she was feeling came through, "Are you kidding? I can't sneak out in the middle of the night. He was probably awakened anyhow from the phone and—"

"I'm not going to stay here and wait for you if you're going to bring him. I've been humiliated enough as it is by men and in front of men. Can't you let me have at least one shred of dignity?"

Tiara's voice bordered on hysteria and Sasha tried to calm her. "Okay. I'll come alone. You better be there when I get there!" she ordered before she hung up.

Sasha stood naked in the bathroom wondering how she was going to leave without upsetting Sexton.

When she walked back into the bedroom he was sitting up in bed.

His jaw was clenched and she knew that he was fuming.

Sasha walked over to her dresser and pulled out her undergarments and put them on. Then she grabbed a pair of shorts and shirt and started pulling them on.

"Where are you going?" Sexton demanded. His arms were folded in front of him as he sat up in the bed, his back against the headboard.

"I won't be gone long," she mumbled, avoiding his stern gaze.

"I asked where you're going." His voice was low, but Sasha was not deceived just because he wasn't yelling.

She drew in a deep breath. "Tiara is down on Sixty-eighth Street at a bar, and she's too smashed to drive. I have to go and get her."

"Why didn't she call Calvin? He doesn't have anything else going on," he said sharply.

Sasha shot Sexton a questioning look taken aback by his statement. "I don't know. I didn't think to ask, and she called me from a pay phone." She stammered, "I won't be long."

Sexton got up and began pulling on the shorts and shirt that he had earlier left on the occasional chair in the corner of the room.

"Sexton," Sasha said, "you can't come. Tiara didn't even want you to know what's going on."

"Too bad. Then she shouldn't have called here!" he snorted derisively.

"Seriously, Sexton, I told her that I wouldn't tell you." Sasha's voice was a few decibels higher.

"Sasha, I'm not going to let you go alone to a bar at three o'clock in the morning to pick up some drunken friend." Sexton slid his feet into a pair of flip-flops. His words were curt and he was obviously gritting his teeth to keep from saying something that he might regret later on down the road. He snatched his keys and wallet from the nightstand and stormed out of the bedroom.

The drive to Shooters was made in complete silence. The look on Sexton's face let Sasha know that conversation was not an option.

Once he pulled into a parking space in front of Shooters, he didn't turn off the engine but shifted it into park and said roughly, "Sit tight. I'll be right back."

For about five minutes Sasha peered anxiously through the darkness watching the entrance to the bar. Then Sexton emerged with a bleary-eyed Tiara shakily walking on his heels.

With a sheepish look at Sasha, she slid into the back seat of the Chrysler. Still without uttering a word, Sexton pulled out into the sparse traffic and they sped down the street. When he headed to the direction of his apartment, Sasha shot him a surprised look. "My place is closer," he said shortly.

Once they reached his parking garage, Sexton shut off the car, and after slamming the door, stomped past Rudy into the apartment building.

Sasha turned to Tiara, who looked as if she were dozing. She took her hand and slightly shook her shoulder. "Wake up!" she ordered sternly.

Tiara opened her eyes and said, "Why didn't you guys take me home?"

"Sexton wasn't doing all that. You'll have to sleep on the couch until you're able to drive."

She led Tiara to Sexton's apartment. After locking the door she went to the bedroom and returned with one of her spare nightgowns and a housecoat. Throwing them to Tiara she said, "We'll talk in the morning."

When she joined Sexton in bed he didn't turn around to acknowledge her. Tentatively she spoke. "I know what you're thinking and I know that you're right. I'm going to sever my relationship with her."

Sexton's back was rigid and his words were hard. "You already did that, and now you've been drawn right back into the middle of her foolishness."

"I felt drawn back into a relationship with her out of sympathy." She hesitated before adding, "At least she's stopped being catty about us. That's an improvement."

Sexton turned to lie on his side facing her. "It amazes me how that one adversity in her life has changed her into someone that no one recognizes. Calvin has made some comments but I guess out of respect for her he's been pretty quiet about what's really going on. When I first met Tiara I would have never figured her to be such a nut case."

"She's just going through a rough time."

"She's too needy. Real men love secure women."

"I'll talk to her in the morning." Sasha moved restlessly in bed and then all of a sudden she said, "There's something at my feet, under the covers."

She slid her hand all the way down to the bottom and withdrew it. She came up with a short blonde wig cut in the style of a bob. She stared at it and then said to Sexton without smiling, "Ha, ha, ha Sexton, very funny! Your timing for this joke is way off, Buddy! I am not in the mood to be trifled with." She tossed it to him and it fell on his stomach. "Get rid of this thing before you're the person in trouble with me and not Tiara."

Sexton lay immobile, his eyes focused on the wig. Then without saying a word he got up and threw it in the wastepaper basket. As Sexton walked back to bed he had a rather peculiar expression on his face.

Interpreting his expression she blurted out, "I said I'll take care of Tiara. Now come on to bed and go to sleep."

The atmosphere in the room was filled with tension and finally Sexton spoke. "I have an early morning meeting so you'll have time alone to talk to her. Just make sure that you do," Sexton instructed tersely. Then he turned his back to her and fell asleep.

When she awoke the next morning, true to his word, Sexton's side of the bed was empty.

She walked into the bathroom and took a shower. She had a tension headache so she made the water temperature the hottest that she could stand. Then she turned the knob and blasted herself with cold water in order to close her pores and finish waking up.

Once she had toweled off, she shrugged into a day dress and ventured into the living room to once and for all settle things with Tiara.

Tiara was seated on the couch in Sasha's bathrobe. One of her feet was propped up on the coffee table. Sliding her bleary eyes away from Sasha's, she mumbled, "Good morning."

"How are you feeling?"

"I have a headache, but it's what I deserve. I'm surprised that I didn't throw up. You know that I can't mix my liquor."

"If you know that, then why did you?" Sasha asked sharply as she began filling the coffee pot with water.

Tiara shrugged and said defensively, "I don't know. I didn't intend to get schnockered. It just happened."

"Getting drunk doesn't just happen. There's supposed to be a little voice in your head that turns on at some point in time and warns you to not have another drink."

"So I got drunk," she said defensively. Her lips were thrust out and she rubbed her red eyes. She looked like someone Sasha had never seen before. "What's the big deal?"

"The big deal is that your antics are infringing on my life and my relationship with my man."

"I said I was sorry." Tiara rolled her eyes and sucked her teeth. "What do you want from me?"

"I want you to grow the hell up!"

"You're making mountains out of molehills."

"You think that what you did wasn't a big deal? Sexton was furious."

"He doesn't want us to be friends, and he's just using last night as an excuse."

"Until lately, Sexton has never had a problem with us being friends. Remember, that's how we met."

"Things have changed."

"For who?" she asked bluntly.

"Never mind. I'd just like to give you a piece of advice. Calvin and Sexton are very close." Tiara drawled her next words. "I think you should know that Sexton's not all you crack him up to be. He may have a secret or two that you might be interested in knowing about."

Sasha slammed her coffee mug down on the counter. "That's enough, Tiara! Anything I want to know about him I will learn from him and not you."

"Oh, so you can talk about my business, but no one can say anything about yours?" Tiara sneered.

"The difference is that I'm not asking anything from you, Tiara. I don't call you in the middle of the night and drag you out of bed. When you and Peter were together I never made negative remarks about him or interfered in your short-lived make-believe fantasy life."

Tiara stood, incensed. "You said things about Peter that made me feel that I couldn't take him back."

"Tiara," Sasha shouted, "does a house have to fall down on you for you to deal with reality? Peter made it impossible for you to take him back. He did that to you and no one else. Peter," she stressed his name, "started the divorce proceedings and Peter didn't even try to fight for you. Stop burying your head in the sand!"

"You're a lousy friend!" Tiara declared venomously.

"You're a lousy friend," Sasha retorted just as venomously. Then she held Tiara's eyes with hers and said with authority, "I am going to expel you from my life. Please leave."

After Tiara left, Sasha sat on the couch, seething. How dare she try to compare Peter with Sexton? She didn't bother to wipe the tears of anger from her cheeks because she was too emotionally drained to make the effort.

∼

Instead of immediately leaving the building, Sexton got off on the fifth floor and rapped sharply on Calvin's door.

It was still early in the morning, and when Calvin opened the door Sexton could tell he had still been asleep, but he didn't care. Instead he closely studied Calvin's face and asked, "Calvin, do you know where the key to my place is?"

"Sure, I keep it on my extra set of keys in my apartment." He reached behind the door and pulled a set of keys off a hook and showed it to him. "They're right here." Then he looked at him curiously. "Why do you ask?"

Sexton sidestepped his question. "Have you let anyone into my apartment?"

Obviously taken aback by the question, Calvin said, "Of course not. Why do you ask?"

"No reason," Sexton answered. "I was just trying to figure something out."

"What's going on?" He motioned for Sexton to enter his apartment, but Sexton declined with a negative shake of his head.

"Nothing," he denied. "By the way, your sister's upstairs with Sasha," he said curtly before he walked off.

CHAPTER 16

"What do you think?" Sasha was holding up a cobalt blue bubble dress made of silk.

"I like that one," Sexton replied.

He reached for an emerald green sleeveless sheath with a slit in the front and handed it to her.

Sasha went into the dressing room at BeBe's and tried on the blue dress. Staring at herself from every angle she could, she then ventured out into the store to stand in front of the full-length triple mirrors.

Sexton came to stand behind her and she looked at their reflection. Even though he towered over her, as they stood close, the mirror gave the illusion that they were one person.

Sexton stared at their image and when he spoke his words sounded full of happiness. "Go and try on the green one."

When she sauntered out of the dressing room in the other dress, Sexton smiled. "We'll take both of them."

Once they left the store Sasha said as she slid her arm in the crook of his, "Thank you for the dresses, Sexton." He was carrying them and she smiled her appreciation.

"You can't go on vacation without a new wardrobe, can you?"

"People do it all the time. I know that I have in the past."

"That was then and this is now. My woman can't be wearing old clothes," he said teasingly.

She started laughing. "I don't know those people. Anything I have on is new to them."

He smiled at her joke and grabbed her hand. As they strolled down Fifth Avenue she said, "Let's go into the Guess store. I can't fit into any of my old jeans."

"Good," Sexton answered, giving her behind a small squeeze. "That's a sign of healthiness."

Sasha tried on over a dozen pairs of jeans before she ended up choosing three pairs in varying lengths.

At the counter she pulled out her credit card and Sexton stopped her. "I'm paying for these."

Sasha protested, "I got this, Sexton."

"Don't take my fun away from me. I enjoy dressing my woman. The players' wives are supposed to be present at several events. Also, while the team is practicing there's a whole itinerary lined up to keep the ladies occupied. There's so much to do in Vegas you could feasibly vacation a month there and not do it all."

"The dresses are enough, Sexton," she replied firmly. "I've been planning to refurbish my wardrobe for some time. I just hadn't gotten around to it," she said, handing her card to the saleswoman.

"All right, Sasha." He put his credit card away.

"Anyhow, I'm not your wife. Are you sure that it's okay for me to go to these things?" she looked at him questioningly.

"I've already made arrangements so that your name is on the VIP lists."

Hours later, Sasha and Sexton were exhausted when they entered his apartment. She sank gratefully into Sexton's sumptuous leather couch and looked over at him sheepishly. "You've been such a good boy all afternoon by not complaining as I dragged you from store to store, dinner's on me. How about me ordering a pizza and wings for dinner?"

"Sounds like a winner to me," Sexton agreed before he closed his eyes to relax until the food arrived.

Sasha was locking her desk when her phone rang. She looked at the clock on the wall, hesitated for a minute, then grudgingly picked up the receiver. "This is Sasha Diamond."

"You must be in love because we never hear from you unless we call you first."

Sasha grinned when she heard Desiree's voice. "I am most definitely in love, and I was going to call you tonight."

"Liar," Dominique piped in.

"No, seriously, I was. I'm going to Vegas in the morning with Sexton."

"You're not planning on getting married in Sin City, are you?" Dominique sounded aghast at the thought of a Diamond girl getting married without a big church wedding.

"No, I'm not planning on getting married. That's kind of like putting the cart before the horse. I heard that you have to be asked first."

"I asked Benjamin. He was too much of a chicken and I was tired of waiting for him to ask me," Dominique replied matter of factly.

"That may have worked for you, but that's not my way. I kind of like the old fashioned ways when it comes to matters of the heart."

"My Lord, Sasha. All our lives you've been pretending to be a trendsetter and you're really just an old-fashioned girl. I must admit I like the softer side of you which Sexton's brought out."

"Then why are you going to Vegas?" Desiree interjected as she rejoined the conversation.

"Sexton's been asked to play on the All Star team and I'm going with him. After the game, we're going to hang out and see some shows."

"That sounds like fun, Sasha. I told you to play with him, but going to Vegas puts new meaning to the words playing with your man."

"I know," Sasha said with a wealth of feeling. "I can really use a break."

"I told you not to become a nurse. You're overworked and underpaid."

"It's not my job, Dominique," Sasha denied. "It's Tiara."

"Problems with her again?" Desiree asked, and now there was a note of suspicion in her voice.

"I thought you got rid of that drama queen?" Dominique said abruptly.

"I thought that I did." Sasha explained with resignation that she had been drawn back into a relationship with Tiara out of pity.

"I wouldn't be bothered with that much nonsense from a girlfriend."

"Dominique's right, Sasha. You can't pick your family, but you can pick your friends."

"Her divorce became final and she called me all down in the mouth so I went to see her. Then she goes to a bar and gets drunk and Sexton and I had to go and get her. He was really mad because she keeps interrupting our lives. Almost every time she calls and ruins the most intimate moments."

"I smell a dead cat on the line," Dominique added emphatically.

"What?" Sasha responded.

"You know what that means. Mom uses that expression when something doesn't quite smell right. For example, if your woman is too familiar with your man, or you catch her flirting with him when she doesn't know that she's being observed," she explained.

Desiree put in her two cents, "Or if she just happens to be in the neighborhood where he works and she's free for lunch."

Sasha gave a small laugh. "Well, that's not the case with Tiara. She doesn't even like Sexton anymore."

"Why?" The Diamond sisters spoke in unison and it would have been kind of funny if the conversation weren't so serious.

"I don't know," Sasha responded slowly.

"That's a clue right there that something's not quite right. If he hasn't given her a reason to dislike him that probably means she's jealous," Desiree said gently.

"Girl, you better wake up and smell the coffee." Dominique made a snorting sound through her nose.

Desiree said brusquely, "I think that this girl is just playing on your sympathy with an ulterior motive."

"So do I!"

"It doesn't matter because I know for a fact that Sexton doesn't respect Tiara, and that's real important to him. Anyhow, I severed the relationship with her for good. So if that's what's going on, problem solved."

"That's for the best," Desiree said.

"Make it stick this time," Dominique ordered.

⟞⟝

"Are you ready to go?" Sexton asked as he stood in the doorway in her loft. He had on a pair of plaid shorts and a green oxford shirt. On his feet were a pair of green jelly Sketchers, and he looked good as he stood and tapped his foot impatiently.

Sasha came to him and stretched up to plant a big, teasing, sloppy kiss on his mouth. When she pulled back his lips were stained a bright red. "You look good enough to eat. I wish I had the time."

"So do I, but you don't." Sexton glanced down at his watch and his expression became a little anxious. "Our plane leaves in just under three hours, and even though we're traveling VIP, there are still quite a few checkpoints that we have to make."

"I'm ready, Daddy!" She smiled at him. "You remind me of him. Whenever we had to travel together as a family, I was on pins and needles because he kept checking on us every five minutes to see if we were ready."

"Planes wait for no one," Sexton replied in a brusque voice.

"All I need to do is go back and check to make sure I didn't leave anything." Just as Sasha turned to give the bedroom one last going over, the telephone rang.

"Don't answer that!" he ordered. But when the caller I.D. identified St. Mary's Hospital she threw him an apologetic look and said, "I have to. It's work, so it probably won't take but a minute. They must need to ask me where a file is or something."

"Yes, this is Sasha. Oh, my God!" she exclaimed.

Sexton strode down the hallway to where Sasha stood with the telephone receiver in her hand.

He watched her and at her look of horror, Sexton dropped the small overnight case he was holding.

"Is she going to die? When? How bad is it? Did you call her brother? No, of course I understand. Thank you. I'll be there as soon as I can." Sasha slowly placed the phone on its base.

"What is it? What's wrong?"

"It's Tiara," Sasha said, staring at Sexton. "She tried to commit suicide."

"That's terrible. That chick has lost her damn mind." Sexton shook his head in disbelief.

"She's at the hospital. They don't know whether she's going to make it." Sasha spoke her words slowly as she tried to process the information. She sat down on the edge of the bed and stared off into space. "I have to go to her. She's asked for me."

Sexton's mouth was set and his eyes were hard. "We have a plane to catch."

"I'll catch a later plane. Take my luggage and I'll meet you in Vegas as soon as possible."

"No." Sexton's expression was uncompromising. "We've been planning this trip for weeks. It's too late to change our plans."

Sasha was quiet as she tried to come up with a solution to her dilemma. "Then I'll meet you at the airport. I'll drive to the hospital, look in on her, and be at the airport as soon as I can."

"Sasha, it's a twenty-five minute drive to the hospital, not including the time it takes to park. Then it's a forty-five minute ride to get to the airport from there."

Sasha's eyes were filled with tears. "I can't leave without going to see her. She may die and I would never forgive myself."

"You can't fix her! Especially in half an hour, which is about all the time you would have to spend with her," Sexton shouted. When tears slid down Sasha's cheeks his expression softened. "Sasha, it's a cry for attention. If you keep feeding into this, in the end you'll only make things worse."

"They say that she might not make it. She needs me. I'm a nurse, Sexton. I can't leave with a clear conscience knowing what I know."

"I told you not to answer the damn phone," he said with a tinge of bitterness.

With his words, Sasha gave him a look filled with trepidation.

He saw that and softened his tone but stated, "Tiara has all the nurses that she needs at the hospital. What she really needs is a damn shrink!"

Sasha nodded her head in agreement with Sexton's statement but she held his eyes with hers, willing him to understand. For a while neither one of them said anything. Sasha could hear the clock ticking in the background.

"Does Calvin know?" he finally asked with a look of gravity on his face.

"They said he couldn't be reached."

"That's probably because he's already in Vegas helping to set up the emergency sports clinic in case there are any injuries sustained in the game."

"I'm so sorry, Sexton."

"You're choosing her over me." His words were filled with disappointment.

"You know that's not true." Sasha walked over to him and slid her arms around his waist.

Sexton's body was rigid and he stepped out of the circle of her arms. His brow was furrowed and his teeth were clenched. "If you are not at the airport when the plane leaves, don't come at all."

"I'll be there," she promised with confidence. "Take my luggage with you," she said, snatching her car keys off the nightstand. "I love you, Sexton," she said as she bolted out the door.

Sasha stood in the darkened room in the psychiatric wing of the hospital and looked down at Tiara. Her wrist was bandaged and the hospital gown she wore had small drops of dried blood that had soaked through the tape. She sadly shook her head, appalled that things had progressed to such a state.

Reaching down, she kissed Tiara's cheek and grabbed her purse. Softly closing the door, she felt relieved when she spied Anita walking towards her with a chart in her hand.

"Do you know her?" she asked, surprised.

"Yes, she's a good friend of mine. I just can't believe that she tried to commit suicide."

"She didn't," Anita responded in a derogatory manner. "She slit her wrists across. If she was serious she would have slit the vein. It was a rather pathetic attempt at suicide if you ask me." Anita eyed Sasha searchingly. "You're a nurse. You should have known that."

"Obviously I wasn't given all the details," Sasha replied.

Anita handed her the chart, "Here, read this. The cuts aren't even deep."

Sasha quickly scanned the information on the chart and intense anger began to build in the very core of her being. Mutely she handed the chart back to Anita. "Someone called me and said that they didn't know whether or not she would make it."

"That was false information. She's in no danger of dying from this injury." She continued with sarcasm, "The only reason the nurses sedated her is because she was so demanding that they needed to calm her down." Then Anita eyed Sasha speculatively. "Aren't you supposed to be on vacation?"

"Yes," Sasha responded curtly.

"Then go. We gave her a combination of ativan and haldol, so she'll be sedated for some time. We usually keep people in these cases for only seventy-two hours but because she's your friend I can pull some strings and keep her under wraps and let her remain here until you get back if you like."

"No thanks." Sasha slammed the folder into Anita's hand and said, "Send her home whenever you want. I'm going on vacation."

Anita said as Sasha turned to leave, "I've been meaning to call you in regards to that other matter we discussed. I hit a wall and wasn't able to find out any information other than what you already knew." She touched her shoulder consolingly. "I'm sorry."

"That's okay, Anita. I appreciate you trying."

CHAPTER 17

Sasha hit the palm of her hand on the steering wheel in frustration as she inched her car little by little along the outside lane. A three-car accident had traffic in every direction crawling at a snail's pace.

Once she was free of the congestion, she drove towards the airport as if the devil himself were on her heels. As she sped up the circular loop of the parking area, she began to frantically search for a parking place in the garage. She wound up on the roof in an obscure corner.

The sun was blinding as she searched for the position of the elevator.

Chewing nervously on her bottom lip, she became even more irritated as the last person to enter the elevator ran over her toes with a baby stroller.

"I'm sorry, ma'am."

Sasha's response was to merely grunt in the woman's general direction and look at her wristwatch.

"The plane should be taking off in about five minutes. I just pray that it's a few minutes late," she muttered to herself. Sasha crossed all her fingers, all the while praying for a miracle. *If you help me to make this flight, I won't be stupid again, I won't be stupid again!* She reiterated the words in her head several times. Once the elevator doors opened she ran towards the terminal. With every step her pocketbook hit her side. Finally clutching it in front of her, she ran to the screener.

Sasha tapped her teeth together in agitation as the screener dumped all of her belongings into a grey plastic container. Then she barely held her tongue when she saw her open her round tube of lip gloss to see if anything was hidden inside. When the screener tried to replace the cap, she dropped it and it fell on the floor and rolled out of sight.

The girl started to bend to try to retrieve it and Sasha said tersely, "For heaven's sake, forget it. It's not that important." After her body was scanned from head to toe several times, she approached the departure board. Her heart sank when she read Flight 1211 to Las Vegas had departed.

A hard knot formed in her stomach and she felt nauseous. Stumbling over to a chair she sank into it and dropped her head between her knees. She remained in that position for about five minutes, and when she weakly lifted her head, she realized to her chagrin that she'd aroused the somewhat nervous curiosity of several onlookers.

Gathering her wits, she went to the customer service window at the Delta counter and said with a slight tremor in her voice, "I missed my flight to Las Vegas. Can I exchange my ticket for a later flight?"

Sasha fumbled around in her pocketbook and then she felt nauseous again when she realized that Sexton had her ticket. "I don't have my ticket. Check under my name, please." Sasha wheedled. "It's Sasha Diamond."

The ticket agent quickly typed in the information. "I'm sorry, ma'am, but there's no ticket under the name Sasha Diamond."

Sasha frantically searched her brain. "Is there one under Sexton Johnson?"

The clerk typed in the information in the computer and said, "Yes ma'am there is. However, the ticket reads Sexton Johnson and passenger." The clerk then gave Sasha a look of sympathy. "I can't prove that you're the passenger he's talking about so I can't let you use it." The attendant saw the look of despair on Sasha's face and said, "Let me see if there is anything I can do for you."

"Never mind. How much is it for a one-way ticket?" Sasha asked, reaching for her wallet.

"Six hundred and ninety-three dollars for a last-minute one-way express ticket. However, there's not another available flight until tomorrow morning at eleven-thirty."

"Damn!" Sasha's nightmare of a day was complete.

"You can try stand-by starting at six o'clock in the morning."

"Thank you," Sasha replied weakly and turned to make the long trek back to her car.

Once she got back into the mainstream of traffic she pulled out her cell phone and punched Sexton's cell phone number. It went straight to voice mail. "Sexton, I missed the plane by ten minutes. I want to come in the morning. You have my plane ticket so I have to fly stand-by. Please call me and let me know if that's okay with you." Her voice sounded nervous, and she knew it.

Hours later, Sasha emerged from the shower and checked her voice mail. A lump formed in her throat when she realized that Sexton still hadn't called. An image of Tiara came to the forefront of her mind once again, and she was consumed with anger.

Later that evening, Sasha sat in front of an uneaten South Beach diet frozen dinner. She looked at the clock and picked up her cell phone, hit redial for his private line, and found herself once again listening to his voice mail. The background music of Stevie's "All I Do" played and she had to blink back tears remembering the night he'd downloaded it and let her listen. "Sexton, I've been waiting to hear from you. I'm sorry I messed everything up. Please call me back if I can come in the morning."

That night Sasha slept fitfully. Every hour on the hour, she awoke and looked at her cell phone as it lay on the empty pillow next to her. She almost felt overcome with an unfamiliar loneliness that she'd never ever experienced before Sexton Johnson had entered her life.

⁓

The phone rang, and Sasha eagerly jumped off the couch before the caller I.D. had a chance to activate. "Hello," she said in a deliberately sexy voice.

"Good morning, this is Island Getaways notifying you that you have the chance to win a four day, three night cruise for two." Frustrated, she slammed down the telephone. She hadn't been out of the house for two days straight and still she hadn't heard from Sexton.

The game was due to be televised in an hour and she took a moment off from mentally kicking herself for her stupidity to send up a prayer for Sexton that he would play well and would be recognized in front of millions for his remarkable talents.

Sasha knew that Sexton had been angry with her when she had insisted on going to see Tiara, but still she was surprised by his lack of response to her phone calls. It was out of character for him to sulk. As a couple he had always been the more level headed one, so she knew that his lack of response meant that he was really angry. She couldn't wait for him to return, and even though she knew that she couldn't change how she had let him down, she could reassure him that she would not let history repeat itself.

That evening, Sasha sat mesmerized in a room illuminated only by the television as she watched the East Coast battle the West in the All-Star game. It was the fourth quarter and the score was tied. Whenever Sexton ran or dribbled down the court, she sat up even straighter on the loveseat and watched his every move. He wore a white jersey with the name Johnson and the number twelve embossed in large, red letters.

Sexton had gotten playing time every quarter, and every time the announcer said the name Sexton Johnson the crowd in Las Vegas echoed the screams she emitted in her living room.

Sexton was being closely guarded by point guard Oscar King. He was the lankiest basketball player that she'd ever seen. Sasha already knew of him because

Sexton had told her that they had played together over-seas. He had been picked up by the NBA one year earlier than Sexton and had already established himself as one of the newer players in the league to watch.

Sasha glared at him, channeling her anger on him. He covered Sexton with an aggressiveness that seemed to cross the line. Even when Sexton wasn't in possession of the ball he was all over him. However, when the cameras gave a close-up of Sexton's face, his expression showed only concentration not annoyance.

The east coast players continued to feed Sexton the ball throughout the game. Sexton was ambidextrous; even though the other team's players knew it, he was still able to catch them off guard and get a clean shot.

The last ten minutes of the game, Sexton's team was two points ahead. They had made the last six baskets while the west had made only three. The tempo of the game had slowed slightly and it was obvious that the players on both teams were tired because they had both fought tooth and nail throughout.

Pride coursed through Sasha's veins as she watched Sexton play. Not only had he contributed by scoring over seventeen points, he had managed to make two out of three baskets at the foul line. She admired the fact that he was a team player. Instead of taking every shot when he had the ball, he passed the ball to teammates who appeared to have a cleaner shot.

In the last five minutes of the game, the east coast's score was up by three points and they bounded down the court towards their goal. Sexton was running parallel with his teammate who was in possession of the ball when suddenly the ball was passed to him. Easily catching it, he dribbled down towards the basket and Oscar King. Switching the ball from his right hand to his left, he went for the lay-up. Just as Sexton released the ball, Oscar King slapped it and instead of it going off to the side, the ball hit Sexton directly in the face with such force he went down and was sprawled out flat on his back on the basketball court.

A gasp of fear mixed with excitement rose from the crowd. The referees' whistles went off as they motioned that the move was a flagrant foul. The east coast coaches ran to the court.

Sasha craned her neck trying to see what was going on. Finally, she spied Calvin as the first person to reach Sexton. The other players deliberately shielded his body from view and Sasha's heart dropped when she saw a stretcher being wheeled out. She wasn't aware that she was now standing. As if from a distance, she heard a voice announce that Sexton Johnson remained unconscious and he was being rushed to the hospital.

Calmly, almost as if in a robotic trance, Sasha stiffly walked over to her kitchen counter, picked up her handbag and walked out of her loft to begin her journey to Las Vegas.

The trip in the taxi was a blur, and when it came to a stop at the terminal, she blindly reached into her pocket-book, withdrew a fifty dollar bill, and walked through the glass doors to the ticket counter. By the grace of God, she managed to secure a seat on the next plane out. There had been a last-minute cancellation, and even though she was in the last seat of the plane by the bathroom, she thanked God to be sitting there.

Once they had leveled off, she used the plane's telephone and tried to contact Calvin. She got no answer so at the sound of the beep she said in a voice bordering on hysteria, "Calvin, this is Sasha. Call me on my cell phone with an update on Sexton's condition as soon as possible. Right now I'm on a plane on my way to him."

Then she called Sexton's cell phone, praying for him to answer. She hit redial over and over again and then finally she decided to leave another message. "Sexton, if you get this message, I saw what happened and I'm on my way to you. Stay strong. I love you so much."

CHAPTER 18

When she emerged from the airport, she gasped and almost toppled over from the wave of heat that hit her. The temperature sign on the bank across the street was flashing 107 degrees. Wiping the beads of sweat off her face with the back of one hand, she hailed a cab with the other. After sinking gratefully into the back seat she said, "Please take me to the Paris Hotel." She felt like ordering him to step on it, but gazing at the bumper-to-bumper traffic she knew that it would be a waste of time. Taking a stab in the dark she asked the driver, "Did you see the All-Star game?"

The driver looked in his rear view mirror and said, "Yeah, it's a shame what happened to that guy."

Sasha's heart dropped and even though she was afraid to ask she did. "Do you mean Sexton Johnson?"

"Yes, ma'am. He was really putting on a show until that guy put him out of commission. I'm glad the east coast won the game even with that Johnson guy being carried out."

Swallowing hard she asked, "Have you heard a recent update on his status?"

"Sure. I heard on the radio he's at University Medical Center with a mild concussion. They say he's going to be okay."

Sasha felt as if the weight of the world had been lifted off her shoulders. "Please take me to University Medical Center instead of the Paris Hotel."

The driver looked at her and curiosity was written all over his face. "Of course."

Once she was in the lobby of the hospital, she clipped on her nurse's badge from work, which coincidentally was the same color worn by the receptionist who had given her directions to Sexton's room.

She strode down the hallway and halted her steps in front of room 517. Remembering the last conversation that she'd had with Sexton and the fact that he had ignored her numerous phone calls, she tried to still the butterflies in her stomach. With trepidation, she pushed open the hospital room door.

It was a private room and Sexton lay back against the pillows. His eyes were closed and the contrast of the white sheets against his dark skin made him look vulnerable. She went to stand at his bedside.

Sensing the presence of someone else in the room, his eyes fluttered open. The first expression that crossed his face was one of joy, but it was quickly masked with an inscrutable one.

Sasha took his hand and lifted it. Gently turning it over, she kissed the inside of his forearm the way he had done hers so many times during their relationship. At the feel of her touch, a smile began to form and his lips twitched.

Without speaking, Sasha walked to the end of his bed and opened his chart and began to read it. Feeling relieved, she slid it back in place. Then she pulled an empty chair next to the bed. Very softly she began to speak. "Sexton, I don't know how to make this up to you or if I can ever make this up to you, but I'm sorry. I should have been here for you, the way you have always been there for me throughout our whole relationship."

Sexton opened his mouth to speak but Sasha held up her hand to stop him. She spoke slowly, not knowing how much his medication would affect how he processed information. "When we parted, I didn't feel as if I was choosing Tiara over you, but I did feel that she needed me and you didn't. You're so strong, Sexton. There's an inner strength that I see in your eyes when I look at you and it makes me feel safe and warm. I feel protected when I'm with you and I realized while we were apart that I need to start having your back the way that you have mine. When you didn't return my calls, I was bereft. You were right, Tiara was just playing games and I fell for it."

Sasha hypnotized him with her eyes. "I know that you love me, Sexton, but I have never been as afraid or lonely as I've been the last couple of days, thinking that maybe you had decided to throw in the towel on us as a couple." She placed her hand over her heart, looked into his deep chocolate brown eyes and said, "I promise that I will never choose another person's welfare over yours again."

Sexton lay motionless in bed, not saying a word.

"Do you still love me?

Mutely he searched her face with his eyes and nodded yes.

"Do you still want me?"

Again he nodded yes.

Nervously she cleared her throat, but her words were loud and clear, "Will you marry me, Sexton?"

Finally, after an endless time, he murmured softly, "Sasha, get my small suitcase from out of the closet."

He pointed to a set of closet doors on the other side of the room and Sasha went to do as she was told.

When she turned back around Sexton was sliding out of bed and she protested, "Don't get out of bed. You're still recuperating!"

"Hush, girl. You're my woman, not my nurse."

A mixture of happiness and optimism surged through Sasha when she heard his words. Crossing back to him, she handed him his small overnight case. After rifling through it, he pulled something out, but because his hands were so huge, she couldn't see what he was concealing.

Then he dropped to one knee and took her left hand in his. "Sasha Diamond, I love you with all my heart."

He opened the box. Inside was the largest princess cut diamond engagement ring she had ever seen.

"Will you marry me?"

Tears coursed down her cheeks and without wiping them away she dropped to her knees in front of him. "Please," she answered before she was enveloped in his embrace.

That night, Sasha sat at Sexton's hospital bedside and smiled wryly at him as he slept in his usual manner. The bandage was gone from his head, and he was lying on his back with his legs spread eagle, exposing himself to any and everyone who might enter the room. She knew from previous experience that he was such a deep sleeper that she could make all the noise she wanted and he would not wake. As she slid in the bed next to him and gently pulled the sheet up to his waist, he still didn't stir.

~

The penthouse suite at the Paris Hotel and Casino was gorgeous. Even after a night's sleep, she was still so tired from overwrought emotion during her plane ride that after taking a quick shower and making sure that Sexton was resting comfortably, she had fallen into a deep sleep.

Now that she had time to give her surroundings a closer inspection, she gave a very unladylike whistle. On one wall there a mural that replicated a Paris scene. The other walls were a light mauve, and the matching carpet was so plush she hadn't felt the need to put on her bedroom shoes. *To think that I almost missed this. God works in mysterious ways. Sexton's accident not only got me my man back for a minute, but for a lifetime.*

She had always wanted to travel to Europe, and as she craned her neck and looked out the window she stared at the scaled replica of the Eiffel Tower and felt as if she were in France.

Crossing to a full length mirror, she placed her left hand over her heart. "Sasha Johnson, Mrs. Sexton Johnson, Mrs. Sexy Sexton Johnson." As she spoke the words aloud to her reflection in the mirror, a thrill went through her. Her engagement ring fit to a tee, and she hadn't taken it off since Sexton had put it on her finger when they were at the hospital.

The sound of the suite's doorbell shook her out of her reverie, and pulling on Sexton's shirt and boxers, she looked through the peephole. She couldn't see the person's face, but she recognized the body posture as that of Calvin. Hurriedly she opened the door and the look of happiness when he saw her eased any fear that she might have felt because he was Tiara's brother.

"I see you made it after all." He gave a knowing grin.

"Damn skippy!" Sasha replied with a saucy tone and smiled as she thrust out her hand and showed the ring.

Calvin gave a whistle that was identical to the one Sasha had uttered moments earlier. "Homeboy really goes all out, doesn't he? I knew he planned to ask you to marry him while you guys were here in Vegas but when you didn't make the plane," Calvin paused and gave Sasha a sideways look, "I didn't know that it would happen."

"I know you didn't think that I would let Sexton go so easily, did you?" Sasha stood with her hand planted on her hips.

"I know that I wouldn't."

She gave Calvin a questioning look and then he explained. "I know from traveling with the team what some of these guys do. Even before the two of you hooked up, he didn't pick up a woman in every city we visited. Don't get me wrong, he was no monk. But a man like Sexton is hard to find. He has some real old-fashioned scruples. " As he spoke these words, Calvin had a somewhat wistful expression on his face.

"I know. His parents did a good job with him."

"Many a night, he'd just hang out in the room, watching tapes of the team he was there to play, trying to hone his craft."

"I always knew I could trust Sexton while he was away on the road because I knew in my heart what kind of man Sexton is. Still, sometimes I would grow fearful that this would end, so when Sexton agreed to marry me I felt that all was right in the world."

Calvin gave her an earnest look. "Then seal the deal with a marriage, Sasha. Las Vegas is the marrying capital of the world. What are you waiting for?"

On his way out the door, he gave Sasha another perceptive look. "By the way, I talked to Tiara today and she's fine, or should I just say she's the usual."

After Calvin left, Sasha sat in the rocking chair by the fireplace and thought about Calvin's advice. She was deep in thought and didn't realize that Sexton was awake and lying there watching her.

"A penny for your thoughts."

"Marry me, Sexton."

"I know that I got hit in the head, but I distinctly remember going over this with you already." He looked at the ring on her finger. "In fact, I'm positive that I did."

"I mean marry me here, in Las Vegas."

"I would, Sasha," he smiled at her softly, "but I know your family will be expecting us to have a really big wedding with all the frills. And I promised my mom that when I got married I would have a church wedding."

Sasha sat quiet and her expression was contemplative. "We can do that on our one year anniversary. That way I'll have enough time and enough of your money to turn it into a real party," she teased gently as she gazed into his eyes. "Sexton, I don't want to wait to be your wife."

He touched his forehead with his index finger. "Are you sure that you want to marry a man with an egg like this on his head?"

"I'd marry you with two eggs on your head," she affirmed.

A broad grin spread across his face and then he responded with, "All right then, Sasha. We'll get married. My mom also told me that a gentleman never keeps a lady waiting."

CHAPTER 19

Sasha looked over at her fiancé and shook him slightly on the shoulder. "Honey, wake up. We have his and her appointments at the spa."

Sexton eyed her wearily. "Why did you make the appointment so early? You know how I like to sleep in."

"It's not that early. It's after ten o'clock." Then she added, "Don't blame me, I didn't know that you would be up half the night gambling. How much of your money did you lose?"

"You mean how much of our money did I lose," he replied, covering his mouth with a yawn. "Let's just say that you might have to work until you're seventy."

"Just so you have dinner ready for me when I get home." She chuckled at the thought of Sexton meeting her at the door sporting an apron.

They walked downstairs to the Paris Mandara Spa. The attendant was the spitting image of Iman and Sasha whispered, "I'll have what she had."

"You look better than her," Sexton whispered back.

"Sure I do!" Sasha scoffed.

"You do to me and that's what matters, isn't it?"

"You always know the right thing to say." She squeezed his hand.

"May I help you?"

"We have reservations for the Paris for Lovers Package."

"What is the name, ma'am?" The attendant's tone was pleasant and she made Sasha feel as if they would be well taken care of.

"Mr. and Mrs. Sexton Johnson." Sasha took a credit card out of her wallet, placed it on the counter, turned to Sexton and gave him a wink.

Several hours later after body massages, pedicures, manicures, and facials, they were walking hand in hand down the Las Vegas strip. They felt and looked like a million bucks.

Throngs of people walked scorching sidewalks and several times Sasha almost lost her footing in her stilettos as she was jostled by intoxicated people hurrying into casinos trying to dodge the heat and reach the gaming tables. They acted as if they had the inside track as to which numbers on the roulette wheels would come up, or which slot machines were going to pay out.

Sexton moved from Sasha's side, grabbed her hand, and led her into Caesar's Palace. "They have any and everything here that we need for the wedding."

Sasha turned to him and said, "You can't go shopping with me for my wedding dress. It's bad luck."

"I know, but we have to get wedding bands. Once that's taken care of, we'll split up and I can get my suit."

Sasha sat in a velvet cushioned chair at the jewelry store. "We want matching wedding bands," she said emphatically. Then she looked over at Sexton in the seat next to hers and asked as an afterthought, "That is what you want, isn't it, Honey?"

"That's want I want." His eyes twinkled at her and she knew that he was thinking that he might as well.

Sasha tried on over a dozen rings and after she had narrowed her decision to three she looked at Sexton and said, "I can't decide. Which do you like best?"

Sexton reached over and picked up the plain twenty-four carat gold wedding band. "I like this one. Its simplicity makes it eye catching, and it won't look as if it's competing with your engagement ring." Then he picked up the matching band. Sexton slid the ring on his hand and it was a perfect fit. He smiled gently at her. "Now I'm living the dream."

Her lips quivered from emotion and the jewelry clerk bowed his head in silent apology for intruding on such an intimate moment.

Sasha dialed Sexton's room number from her suite in the Venetian Hotel. She had been stunned, yet charmed, when Sexton had insisted that they separate until they were married. "When our daughter asks us about our wedding day, I don't want to have to tell her mommy rolled over and told me it was time to get up."

At twelve o'clock Sasha and Sexton stood together in the Venetian Wedding Chapel. Calvin and the minister's wife stood off to one side to witness the union.

She had purchased a white wedding dress that was cut close to her ankles and matching pumps from the shops in Caesar's Hotel. In her arms she held a bouquet of white calla lilies. Sexton looked debonair in a crisp white shirt and a black double-breasted suit.

Throughout the ceremony, Sasha and Sexton's eyes never wavered from each other's. In her subconscious, she heard the serious tone of the minister but her full concentration was on Sexton. Her eyes filled with tears of happiness at the beginning of the ceremony but she didn't attempt to wipe them away, preferring to let them slide down her cheeks as testimony to how much she loved the man standing beside her.

At the close of the ceremony, Calvin produced a broom and placed it on the floor in front of them. Sexton took his hands in hers and together they jumped over it. The minister smiled and said, "I now pronounce you man and wife."

Sexton turned to Sasha and she melted in his arms. He bent his head to her and when his lips touched hers, she slid her arms around his neck. Sexton explored her lips as if it were the first time they had ever kissed and when he finally withdrew his mouth from hers she felt her face grow hot when she remembered that there were other people in the room.

Calvin gave a discreet cough, and when they looked at him he teased, "Man, you act as if this is the first time you've kissed her."

Sexton put his arm around Sasha's shoulders and said smiling, "This is the first time I've ever kissed her as my wife."

Calvin grinned, held out his hand and vigorously shook Sexton's. Then he turned to Sasha and gave her a kiss on the cheek. "Congratulations. May you have a long and happy marriage."

"Thank you." Sasha's voice was husky from emotion.

"I have to go now because my plane leaves in about an hour. I was due back home yesterday, but I refused to not be here for the big day."

"Thanks, Calvin, you're a good friend." Sexton sounded choked up.

"You can thank me by naming me godfather of your first child," he declared, picking up the suitcase that he had hidden in the back of the chapel during the wedding.

"Absolutely," Sexton spoke to Calvin's retreating back.

That afternoon, Sasha leaned on Sexton as they rode in their private gondola in the green canals of the Venetian Hotel. The gondolier sang as he paddled his gondola and between the combination of his music and the murals of Venice it was easy to forget that they were in the States and not Italy.

Hours later, Sasha sat in their hotel room at a round table lit with candles. She was dressed in a cream negligee with matching satin slippers, and as Sexton gazed at her he thought that she was the loveliest vision he had ever seen.

"I never thought that I could be so happy. I love you very much, Mr. Sexton Johnson," Sasha murmured.

"We're going to be very happy together, Sasha." Sexton picked up his glass of champagne and raised it, motioning for Sasha to do the same.

"I love you," he vowed, "for today, tomorrow, and forever."

The clinking of the glasses was the only sound in the room. Sasha emptied her glass in one draught.

Sexton smiled, "Don't get too tipsy. I have more in store for you tonight."

"I'm eagerly looking forward to it, young man. You haven't slept next to me for three days," she complained. "I think that's the longest time we've ever spent apart when you weren't traveling."

"Well, you're mine now, Sasha Johnson, and I'm never going to let you go."

Sexton stood and let fall the brocade robe that Sasha had purchased for him the day she'd bought her wedding dress. He stood there, naked and glistening, unabashed that his body showed how much desire he had for her. He leaned over and blew out the candles. Then with cat-like steps, he went to stand in front of Sasha. He held out his hand to help her to her feet, then bent and picked her up in his arms and cradled her as if she were a baby.

"Oh, my!" she gasped.

Sexton pivoted and walked with her to the bedroom and kicked the door closed. Then he gently laid her on the bed that was covered with rose petals and joined her, covering her body with his.

———

Very late the next morning, Sasha opened her eyes and they focused on a note leaning against the lamp on the nightstand. She knew without turning over that she was alone in the king size bed because she didn't hear the familiar light snore that she had become so used to during the last few months.

Reaching for the note, she read Sexton's words:

"I didn't want to disturb you so I went to the gym to work out. We have tickets to Cirque de Soleil at five o'clock. I'll be back no later than three so we can go to a late lunch before the show. Love, your husband, Sexton."

Glancing at the clock on the wall, Sasha knew she had a couple of hours before he would return, time for a long, leisurely bath.

The doorbell rang and Sasha pulled on the negligee she had worn the previous night and padded barefoot to the door. Looking through the peephole, all she could discern was a Federal Express emblem. Leaving the chain bolt across the door she opened it barely an inch. "May I help you?"

The man's voice was deep and gravelly. "I have a certified package for Sasha Diamond."

"I'm Sasha Diamond Johnson." Opening the door completely, she signed the register with one hand and took the manila envelope in the other. Smiling at him as he tipped his hat, she closed the door and walked back into the living room.

Curiously tearing open the package, she emptied the contents onto the table that still had the champagne glasses she and Sexton had drunk from the previous night.

Several pictures and a white envelope fell out and she reached for one of the pictures first. Sasha stared at the picture for five whole minutes before she slumped in an unconscious heap. Her head barely missed full contact with the glass table.

Sasha's eyes fluttered open. She didn't know how long she had been unconscious; she lay on the floor, unable to will her body to move. She only knew that she felt tightness in her chest and that she was having difficulty breathing. Gingerly, she sat up and moved her limbs, hoping she hadn't bruised or even broken something in her fall. Trying to gather her wits and to fully comprehend the picture she'd seen before she fainted, she shook her head from side to side in disbelief.

They lay on the floor like dead leaves from a tree struck by lightening. Not trusting herself to stand, she sucked in her breath and reached for the pictures. One by one she stared at them, transfixed.

One was of Sexton flat on his back, butt naked in bed in his apartment. Sasha knew this was his usual posture after a heated session of lovemaking. Another had him lying on his back; facing him was Tiara, who was also naked. She was wearing the blonde bob wig Sasha had found in Sexton's bed. Tiara's expression looked sly and triumphant at the same time. The third picture had Sexton sitting in a chair, naked, with his thighs sprawled open. His back was to the camera so she couldn't see his face, and Tiara was on her knees in front of him with her head bent, wearing the blonde wig and obviously performing fellatio on him.

Still not wanting to believe what she saw, she rubbed the pictures, hoping the ink would wipe off and show her that they were not real, but a cruel joke by someone who hated her. The pictures remained intact. She reached for the envelope. Tearing it open, she recognized Tiara's childlike cursive. "I've done everything possible other than hitting you over the head with a sledge hammer to clue you in as to what kind of man Sexton really is. When Calvin told me that Sexton was going to propose to you in Las Vegas, I thought that you should know the real deal on your boyfriend before you made the same mistake I did. I'm ashamed to admit that I've been sleeping with him, but I felt that I owed him because he gave me money."

Sasha then looked at a copy of Sexton's canceled check made out to Tiara for thirty thousand dollars.

"Sexton made me wear the wig when I went to his apartment in order to keep people from recognizing me. He made me promise not to tell you, but I can't keep quiet anymore. Please forgive me, Sasha. I'm telling you this because I love you. Your friend to the end, Tiara."

Zombie-like, Sasha stood and walked to the closet that held her clothes. She began haphazardly throwing them into her suitcases before grabbing a pair of jeans, a tee shirt, and sneakers and pulling them on.

Less than twenty minutes later, she looked around the suite and found a tablet inside the dresser drawer. Dry-eyed, she scratched out the words, "I don't ever want to see you again, Sexton." Tugging off her engagement and wedding rings, she placed them on the table next to the note. Next, even more enraged, she slammed down the cancelled check. Without looking, she shoved the photographs into one of the pockets of her suitcase. "I'll keep them to remind me in the future of how stupid I am about people," she muttered to herself as she walked out to the door to catch a plane and put as much distance as she could between herself and the man who had truly broken her heart.

⚊⚊

Sexton entered the empty honeymoon suite and surveyed the room, shocked by the disarray. The drapes across the sliding glass doors were completely open the way the maid usually left them, yet the bed was still unmade and the dining area was a disaster. "Sasha?" he called out before crossing over to the bathroom.

Sexton knocked on the door and when he received no response, opened it. Quickly opening the vanity doors, he saw the ones that had held Sasha's toiletries were now empty. His brow furrowed with confusion, he crossed over to the closet and flung open the doors to find it now held only his clothes. He spied a tablet on the bedside table with writing on it. He lifted it, and read the note several times before seeing a copy of the cancelled check he had given Tiara on the table.

A closed expression settled on Sexton's face and light faded from his eyes. With his jaw clenched, he walked over to the other side of the room to the gas fireplace and hit the switch. Once the flames flared, he threw Sasha's note on them and watched it burn. Next, he picked up Sasha's rings, pulled off his wedding band, and threw them in the fireplace to watch them become enveloped in flames.

CHAPTER 20

Sasha had been home for days without talking to anyone. Upon her return from Las Vegas, she had placed a block on her telephone for Tiara's home and cell number. She hadn't done the same for Sexton, but she wasn't surprised when he didn't call. What could you say when caught with your hand in the cookie jar?

She hadn't been able to sleep and she'd had plenty of time to think of the clues that she should have seen a long time ago. From Sexton wanting her to drop Tiara as a friend to his silence when she had tossed him the wig at his apartment, not to mention Tiara's sudden pretended dislike for Sexton.

Yes, they had certainly played her for a fool, and she was afraid of what she would do to Tiara if she saw her. She decided that her best course of action was to pretend that Tiara didn't exist, and maybe that avenue would keep her out of jail for assault.

The sudden sound of the telephone ringing startled her out of her dark thoughts. Cocking her head to listen for the caller, she gave a sigh when she heard the name Dominique James. She picked up the telephone receiver.

"Hello," she said dully.

"What's the matter with you? Are you sick or something? You sound terrible," Dominique fired off the minute she heard Sasha's voice.

Without hesitation Sasha poured out her heart. "Sexton and I broke up. He's been sleeping with Tiara behind my back." For the first time since she had seen the pictures and read the letter, Sasha began to cry. At first she made small gulping sounds. Then letting go, a deluge of tears coursed down her face. She began to cough, making choking sounds as she gasped for air.

"Don't cry!" Dominique ordered sharply.

"Let her cry if she wants to. She certainly has a right," Desiree said sharply.

Her sisters were silent as they listened to her sob uncontrollably.

Finally, when the tormented sounds stopped, Dominique said roughly, "I'm coming over."

"Please don't!" Sasha begged. "I just want to be alone."

"You should be with family, not alone."

"Let her be!" Desiree cautioned Dominique. "Sometimes people need alone time to adjust without people staring at them."

"We're not people, we're family," Dominique argued.

"And if Sasha wanted us there, she would have called us, not the other way around," Desiree countered.

"How did you find out?" Dominique asked.

"While Sexton and I were in Vegas, Tiara sent me pictures of the two of them in bed with a letter stating that she thought I should know the truth before I made the mistake that she had."

"Damn! She knew that you were in Vegas and she just had to go and ruin it. She probably was scared to death that the two of you were going to get married and had to find a way to stop it. That's why I don't have any girl-friends," Dominique stated with firmness. "They're like crabs in a jar. When they think one is going to get out they pull them back in."

Sasha kept silent. Dominique always had a knack for hitting the nail on the head. She didn't want to tell her sisters the humiliating fact that she had indeed made that colossal mistake while in Vegas.

"If she gave a crap about you she wouldn't have told you the way she did. They say that there's a right way and a wrong way to do things. I don't know if in this situa-tion there is a right way, but if there is she certainly didn't choose it. How cowardly is that? Sending her best friend a letter. That's so tacky. Tiara has too much time on her hands. That chick needs a hobby."

"I must say that I'm surprised at Sexton. He didn't strike me at all as a run-around. Go figure." Dominique mulled over these revelations.

"What did he say when you confronted him?" Desiree queried.

"I didn't confront him. I just took off. I couldn't stand to see him." Her voice was hoarse from crying.

"Are you telling me that you didn't have it out with him?" Dominique sounded appalled.

"What could he say? There's no explanation for that."

Desiree rejoined the conversation, and she also sounded stunned that Sasha hadn't given Sexton the chance to explain. "Sasha, you don't know when those pictures were taken. It could have been before the two of you got together."

"Still," Sasha exclaimed weakly, "he gave her thirty thousand dollars after we were together."

"So what? From what you told us, she's been going around begging since her husband left her. Thirty thousand dollars isn't over the top if he views her as a charitable donation," Desiree retorted sarcastically.

"I never thought of that," Sasha answered weakly. "But still, it's disgusting, Sexton having slept with my best friend."

"She's not your best friend," Desiree stated emphatically. "In fact, she's not your friend at all."

"Grow up, Sasha!" Dominique instructed sharply. "Women sling that thang at men all the time and they don't always turn it down. More times than not, sex is simply a physical release for them." She paused. "So what if Sexton slept with Tiara. If it was before you and he wasn't sleeping with the two of you at the same time, it doesn't matter. Everyone has a history. Obviously it didn't mean anything to him or he wouldn't have pursued you the way that he did."

"Sasha, you need to talk to Sexton and find out the truth," Desiree advised.

"Yes, you need to check with your man!" Dominique ordered.

Sasha sat in her darkened living room thinking about the telephone conversation she'd had with her sisters. She hadn't been to work in days and had gotten used to being a recluse, so when her doorbell rang, she jumped with surprise. Looking at the clock, she realized that it was late evening; fearful as to who would be coming to her place at that time of night, she tiptoed down the hall to peer through the peephole. Spying Calvin, she held her breath and had turned to tiptoe away when she heard his voice through the door.

"Sasha, Desiree called me. Let me in so we can talk."

Sasha stood holding her breath, waiting for him to leave.

"I know that you're in there. I'm just trying to help."

"I don't ever want to see you or your sister again," she shouted back at him.

"That's not fair, Sasha," he scolded. "I am not my sister's keeper."

Upon hearing this, Sasha unlocked her door and threw it open. It hit the back wall.

Calvin stood staring.

Sasha's hair was sticking out on top of her head and she looked as if she had been through the wringer. Because her skin was so fair, it was easy to detect the beginning of dark circles forming under her eyes. Those eyes looked accusatory as they met his.

Her stance was defiant. "Are you trying to tell me that you didn't know about the affair that Sexton and your sister were having and that you didn't help engineer a cover-up by pretending that you and he were good friends so that Tiara could have the inside track to make herself available to him?"

"I did no such thing." Calvin walked past her into the loft. He tapped the light switch on the wall and it flooded the area with light. Then he turned and gave her a stern look. "I am Sexton's friend, which is one of the reasons I'm here. The other reason I'm here is because I also thought that I was one of your friends."

Sasha shrugged her shoulders and replied sarcastically, "If I were you, I wouldn't put too much stock in friendship anymore. I know that I don't."

"Where are the photos that my sister sent you? I want to see them," he demanded in a tone that brooked no argument.

Sasha stood in front of Calvin with her hands planted firmly on her hips. "Why don't you go and get them from Tiara? I'm sure she has copies."

"I've tried to reach Tiara, but she hasn't returned my calls and she wasn't at home when I went over there to talk to her."

"How convenient. Maybe she's gone into seclusion. I know that I would have, if I was her."

Calvin didn't respond to that. He only reiterated, "Go and get the pictures Desiree told me about. I want to see them."

Sasha walked over to the couch in the den and lifted the cushion. She withdrew the manila envelope and handed it to Calvin, who'd followed her into the room. "Your sister's disgustingly naked. I don't know if you're prepared for that," she added sarcastically.

"In my line of work, I see naked people all the time. I'll just pretend that she's not my sister. Under the circumstances that's quite easy to do," he returned, not at all put off by Sasha's attitude.

He sat down on the couch and Sasha sat on the cushion farthest away from him with her arms folded and head turned in the opposite direction as Calvin solemnly scrutinized the pictures. Not being able to hold the question that had been plaguing her since Calvin had entered her loft she asked, "Has Sexton said anything to you about this?"

Calvin momentarily took his eyes from the photos. "I knew something was wrong the minute that I saw his face at the gym. I asked him what was wrong and he refused to answer me. I had no idea it was this serious until Desiree called me." He gave her a quick look, "Sasha, do you have a magnifying glass?"

"I have that gadget that helps you read prescription labels, why?"

Looking up from the picture he was holding he said brusquely, "Go get it."

Mutely, Sasha walked down the hall to the bedroom, returning with a small magnifying card in her hand.

Calvin took it and held it to the picture, turning the card in several directions. Then he handed her the photo of Sexton sitting in a chair with Tiara at his feet. "That isn't Sexton."

"Unfortunately, it is." Sasha tried to hand it back to him.

"Sasha, look closely and pay attention." His tone was abrupt. "That person has a scar across the base of his neck. Sexton doesn't have a scar there."

Sasha slid closer to Calvin and slowly took the picture from his hand. She stared at it with the magnifying glass. "The cut is so small. How can you be sure?"

"The cut is small but long. I'm the team's trainer. I've seen every inch of every player's body. I don't know who that man is, but it isn't Sexton," he confirmed with authority.

Hope began to flicker inside her, then died just as quickly. "How about the money and the other pictures?"

"I can't really say with certainty how those other pictures came to be, but I do know that one morning, I got an early morning visit from Sexton and he asked me if I knew where my spare key was. Once I showed it to him, he left with a very strange look on his face and no explanation.

"As to the money, Sexton gives money to people and helps out a lot of causes. He just doesn't talk about it." A hard look settled on his face. "I know how manipulative Tiara can be. My eyes have been opened to my sister for some time now."

"How could she have done this to me? I've been a good friend to her for years. To sleep with my man and send me a letter on my honeymoon . . ."

"Tiara is not the person you met years ago, though it pains me to say that. I love her, but I can't defend what she's done or even come up with a explanation."

"You are not your sister's keeper." Sasha echoed the words he had used to her less than an hour earlier.

Calvin gave her a slight smile, feeling grateful that she understood his dilemma. "I don't get it. I've tried to introduce her to men of means since her divorce, but she's always brushed my attempts aside."

"She didn't have time for that!" Sasha replied caustically. "She's been too busy trying to mess up my relationship with Sexton."

"I don't understand her fascination with Sexton."

"I do," Sasha answered emphatically. "Only a woman could though."

They sat together on the couch, neither talking, each lost in thought, and then Sasha broke the silence. "I want to thank you, Calvin." She took his hand in hers. "I know it must have been hard to come here and out your sister. She's family and I'm not."

"I think I owe it to Desiree. After all, she never broke the trust that I gave her the night we met at Tiara's party."

Sasha lifted an eyebrow at Calvin's words. "What do you mean?"

"The fact that I'm gay," he said without preamble. "Desiree confided in me that she had been hiding the fact that she was involved in an interracial relationship. And I confided in her that Tiara was having a hard time coming to terms with my sexuality."

An incredulous look crossed Sasha's face. "Tiara has been trying to hook us up ever since I got with Sexton."

Now it was Calvin who looked shocked and then resigned. "She's still trying that? She thinks that because I'm divorced, my chosen lifestyle is a phase which, with the right woman, I can recover from." Calvin captured Sasha's eyes with his. "In fact, I told her that if I was to ever love and marry another woman, it would be someone like you."

Sasha blushed at the unexpected compliment. Time seemed to stand still as Sasha had an epiphany as to why Tiara had been so hell bent on sabotaging her life with Sexton.

"But I know," he said, finishing gently, "that solution would be like putting a Band-Aid on an open sore and only a temporary fix."

After Calvin left, Sasha's blood boiled at the thought of what Tiara had done to her. Because of her, she had done the unforgivable. She had run out on her husband on their honeymoon. She had made a horrible mistake by taking off and not giving Sexton a chance to explain.

Sasha held the small magnifying card to the remaining unexplained picture. And then a moment of clarity came to her. Tiara had stolen stole Calvin's key to Sexton's apartment and taken pictures of him while he slept. He hadn't been aware that he was being photographed. Somehow, somewhere, Tiara had had those photos doctored and she was going to get to the bottom of it. *For months I've been trying to fool myself into thinking that Tiara's changed because of what Peter did to her. But she's always been like this. She's always had to be on top. The minute she lost her man, the real Tiara came out and she has been instrumental in ruining the best thing that has ever happened to me.*

～

The bell rang and the students quickly ran out of the building and down the steps. Bumping into each other as they laughed and talked, some hurriedly boarded the buses that idled nose-to-nose behind each other in a circular formation. Others jumped into waiting cars, waving good-bye to friends whose rides hadn't arrived yet.

Sasha stood to one side of the building and waited. Eventually Tiara exited the glass doors, and with bent head, was digging into her purse, obviously searching for her car keys. Finally she withdrew a set of keys. Noiselessly, Sasha walked up behind her. "What did I ever do to you to make you want to destroy my happiness?" Her voice was harsh and her body language was warlike.

Whirling around to face her, Tiara's face registered shock and then fear.

Sasha noted to her immense satisfaction that fear that was the most dominant.

"You can't come on my job like this, Sasha." Tiara groped for something else to say as she shifted uncomfortably from one foot to the other.

"Why did you do it? I want an answer and I want it now."

Sasha looked Tiara up and down, and her eyes glittered in a way that Sasha had never seen before.

"I didn't make him sleep with me," Tiara answered sharply.

"He didn't sleep with you," Sasha retorted with certainty.

"Are you trying to tell me that you don't believe your own eyes?" Tiara's eyes snapped angrily before they slid away, unable to stand the accusations she saw.

"The man in the picture with you down on your knees isn't even Sexton." Sasha's voice rose and attracted the interest of the remaining students at the curb.

A wary look crossed Tiara's face. Then she asked derisively, "How can you be so sure?"

"Sexton doesn't have a scar across the base of his neck. That's some other man you were probably pimping yourself to in order to get some cash."

"You're turning on me because your man is a cheat!" Tiara exclaimed hotly.

"Sexton is not the cheat. You are!" Instead of Sasha's anger diminishing, it only flared more at Tiara's continued lies about Sexton. "You had somebody doctor those pictures or tell you how to." Then even more contemptuously Sasha said, "In order to get the naked pictures of Sexton, you stole Calvin's key to Sexton's apartment, and again stole them in order to plant that tacky-ass blonde wig," she ended scathingly.

Tiara quickly masked a look of consternation before blustering, "You're grasping at straws, Sasha."

"No I'm not," Sasha denied. "For the very first time, I see you for what you are." Her eyes captured Tiara's, as if she could see into her very soul.

"Throughout our friendship you've always had to be the center of attention. If you had a steady boyfriend and I didn't, you were happy. If we both had boyfriends, but you thought yours was better, you were happy. The only reason you never interfered in my relationship with Abdul was because you felt that it wasn't going anywhere so you didn't feel threatened."

"Shush, Sasha. People are watching," Tiara said, furtively looking at the small crowd.

"Good, maybe they should know what kind of substitute teacher works here. I don't think that you should be around children. You're a horrible role model."

The group of students watching the scene started laughing, amused to see a real life soap opera being acted out practically on the school's steps.

Tiara's body stiffened and she shot Sasha a look of arrogance. "That's not for you to decide."

"Don't worry, Tiara," she warned. "I'm not going to drop the dime on you. I know how much you need money since Peter dumped you," she added snidely. "Stay away from me and stay away from Sexton. If you don't you'll be sorry," Sasha advised with a cautionary tone in her voice before she turned to leave.

"I'm not afraid of you, Sasha. You're all mouth. You always have been."

"Don't be too sure, Tiara." She repeated her warning. "I'm at the end of my rope with you and your shenanigans."

"All you had to do was cooperate," Tiara added, exasperated. "You act as if there are a lot of eligible men out there. Calvin really liked you. You could have gone out with him and Sexton and I—"

Finally losing all control Sasha yelled, "Calvin is gay! Your brother is a homosexual. Don't you get that?"

The group of students now laughed so hard they didn't even try to pretend to hide it. Some were doubled over holding their stomachs.

Seeing this, Tiara became livid and spat out, "How dare you!" Then she lunged for Sasha.

Sasha quickly stepped to one side and avoided Tiara's attempt to assault her. When Tiara straightened, Sasha slapped her across the face with an open palm. The sound of the blow filled the air. Sasha stared at Tiara as she stood with her hand to her cheek and a stunned look on her face.

A young Hispanic teenager had his fist to his closed mouth but he yelled out from behind it, "Damn! Missy got smacked down."

Very calmly, Sasha looked at Tiara, whose eyes were filled with shock and tears and said, "I warned you," before she turned and headed to her car.

CHAPTER 21

Sasha lifted a shaky hand and dialed Sexton's number for the thirtieth time, hoping that this time it wouldn't go to voice mail.

Once it did, she tremulously spoke into the receiver, "Sexton, this is Sasha. I really need to talk to you. No apology is good enough for running out on you, but please give me a chance to explain. After that, if you don't want to see me again, I'll understand." Then she dialed his home telephone number. The impersonal message, "The owner has put a block on his phone and is not receiving calls from this telephone number," echoed in her ears.

Taken aback, Sasha dropped the phone as if it were a hot coal and it clattered onto the tile of the kitchen floor and broke into sections.

She stumbled to the bathroom. There she picked up a washcloth and ran cold water over it. After wringing it out, she stretched out on her bed with it on her forehead. Sasha lay in the darkness, cursing herself for her stupidity and cursing Tiara. At the thought of her, an intense hatred that she had never felt for another human being surfaced. *I'm not going to let her win.*

Sasha recklessly drove to Sexton's apartment. Once she parked her car in the garage next to Sexton's Escalade, she smiled hesitantly at Rudy when she noticed the look of surprise he tried to conceal once he saw her.

"May I go up?" She was afraid, and her expression showed it.

Rudy hesitated and then responded quietly, "Mr. Johnson went out a couple of hours ago and he hasn't returned yet."

"Thank you," she whispered despondently, now noticing that Sexton's Mercedes was missing.

As she drove out of the garage, her chest felt constricted and she couldn't breathe. She pulled into a vacant parking spot on the street, and bent her head in order to still an impending panic attack. Once the feeling passed, she lifted her head and saw Sexton driving into his garage with a woman she had never seen before. She was talking and he had a grin on his face in response to whatever she was saying.

"Oh, my God!" she spoke aloud before she opened her car door and shielding her face from the cars driving by, dropped her head and vomited. After she'd emptied her stomach, she continued to have dry heaves until all of her energy was spent.

Sasha moved her car to a parking spot at the entrance of the garage. *I don't want to make a scene. I don't even have a right to be here, so I'll wait. Once she leaves, I'll go back and try to explain.*

She dozed off and woke up hours later. Using the darkness as her protection, she quietly crept from her car and walked towards the area where Sexton parked his automobiles and saw the Mercedes. Staring at them, she knew that he hadn't moved any of them. *He's still up there with her.* With tears coursing down her face, she returned to her car, turned the ignition key, gunned the gas pedal, and peeled off with screeching tires.

⟞⟝

The next day, she sat on Desiree's sofa staring desolately at a cup of herbal tea. "I've tried to call him and he won't return my calls."

Desiree stared at her bent head. "Make him talk to you."

"I tried, but I saw him arriving home with another woman."

"So what?" she gently scolded her. "I thought that you learned your lesson about jumping to conclusions."

"I have, but I waited around and she never left. She stayed the night with him."

Sasha's last words were muffled and Desiree could barely hear her. She gave Sasha a look filled with understanding. "I know that must hurt you, but it's to be expected that he'd turn to another woman for comfort. That doesn't mean he's over you." Now she gave Sasha a stern look, "Maybe he's decided that you're too high maintenance and he prefers to be with a woman who appreciates him and doesn't doubt his integrity. There are a lot of good black men out there, Sasha. Don't doubt the love that he showed you."

"I miss him so much, Sasha. I can't eat, I can't sleep."

Desiree gave Sasha's slender form a once-over. "I can tell." Sasha's bottom lip quivered and Desiree felt as if could see the pain she was feeling in her heart.

"I took some time off from work and I think that was a mistake. I've had too much time to sit and brood. I'm going back in tomorrow."

"Are you going to try to see Sexton again?"

"Yes," she answered. "He knows that I've been trying to talk to him from the numerous messages he's chosen not to return. I'm not ready to give up. I have to try to make him understand why I took off the way I did."

Desiree placed her arm comfortingly around her sister's shoulder. "I know things look dismal, but Sexton wanted you from the first time that he saw you. Remember, I was there. I don't think that a person gets over a powerful attraction that grows into love in the short length of time you've been separated. After the two of you left Dominique's house we talked about the expression Sexton had in his eyes every time he looked at you. He didn't try to hide it or act as if he wasn't in love with you. And I've never seen you as happy or light-hearted with another man as you were with him. We knew that the two of you had something special.

"But you hurt him badly, Sasha. Now you have to get him to see you are still the person he fell in love with even though you made a terrible mistake by believing the worst about him. You know the kind of man he really is and you'll just have to do whatever it takes to get him back."

Sasha drew in a deep breath filled with unhappiness and exhaustion. "I'm going to give him some more time to cool off."

"Don't give him too much time," Desiree cautioned. "My ex did that, and by the time he worked up the courage to see me I was already head over heels in love with another man, a man who I ended up marrying."

As she left Desiree's house, Sasha was mindful of her advice and once again drove to Sexton's apartment. She knew that it was useless to try and call him again since he'd made it clear that he was not going to make himself accessible to her. Sasha was sitting at the light, waiting for the green, when she saw Sexton's Escalade driving down the ramp. Once again he was not alone. The same woman who had been in the car with him the previous night was in the car, grinning.

As Sexton drove past her, his eyes locked with hers, and then he coldly turned his head in the opposite direction.

Sasha dropped her head to let it rest on the steering wheel. She quelled tears, knowing they were no good to her. Only the honking of the cars behind her prodded her into action. Instead of pulling into the garage so that she could turn around she made a U-turn and ignoring the car horns of angry motorists, she drove in the direction that Sexton had gone.

The traffic was heavy as usual, but she easily spied Sexton's SUV ahead of her. There were several cars and a city bus between them, and while keeping a distance, Sasha craned her neck to not lose sight of them.

Suddenly, Sexton pulled out of traffic and parked in a space in front of the movie theatre they had frequented as a couple. Agilely, he jumped out of the driver's side and walked around and opened the door.

Traffic was now at a standstill and Sasha slid a little ways down in her seat, embarrassed at herself for spying.

Sexton held his hand out, and smiling at him with a loving look, the woman placed hers in his. Sasha could see that the woman was unusually tall and stood eye level to Sexton. As they walked together towards the entrance of the movie theatre, Sasha watched dazed as the woman slid her arm into the crook of Sexton's. After purchasing tickets at the window, they disappeared inside, arm in arm.

Sasha sat stupefied, wishing she had never followed him. Then swallowing hard, once again she pulled out into traffic.

Once she arrived back home, bereft, she slid naked into bed, curled into the fetal position, and pulled the covers completely over her head.

⌒

Sasha aimlessly pored over the budget reports that were due to be completed before she left work that day. She ran one hand listlessly through her hair and, with a sudden feeling of intuition, felt the hairs on her neck stand. She looked up and her eyes locked with Sexton's as he stood in the doorway of her office.

He was dressed in black from head to toe and his eyes glittered with a force that made her feel apprehensive.

"Sexton, you came." Her voice was faint and her lips quivered with apprehension.

"I have an appointment at the sports medicine clinic." Sexton's terse voice gave no indication of emotion, and the rigidity of his body dashed any hope that might have been ignited in Sasha by his appearance.

She was at a loss to reply with anything but, "Oh."

"I felt that since I had to come here, I might as well kill two birds with one stone." Sexton reached into his pocket and withdrew a few sheets of paper stapled together. He handed them to her and said bleakly, "These are our annulment papers. All you have to do is sign them. I'll take care of the rest."

Sasha's heart dropped to her feet, but she took the papers from him. Quickly scanning them she handed them back to him and said, "I can't sign it."

Sexton coldly asked, "Why not?"

"Annulments are for people who've never had sex. We had sex the night we were married. It wouldn't be right or legal."

Sexton's eyes were hard and his words dripped with sarcasm. "Since when did you decide to do the right thing, Sasha?"

Sasha recoiled from the severity of his words. "Can we please talk, Sexton?" she softly pleaded.

He rocked back and forth on his heels and Sasha could see that his fists were balled in his pockets.

She pointed to the chair in front of her desk and reiterated her request. "Please hear me out."

In one quick motion, Sexton kicked her office door shut with his foot and lowered his long frame into the chair, stretching his legs out in front of him.

"Saying I'm sorry for running out on you in Vegas is obvious. Changing what I did is impossible, but trying to make it up to you for the rest of my life is possible."

"You can't make up for the past, Sasha." Sexton stared at a spot on the wall behind her, obviously now loath for their eyes to connect.

"I made a mistake. Married people do it all the time, and they move on and try to forgive."

"They have a foundation, Sasha. We have nothing. You ruined things before we even got our feet wet," he replied bluntly.

"We're married, Sexton. That means something."

"Obviously not to you. You showed me what you really felt for me when you ran out on me on our honeymoon. You proposed to me, married me, and then took off." His teeth gritted with every word.

The sickening feeling in Sasha's stomach intensified and she looked away out of guilt before she whispered, "Who is that woman that I saw you with?"

"None of your business." His words were harsh to her ears and she had to blink back tears.

She couldn't stop the jealousy in her voice. "Is she the reason you won't give us another chance?"

"You are the reason I won't give us another chance. It's all about you, Sasha!"

She choked back tears.

His voice was raw with emotion that he couldn't conceal. "Can you imagine how I felt when I returned to an empty suite? That was the most humiliating experience in my whole life, and I'm not going to give you the power to ever hurt me again."

His manner was contemptuous, but Sasha could see the pain and anguish he was feeling as he bitterly relived the scene he had encountered after she had run out on him on their honeymoon.

She didn't attempt to dry the tears on her face. "I'm sorry, Sexton. But when I got that envelope from Tiara, I was so distraught I wasn't thinking straight and I panicked."

"Yes, Tiara." Sexton bit off his words and continued harshly, "So what if I gave her money. It is mine, you know," he drawled. "We weren't married and I didn't know that sleeping with you meant that I was supposed to give you an itemized statement of what I did with my own money."

"I didn't leave because of the money that you gave her. I know how generous you are. It was the thought of the two of you sleeping together, that's what I couldn't handle."

"What in the hell are you talking about?" Sexton's voice exploded in the room and she thought the window might shatter from the force. "I have never slept with Tiara." He tapped his chest with his index finger with each word.

"I know that now. She sent me some doctored pictures that made it appear that the two of you were lovers."

"And you believed that? The fact that you did only adds insult to injury."

"I'm not making excuses for myself or for what I did, but if you saw them, maybe you would understand how seeing something like that on your honeymoon would throw you for a loop."

"I don't want to hear any more of this nonsense, and I'm not interested in seeing them," Sexton retorted with disgust in his voice. "I warned you about her, and you wouldn't listen."

"I know, Sexton, but I'm listening now." Her eyes begged him to forgive her.

He spat out harshly, "It's too late." Then he pointed at her. "What you did was juvenile." He put his index finger on his chest. "I don't want to be bothered. You make life too hard."

She swallowed hard. "Please, Sexton, give me another chance. Give us another chance." Sasha clasped her hands together and tried to steady them.

"You just don't get it, do you? What you did to me is worse than what my birth mother did." Pain and anguish were etched on his face. "She too abandoned me, but I've always told myself that if she had given herself a chance to know me, she wouldn't have. You know me, the real me, and yet you still left. That's worse." He drew in a deep breath, stood, and walked to the door. "I'll contact my lawyer and have divorce papers drawn up. I'll put a rush on them."

After Sexton left, Sasha buried her face in her arms and wept uncontrollably.

＝

"I have something to tell you, but you have to promise not to tell anyone, especially Dominique."

"Okay, I promise."

Sasha could hear the apprehension in Desiree's voice over the telephone.

"There's something I've been keeping a secret. Sexton and I were married in Vegas."

An astounded gasp was Desiree's reply.

"He came to my job today and wanted me to sign annulment papers, but I wouldn't because we consummated our marriage in Vegas. Annulment is not an option. I saw that on *Friends*."

"You're absolutely right," Desiree confirmed. "What did Sexton say when you refused?"

"He said that he would have divorce papers drawn up and have them sent to me."

Desiree was quiet, obviously mulling over what Sasha had said. "You don't have to sign them, either. New York is one of the few states left in the country that doesn't recognize no-fault divorce. You have to agree. You can pretty much keep him married to you forever, or at least until they change the law. The state officials are working on that as we speak."

"But I don't want to stay married to someone who doesn't love me or want to stay married to me," Sasha whined.

"Then why did you call me to tell me this?" Desiree asked sharply.

"I want your advice."

Sasha sounded so miserable that Desiree's heart went out to her. "I know you still love Sexton, but could you get an impartial read on him at all as to how he feels about you?"

"No, he's so angry. It was as if he was a different person."

"Good," Desiree said with satisfaction. "People don't hold on to anger if it's for someone that they don't care about. When I almost lost Tyler, he took off and I couldn't even find him."

"I remember. Then he showed up at the hospital thinking you'd been in an accident. Maybe I should pretend to get in an accident," Sasha said half joking, half seriously.

"Don't play games with him, Sasha," Desiree admonished her. "You're in enough trouble as it is."

"I didn't really mean that," she stuttered. "I just don't know what to do."

"This is what I would do. Because you're married, you have some leverage. Once I got the papers, I would take them to him unsigned. His lawyer probably will tell him exactly what I just told you. Tell him that if in six months he still wants a divorce you'll sign them. That should give him some time to come to terms with what you did."

"What kind of marriage is that?" Sasha exclaimed. "Him living in one place and me in another."

"I don't know what else to tell you, Sasha. As usual, your impetuous nature has gotten you into trouble. You married Sexton in Vegas, obviously a spur of the moment decision, and then you take off and leave him without talking to him. Another spur of the moment decision. Now you say that you'll give him what he says he wants without thinking that through, either. You need to take a step back and do nothing. Maybe when things settle down he'll be more receptive to working things out."

"Yes, ma'am." Chastened she hung up the phone.

———

Saturday morning the doorbell rang. Sasha turned the stove off and slid her ham and cheese omelet to a cool burner. Throwing open the door, she silently took the Federal Express envelope, signed the receipt, and closed the door.

True to his word, Sexton had quickly sent the divorce papers to her. He had even made check marks at the places for her to sign.

She slammed the papers down on the kitchen counter, picked up her frying pan, which held her breakfast, and emptied the contents in the trash can before she went to douse her face under the bathroom faucet. Hours later, she was sipping her third glass of wine as she mulled over Desiree's advice. *I might as well do what Desiree told me to. After all, I haven't made smart decisions by relying on my own thought processes.*

Standing suddenly, she felt unsteady and realized that the cause was the third glass of wine she had drunk. Realizing she was too tipsy to drive to Madison Square Garden, she decided to take the bus. The bus ground to a stop in front of Madison Square Garden, and once she cautiously descended the stairs, she felt buoyed at the sight of Stefan.

"Hello, Stefan." Her voice was quiet. She was uncertain as to how to go about asking for Sexton's whereabouts.

Stefan was putting the finishing touches of polish on a limousine, and the smile he gave her was genuine. "How are you doing, Miss Diamond?"

Sasha knew that it was a rhetorical question and he wouldn't want to know the real answer so she lied.

"I'm fine, Stefan. Is Mr. Johnson around?"

"You just missed him. I heard him tell Mr. Calvin that he was going to lunch at Mario's."

She asked tentatively, "Was he alone?"

Stefan looked at her, surprised. "Of course. Would you like me to take you over there?"

"No thanks, Stefan, I don't want to impose."

"It's no problem," he replied, looking up at the sky. "Looks like rain, and by the time the bus got you there, he'd probably be gone."

Still, Sasha hesitated.

Stefan opened the door and said conspiratorially, "I won't tell anyone."

She gave him a grateful smile and said softly, "Thank you, Stefan."

Stefan lowered the partition window and offered with a wink, "Have a drink as a lunch appetizer."

Sasha hesitated, but her mouth was dry from nervousness about her impending conversation with Sexton. The effects of her early afternoon happy hour had slightly waned, and she felt that she could use just a little more Dutch courage, so she poured herself a generous glass of wine.

The ride to the restaurant took less than fifteen minutes and once they arrived, she handed Stefan a twenty-dollar bill. When he started to protest she said, "I insist."

Mario's was a small café that she and Sexton had frequented many times. In the fifties it had been a notorious mob hang out, and on the walls there were black and white pictures of many prominent heads of Mafia families. They served homemade pasta dishes that restaurant chains couldn't compete with.

Sasha spied Sexton sitting in a back booth and began to walk over to him. There was a man sitting in the booth across from him and when she got closer she realized that it was Kendall. Just then, emerging from the ladies' room was the woman that Sasha had seen in Sexton's car. The woman halted in front of the booth, and Sexton slid out in order to let her sit on the inside. Smiling at her, he sat back down, resting his arm along the back of the booth behind her shoulders.

Sasha was flabbergasted to find herself in a situation she had hoped to avoid at all costs. *He's introducing her to his brother. He's really over me. I blew it.*

Just as she turned to leave, Sexton's eyes suddenly pinned hers. Then she saw two other pairs of eyes were also staring at her. Not knowing what else to do, Sasha walked towards them. To make matters worse, on her way over to the table, the heel of her shoe turned, and Sasha barely righted herself before falling. She could feel her color run when some people at a nearby table snickered.

Sexton was watching her carefully, his eyes narrowed, his expression bland.

Once she reached the table, she nodded at Kendall and he returned her greeting in the same manner. Then she looked at the woman seated at the table. Now that she was able to examine her so closely, the woman looked eerily familiar and Sasha racked her brain trying to figure out if she had ever really seen her before or whether her mind was working overtime because of the embarrassing situation she had put herself in.

Sasha turned to Sexton and said without preamble, "I got your papers this morning."

Sexton didn't answer her. Gathering her wits, she mustered up all her strength to finish the ordeal she had engineered. "I'm sorry to intrude, but I expected to find you alone." She shot an antagonistic look at the woman and was caught off guard by the expression she now encountered because it was one of kindness. Glancing at Kendall, she saw that he had put down the menu and sat back, looking like Sexton when he was very interested in something.

"In New York, married people have to agree to the divorce. I came to tell you that I wasn't going to sign the papers. I was going to ask you to hold off for six months."

Upon hearing this, Sexton gave a small start of surprise.

"But after my arrival . . ." Again she looked at the woman, only to be met this time with a look of pity. This riled Sasha, but she knew that she needed to keep her cool so that she didn't look as stupid as she felt. "I've decided that I don't want to be married to someone who doesn't want me and has clearly moved on." She reached in her pocketbook and gently placed the papers down on the table. Quickly she signed them and then held out her car keys to Sexton.

For the first time since she had approached them Sexton spoke. "I don't want the car back." His manner did not reveal what his thoughts were.

"I don't feel right about keeping it. It's parked in the garage waiting for you. Take care." Without looking back, Sasha stalked out of the restaurant with her head held high.

CHAPTER 22

Sasha stared at her at her naked body in the bathroom mirror. She smelled because she had been caught in the rain and her body had air dried before she had reached her loft. Once there she had walked in the dark straight to the bathroom, not turning on a light to help her find her way. Now, as she looked in the mirror, she felt and she looked like crap. She hadn't given herself a beauty treatment since getting home from Vegas. She hadn't really felt the energy or need to.

She reached under her vanity table and withdrew a basket that held her beauty products and took out her jar of sea salt scrub, a loofah, pumice stone, and face polisher. She climbed into the shower and doused herself under the hot, stinging spray.

She grabbed a bottle of shampoo from the side of the tub and, as she scrubbed her hair, she hummed the lyrics to a musical she had seen years ago. Thinking aloud she said, "I really wish that I could wash that man out of my hair."

Sasha scrubbed, polished, rinsed, and gave attention to each inch of skin she was able to reach. *If Sexton was here, this is the time I would call him to exfoliate my back for me.* She pushed those somber thoughts away. She had to get used to not having him around to pamper her. She stepped from the shower and reached for a large, fluffy towel. After drying off she cleansed her face with astringent and finished off with a small dab of moisturizing lotion. Then she squirted a generous amount of body oil into the palm of her hand and in small, circular motions, covered every inch her skin.

She again stared at her reflection. Her skin glowed and was soft to the touch. She looked better and even felt a little better. *Too bad I have no one to share this with. I'm not in the mood to share it with myself. Talk about a glass being three-quarters empty.*

Wrapping a large, fluffy towel around her, she padded back into the darkened bedroom.

"What took you so long to get home?"

Sasha whirled around, dropping the towel. Her eyes followed the unexpected sound of Sexton's stern voice. He sat in the occasional chair in the corner. She bent to retrieve the towel that had slipped from her body in an effort to cover her nakedness.

"Leave it." Sexton's tone gave no room for her to not do what he said.

She obediently stood before him, unsuccessfully attempting to cover her breasts with the palms of her hands.

He rephrased his initial question. "What took you so long to get here after you stormed out of the restaurant?"

"I took a ride on the Long Island Ferry," she responded in a voice so low he could barely catch her words.

"What made you go there?"

"Memories," she replied honestly. "The first time I realized just how much I love you was on the ferry." Sasha hoped that Sexton could see as she stood before him completely naked that she was also baring her soul to him. She hoped that he could see what she was feeling inside.

He sat there silently for what felt like an eternity. She could hear the ticking of the clock on the wall.

"Sasha, I don't know what I'm going to do with you." Clearly exasperated, he said, "To run out on your husband during your honeymoon. Who do you think you're supposed to be, Julia Roberts in *The Runaway Bride*?"

She hung her head in mortification, knowing that he only spoke the truth. "I think that there was a small part of me that was insecure about us anyhow." She mumbled the words, not looking up.

"Why are you so insecure? I've never given you any reason to distrust me."

His tone had mellowed slightly and Sasha began to feel a flicker of hope.

"I know. It's just I know The All-Star game really put you on the map and you're getting ready to blow up. It's unusual for superstars to be faithful to one woman."

"I already have more money and prestige than I ever thought I would," he said wryly. "If I'm not insufferable yet, what would make you think that I would change later?"

Sasha's answer was to stare at the floor.

"Don't believe the hype you see on television. It's an insult to me and all black men if you believe that

317

monogamy is an impossible standard for us. Good black men are out there, we just don't get press in the paper."

"I believe you," she replied softly, "my dad's one of them."

"So was mine." Curiosity was evident in his voice as if he was trying to get inside her head. "Don't you believe that people are a product of their environment?"

"Yes, I believe that they are more times than not." She shook her head sadly. "But those pictures. And after what Abdul did to me." She gave him a measured look, willing him to try and understand. "He didn't even have anything going for him, yet he was unfaithful." She shuddered with distaste. "Those pictures Tiara sent me fed a small niggling doubt that I had in the back of my mind, not only about you but doubts about myself."

"This morning, Calvin wouldn't leave my place until he showed me the negatives of the pictures Tiara sent you. I have to admit, they were quite damning. But how could you have not given me a chance to explain?"

"My insane jealousy, Sexton." She walked over to stand in front of him. "I'm sorry."

Sexton ran his eyes up the length of her body and said gently, "I know that you are."

"Does this mean that you're willing to give our marriage a try?" She tried to contain her excitement, not wanting false hope.

"I guess I'll have to. But let me say this, Sasha. You are a pain in the ass." He severely cautioned her, "If you ever pull another stunt like that again—" He took his hand and slapped her bare bottom.

She felt the small sting and she knew it was meant to warn and not hurt. "I won't," she promised. "I'll be the perfect wife."

He grimaced and said, "I doubt that, but everyone has a mission in life, and it appears that you're mine."

Once she heard the slight mockery in his voice, Sasha sat down on Sexton's lap, wound her arms around his neck and whispered, "I want to start being your wife again, right now."

Sexton stood, and drawing her close, he encircled her in his arms and squeezed her.

The next morning she lay nestled in the security of Sexton's arms. She had been lying there quietly, thanking God for giving her a second chance and letting them start their marriage with a clean slate. All of a sudden, her stomach growled. For the first time in weeks, she was hungry.

Suddenly, Sexton pushed Sasha slightly up and spoke. "It's time to get up if you want me to take you to breakfast."

Sitting up in a hurry, she rushed to the shower.

Sasha glanced at Sexton as he maneuvered in and out of traffic. "Where are we going to eat breakfast?"

Sexton didn't answer her, but she surmised as they headed towards Harlem that they were going to his favorite hang out. "Do you still want me to move into your apartment?"

He smiled at her and said, "I think that it would be better if I moved into your place. We'll start looking for something bigger this week."

"What are you going to do with your place? Rent it out?

He gave her an enigmatic look. "I don't think so." Then with an abrupt change of subject he said, "Are you still going to work at the hospital?"

"I plan on it until the babies come." She smiled shyly.

Sexton's cell phone rang and interrupted their conversation. "Hello. Yes, I'm almost there."

Before Sasha could ask him who was on the phone they arrived at Sylvia's. Smiling, she followed him up the walk.

Surprised, she saw Teddy sitting in the largest booth in the restaurant. Next to him was Kendall. When she reached the table, she smiled at them and then froze. Sitting across from them was the woman Sexton had been seeing during their estrangement.

Sexton turned to Sasha and said, "Sasha, this is my sister, Destiny. Destiny, this is my wife."

Sasha felt as if her heart was in her throat as she stared into the eyes that had seemed so familiar before.

There was a look of amusement on Destiny's face and her lips twitched as she watched a myriad of expressions cross Sasha's face, with the last being one of relief.

Sexton said somewhat sheepishly, "It never occurred to me when I read my birth certificate that my twin would be a girl. But I'm happy the way things turned out. Now I have two brothers and a sister. A person couldn't ask for more."

Destiny held out her hand to Sasha and, as they shook, she shot a look of adoration at Sexton.

"It's very nice to meet you." Sasha spoke first and Destiny echoed the sentiment.

As Sexton and his brothers devoured every bit of their breakfast, Sasha picked at hers and surreptitiously watched Destiny.

Astutely interpreting her thoughts, Destiny looked directly at Sasha and said, "Sexton had a private eye find me. After the death of our maternal grandmother, I looked for years for my missing brothers but I had to give up after I exhausted the small insurance policy that was left to me."

Sexton wiped his mouth and explained, "Destiny is going to live in my apartment, which is why we have a change of plans as to our temporary residence."

"Oh, I see," Sasha replied, giving no indication as to what she was thinking.

She was aware of Teddy and Kendall watching her closely as they tried to gauge her true feelings about all she'd heard since she and Sexton had arrived at Sylvia's.

"You can't believe how blown away I was when I realized that my brother was Sexton Johnson the basketball player. I've had no family for years, and now I have two brothers, two sisters-in-law and a niece and nephews. My cup runneth over."

Sasha sipped her cup of coffee and scrutinized Destiny. She was tall with eyes like Sexton's. She seemed to possess his easygoing demeanor, but was that enough? She didn't dare voice her concerns because they'd already accepted her as family. Who was she to dispute it?

Then Destiny picked up the coffee pot. Filling a cup she switched the pot to the other hand to refill Sasha's cup. As she did, Destiny gave her a knowing look. "I'm ambidextrous," she paused for effect, "just like my twin brother."

A huge relief flooded Sasha's body. She reached across the table and placed her hand over Destiny's. "Welcome to the family, Sister."

After breakfast, Sasha and Sexton held hands as they stood outside on the sidewalk. "Anyone need a lift?"

"Naw, man, I got it. We're all riding together." Kendall pointed to an F-150 that was pulled into a parking place near the entrance.

"Talk to you soon?" He looked at Sexton.

"You can count on it."

Destiny leaned over and kissed Sexton on the cheek. With a smile that included Sasha, she said, "I'll see you later this week?"

"You can bet on it," Sexton answered.

They watched as she walked over to the open car door Teddy held out.

Kendall gave Sexton a look of gratitude. "Thank you for finding her." He gave Sasha a wink before he went to his truck, got in, and drove off.

As Sasha and Sexton watched his family drive away, he turned to her and said with a little tremor in his voice, "Yesterday's the past and tomorrow's the future, but today is a gift and that's why it's called the present. I feel as if my life has gone full circle."

Sasha felt overwhelmed by Sexton's words and with a catch in her voice she stated with brutal honesty, "I love you, Sexton Johnson."

"I love you too, Sasha Johnson. Now let's go home, Wifey."

Sasha took the car keys out of Sexton's hand and opened the car door for him to get him.

Smiling, he nodded at her and slid in.

After closing the door, she strode to the other side, got in and cranked the car, gave him a smile of supreme happiness, and pulled out into traffic.

2008 Reprint Mass Market Titles

January

Cautious Heart
Cheris F. Hodges
ISBN-13: 978-1-58571-301-1
ISBN-10: 1-58571-301-5
$6.99

Suddenly You
Crystal Hubbard
ISBN-13: 978-1-58571-302-8
ISBN-10: 1-58571-302-3
$6.99

February

Passion
T. T. Henderson
ISBN-13: 978-1-58571-303-5
ISBN-10: 1-58571-303-1
$6.99

Whispers in the Sand
LaFlorya Gauthier
ISBN-13: 978-1-58571-304-2
ISBN-10: 1-58571-304-x
$6.99

March

Life Is Never As It Seems
J. J. Michael
ISBN-13: 978-1-58571-305-9
ISBN-10: 1-58571-305-8
$6.99

Beyond the Rapture
Beverly Clark
ISBN-13: 978-1-58571-306-6
ISBN-10: 1-58571-306-6
$6.99

April

A Heart's Awakening
Veronica Parker
ISBN-13: 978-1-58571-307-3
ISBN-10: 1-58571-307-4
$6.99

Breeze
Robin Lynette Hampton
ISBN-13: 978-1-58571-308-0
ISBN-10: 1-58571-308-2
$6.99

May

I'll Be Your Shelter
Giselle Carmichael
ISBN-13: 978-1-58571-309-7
ISBN-10: 1-58571-309-0
$6.99

Careless Whispers
Rochelle Alers
ISBN-13: 978-1-58571-310-3
ISBN-10: 1-58571-310-4
$6.99

June

Sin
Crystal Rhodes
ISBN-13: 978-1-58571-311-0
ISBN-10: 1-58571-311-2
$6.99

Dark Storm Rising
Chinelu Moore
ISBN-13: 978-1-58571-312-7
ISBN-10: 1-58571-312-0
$6.99

2008 Reprint Mass Market Titles (continued)
July

Object of His Desire
A.C. Arthur
ISBN-13: 978-1-58571-313-4
ISBN-10: 1-58571-313-9
$6.99

Angel's Paradise
Janice Angelique
ISBN-13: 978-1-58571-314-1
ISBN-10: 1-58571-314-7
$6.99

August

Unbreak My Heart
Dar Tomlinson
ISBN-13: 978-1-58571-315-8
ISBN-10: 1-58571-315-5
$6.99

All I Ask
Barbara Keaton
ISBN-13: 978-1-58571-316-5
ISBN-10: 1-58571-316-3
$6.99

September

Icie
Pamela Leigh Starr
ISBN-13: 978-1-58571-275-5
ISBN-10: 1-58571-275-2
$6.99

At Last
Lisa Riley
ISBN-13: 978-1-58571-276-2
ISBN-10: 1-58571-276-0
$6.99

October

Everlastin' Love
Gay G. Gunn
ISBN-13: 978-1-58571-277-9
ISBN-10: 1-58571-277-9
$6.99

Three Wishes
Seressia Glass
ISBN-13: 978-1-58571-278-6
ISBN-10: 1-58571-278-7
$6.99

November

Yesterday Is Gone
Beverly Clark
ISBN-13: 978-1-58571-279-3
ISBN-10: 1-58571-279-5
$6.99

Again My Love
Kayla Perrin
ISBN-13: 978-1-58571-280-9
ISBN-10: 1-58571-280-9
$6.99

December

Office Policy
A.C. Arthur
ISBN-13: 978-1-58571-281-6
ISBN-10: 1-58571-281-7
$6.99

Rendezvous With Fate
Jeanne Sumerix
ISBN-13: 978-1-58571-283-3
ISBN-10: 1-58571-283-3
$6.99

2008 New Mass Market Titles

January

Where I Want To Be
Maryam Diaab
ISBN-13: 978-1-58571-268-7
ISBN-10: 1-58571-268-X
$6.99

Never Say Never
Michele Cameron
ISBN-13: 978-1-58571-269-4
ISBN-10: 1-58571-269-8
$6.99

February

Stolen Memories
Michele Sudler
ISBN-13: 978-1-58571-270-0
ISBN-10: 1-58571-270-1
$6.99

Dawn's Harbor
Kymberly Hunt
ISBN-13: 978-1-58571-271-7
ISBN-10: 1-58571-271-X
$6.99

March

Undying Love
Renee Alexis
ISBN-13: 978-1-58571-272-4
ISBN-10: 1-58571-272-8
$6.99

Blame It On Paradise
Crystal Hubbard
ISBN-13: 978-1-58571-273-1
ISBN-10: 1-58571-273-6
$6.99

April

When A Man Loves A Woman
La Connie Taylor-Jones
ISBN-13: 978-1-58571-274-8
ISBN-10: 1-58571-274-4
$6.99

Choices
Tammy Williams
ISBN-13: 978-1-58571-300-4
ISBN-10: 1-58571-300-7
$6.99

May

Dream Runner
Gail McFarland
ISBN-13: 978-1-58571-317-2
ISBN-10: 1-58571-317-1
$6.99

Southern Fried Standards
S.R. Maddox
ISBN-13: 978-1-58571-318-9
ISBN-10: 1-58571-318-X
$6.99

June

Looking for Lily
Africa Fine
ISBN-13: 978-1-58571-319-6
ISBN-10: 1-58571-319-8
$6.99

Bliss, Inc.
Chamein Canton
ISBN-13: 978-1-58571-325-7
ISBN-10: 1-58571-325-2
$6.99

2008 New Mass Market Titles (continued)

July

Love's Secrets
Yolanda McVey
ISBN-13: 978-1-58571-321-9
ISBN-10: 1-58571-321-X
$6.99

Things Forbidden
Maryam Diaab
ISBN-13: 978-1-58571-327-1
ISBN-10: 1-58571-327-9
$6.99

August

Storm
Pamela Leigh Starr
ISBN-13: 978-1-58571-323-3
ISBN-10: 1-58571-323-6
$6.99

Passion's Furies
AlTonya Washington
ISBN-13: 978-1-58571-324-0
ISBN-10: 1-58571-324-4
$6.99

September

Three Doors Down
Michele Sudler
ISBN-13: 978-1-58571-332-5
ISBN-10: 1-58571-332-5
$6.99

Mr Fix-It
Crystal Hubbard
ISBN-13: 978-1-58571-326-4
ISBN-10: 1-58571-326-0
$6.99

October

Moments of Clarity . . .
Michele Cameron
ISBN-13: 978-1-58571-330-1
ISBN-10: 1-58571-330-9
$6.99

Lady Preacher
K.T. Richey
ISBN-13: 978-1-58571-333-2
ISBN-10: 1-58571-333-3
$6.99

November

This Life Isn't Perfect Holla
Sandra Foy
ISBN: 978-1-58571-331-8
ISBN-10: 1-58571-331-7
$6.99

Promises Made
Bernice Layton
ISBN-13: 978-1-58571-334-9
ISBN-10: 1-58571-334-1
$6.99

December

A Voice Behind Thunder
Carrie Elizabeth Greene
ISBN-13: 978-1-58571-329-5
ISBN-10: 1-58571-329-5
$6.99

The More Things Change
Chamein Canton
ISBN-13: 978-1-58571-328-8
ISBN-10: 1-58571-328-7
$6.99

Other Genesis Press, Inc. Titles

A Dangerous Deception	J.M. Jeffries	$8.95
A Dangerous Love	J.M. Jeffries	$8.95
A Dangerous Obsession	J.M. Jeffries	$8.95
A Drummer's Beat to Mend	Kei Swanson	$9.95
A Happy Life	Charlotte Harris	$9.95
A Heart's Awakening	Veronica Parker	$9.95
A Lark on the Wing	Phyliss Hamilton	$9.95
A Love of Her Own	Cheris F. Hodges	$9.95
A Love to Cherish	Beverly Clark	$8.95
A Risk of Rain	Dar Tomlinson	$8.95
A Taste of Temptation	Reneé Alexis	$9.95
A Twist of Fate	Beverly Clark	$8.95
A Will to Love	Angie Daniels	$9.95
Acquisitions	Kimberley White	$8.95
Across	Carol Payne	$12.95
After the Vows	Leslie Esdaile	$10.95
(Summer Anthology)	T.T. Henderson	
	Jacqueline Thomas	
Again My Love	Kayla Perrin	$10.95
Against the Wind	Gwynne Forster	$8.95
All I Ask	Barbara Keaton	$8.95
Always You	Crystal Hubbard	$6.99
Ambrosia	T.T. Henderson	$8.95
An Unfinished Love Affair	Barbara Keaton	$8.95
And Then Came You	Dorothy Elizabeth Love	$8.95
Angel's Paradise	Janice Angelique	$9.95
At Last	Lisa G. Riley	$8.95
Best of Friends	Natalie Dunbar	$8.95
Beyond the Rapture	Beverly Clark	$9.95

Other Genesis Press, Inc. Titles (continued)

Blaze	Barbara Keaton	$9.95
Blood Lust	J. M. Jeffries	$9.95
Blood Seduction	J.M. Jeffries	$9.95
Bodyguard	Andrea Jackson	$9.95
Boss of Me	Diana Nyad	$8.95
Bound by Love	Beverly Clark	$8.95
Breeze	Robin Hampton Allen	$10.95
Broken	Dar Tomlinson	$24.95
By Design	Barbara Keaton	$8.95
Cajun Heat	Charlene Berry	$8.95
Careless Whispers	Rochelle Alers	$8.95
Cats & Other Tales	Marilyn Wagner	$8.95
Caught in a Trap	Andre Michelle	$8.95
Caught Up In the Rapture	Lisa G. Riley	$9.95
Cautious Heart	Cheris F Hodges	$8.95
Chances	Pamela Leigh Starr	$8.95
Cherish the Flame	Beverly Clark	$8.95
Class Reunion	Irma Jenkins/	
	John Brown	$12.95
Code Name: Diva	J.M. Jeffries	$9.95
Conquering Dr. Wexler's Heart	Kimberley White	$9.95
Corporate Seduction	A.C. Arthur	$9.95
Crossing Paths, Tempting Memories	Dorothy Elizabeth Love	$9.95
Crush	Crystal Hubbard	$9.95
Cypress Whisperings	Phyllis Hamilton	$8.95
Dark Embrace	Crystal Wilson Harris	$8.95
Dark Storm Rising	Chinelu Moore	$10.95

Other Genesis Press, Inc. Titles (continued)

Daughter of the Wind	Joan Xian	$8.95
Deadly Sacrifice	Jack Kean	$22.95
Designer Passion	Dar Tomlinson	$8.95
	Diana Richeaux	
Do Over	Celya Bowers	$9.95
Dreamtective	Liz Swados	$5.95
Ebony Angel	Deatri King-Bey	$9.95
Ebony Butterfly II	Delilah Dawson	$14.95
Echoes of Yesterday	Beverly Clark	$9.95
Eden's Garden	Elizabeth Rose	$8.95
Eve's Prescription	Edwina Martin Arnold	$8.95
Everlastin' Love	Gay G. Gunn	$8.95
Everlasting Moments	Dorothy Elizabeth Love	$8.95
Everything and More	Sinclair Lebeau	$8.95
Everything but Love	Natalie Dunbar	$8.95
Falling	Natalie Dunbar	$9.95
Fate	Pamela Leigh Starr	$8.95
Finding Isabella	A.J. Garrotto	$8.95
Forbidden Quest	Dar Tomlinson	$10.95
Forever Love	Wanda Y. Thomas	$8.95
From the Ashes	Kathleen Suzanne	$8.95
	Jeanne Sumerix	
Gentle Yearning	Rochelle Alers	$10.95
Glory of Love	Sinclair LeBeau	$10.95
Go Gentle into that Good Night	Malcom Boyd	$12.95
Goldengroove	Mary Beth Craft	$16.95
Groove, Bang, and Jive	Steve Cannon	$8.99
Hand in Glove	Andrea Jackson	$9.95

Other Genesis Press, Inc. Titles (continued)

Hard to Love	Kimberley White	$9.95
Hart & Soul	Angie Daniels	$8.95
Heart of the Phoenix	A.C. Arthur	$9.95
Heartbeat	Stephanie Bedwell-Grime	$8.95
Hearts Remember	M. Loui Quezada	$8.95
Hidden Memories	Robin Allen	$10.95
Higher Ground	Leah Latimer	$19.95
Hitler, the War, and the Pope	Ronald Rychiak	$26.95
How to Write a Romance	Kathryn Falk	$18.95
I Married a Reclining Chair	Lisa M. Fuhs	$8.95
I'll Be Your Shelter	Giselle Carmichael	$8.95
I'll Paint a Sun	A.J. Garrotto	$9.95
Icie	Pamela Leigh Starr	$8.95
Illusions	Pamela Leigh Starr	$8.95
Indigo After Dark Vol. I	Nia Dixon/Angelique	$10.95
Indigo After Dark Vol. II	Dolores Bundy/ Cole Riley	$10.95
Indigo After Dark Vol. III	Montana Blue/ Coco Morena	$10.95
Indigo After Dark Vol. IV	Cassandra Colt/	$14.95
Indigo After Dark Vol. V	Delilah Dawson	$14.95
Indiscretions	Donna Hill	$8.95
Intentional Mistakes	Michele Sudler	$9.95
Interlude	Donna Hill	$8.95
Intimate Intentions	Angie Daniels	$8.95
It's Not Over Yet	J.J. Michael	$9.95
Jolie's Surrender	Edwina Martin-Arnold	$8.95
Kiss or Keep	Debra Phillips	$8.95
Lace	Giselle Carmichael	$9.95

Other Genesis Press, Inc. Titles (continued)

Last Train to Memphis	Elsa Cook	$12.95
Lasting Valor	Ken Olsen	$24.95
Let Us Prey	Hunter Lundy	$25.95
Lies Too Long	Pamela Ridley	$13.95
Life Is Never As It Seems	J.J. Michael	$12.95
Lighter Shade of Brown	Vicki Andrews	$8.95
Love Always	Mildred E. Riley	$10.95
Love Doesn't Come Easy	Charlyne Dickerson	$8.95
Love Unveiled	Gloria Greene	$10.95
Love's Deception	Charlene Berry	$10.95
Love's Destiny	M. Loui Quezada	$8.95
Mae's Promise	Melody Walcott	$8.95
Magnolia Sunset	Giselle Carmichael	$8.95
Many Shades of Gray	Dyanne Davis	$6.99
Matters of Life and Death	Lesego Malepe, Ph.D.	$15.95
Meant to Be	Jeanne Sumerix	$8.95
Midnight Clear (Anthology)	Leslie Esdaile Gwynne Forster Carmen Green Monica Jackson	$10.95
Midnight Magic	Gwynne Forster	$8.95
Midnight Peril	Vicki Andrews	$10.95
Misconceptions	Pamela Leigh Starr	$9.95
Montgomery's Children	Richard Perry	$14.95
My Buffalo Soldier	Barbara B. K. Reeves	$8.95
Naked Soul	Gwynne Forster	$8.95
Next to Last Chance	Louisa Dixon	$24.95
No Apologies	Seressia Glass	$8.95
No Commitment Required	Seressia Glass	$8.95

Other Genesis Press, Inc. Titles (continued)

Other Genesis Press, Inc. Titles (continued)

Other Genesis Press, Inc. Titles (continued)

Sweet Tomorrows	Kimberly White	$8.95
Taken by You	Dorothy Elizabeth Love	$9.95
Tattooed Tears	T. T. Henderson	$8.95
The Color Line	Lizzette Grayson Carter	$9.95
The Color of Trouble	Dyanne Davis	$8.95
The Disappearance of Allison Jones	Kayla Perrin	$5.95
The Fires Within	Beverly Clark	$9.95
The Foursome	Celya Bowers	$6.99
The Honey Dipper's Legacy	Pannell-Allen	$14.95
The Joker's Love Tune	Sidney Rickman	$15.95
The Little Pretender	Barbara Cartland	$10.95
The Love We Had	Natalie Dunbar	$8.95
The Man Who Could Fly	Bob & Milana Beamon	$18.95
The Missing Link	Charlyne Dickerson	$8.95
The Mission	Pamela Leigh Starr	$6.99
The Perfect Frame	Beverly Clark	$9.95
The Price of Love	Sinclair LeBeau	$8.95
The Smoking Life	Ilene Barth	$29.95
The Words of the Pitcher	Kei Swanson	$8.95
Three Wishes	Seressia Glass	$8.95
Ties That Bind	Kathleen Suzanne	$8.95
Tiger Woods	Libby Hughes	$5.95
Time is of the Essence	Angie Daniels	$9.95
Timeless Devotion	Bella McFarland	$9.95
Tomorrow's Promise	Leslie Esdaile	$8.95
Truly Inseparable	Wanda Y. Thomas	$8.95
Two Sides to Every Story	Dyanne Davis	$9.95
Unbreak My Heart	Dar Tomlinson	$8.95

Other Genesis Press, Inc. Titles (continued)

Uncommon Prayer	Kenneth Swanson	$9.95
Unconditional Love	Alicia Wiggins	$8.95
Unconditional	A.C. Arthur	$9.95
Until Death Do Us Part	Susan Paul	$8.95
Vows of Passion	Bella McFarland	$9.95
Wedding Gown	Dyanne Davis	$8.95
What's Under Benjamin's Bed	Sandra Schaffer	$8.95
When Dreams Float	Dorothy Elizabeth Love	$8.95
When I'm With You	LaConnie Taylor-Jones	$6.99
Whispers in the Night	Dorothy Elizabeth Love	$8.95
Whispers in the Sand	LaFlorya Gauthier	$10.95
Who's That Lady?	Andrea Jackson	$9.95
Wild Ravens	Altonya Washington	$9.95
Yesterday Is Gone	Beverly Clark	$10.95
Yesterday's Dreams, Tomorrow's Promises	Reon Laudat	$8.95
Your Precious Love	Sinclair LeBeau	$8.95

Order Form

Mail to: Genesis Press, Inc.
P.O. Box 101
Columbus, MS 39703

Name _____
Address _____
City/State _____ Zip _____
Telephone _____

Ship to (if different from above)
Name _____
Address _____
City/State _____ Zip _____
Telephone _____

Credit Card Information
Credit Card # _____ ☐ Visa ☐ Mastercard
Expiration Date (mm/yy) _____ ☐ AmEx ☐ Discover

Qty.	Author	Title	Price	Total

Use this order form, or call 1-888-INDIGO-1	**Total for books** _____ **Shipping and handling:** $5 first two books, $1 each additional book _____ **Total S & H** _____ **Total amount enclosed** _____ *Mississippi residents add 7% sales tax*